D0403234

CANCELLED AND
DISPOSED OF BY
THE EDMONTON PUBLIC LIBRARY

FICTIONS *and* LIES

Other books by the author
in English-language editions

SHORT STORIES
A Tale of Three Heads

NON-FICTION
Grey is the Colour of Hope

AUTOBIOGRAPHY
In the Beginning

NOVEL
The Odessans

POETRY COLLECTIONS
No, I'm Not Afraid
Beyond the Limit
Pencil Letter
Dance with a Shadow

FICTIONS
and LIES

A Novel

IRINA RATUSHINSKAYA

Translated from the Russian by
ALYONA KOJEVNIKOVA

JOHN MURRAY
Albemarle Street, London

© Irina Ratushinskaya 1999

English translation © Alyona Kojevnikova 1999

First published in 1999
by John Murray (Publishers) Ltd,
50 Albemarle Street, London W1X 4BD

The moral right of the author has been asserted

All rights reserved. No part of this publication may be
reproduced in any material form (including photocopying
or storing it in any medium by electronic means and
whether or not transiently or incidentally to some other use
of this publication) without the written permission of the
copyright owner, except in accordance with the provisions
of the Copyright, Designs and Patents Act 1988 or under the
terms of a licence issued by the Copyright Licensing
Agency, 90 Tottenham Court Road, London W1P 9HE.
Applications for the copyright owner's written permission
to reproduce any part of this publication should be
addressed to the publisher.

A catalogue record for this book is available from the British Library

ISBN 0–7195–5685–6

Typeset in Palatino by Servis Filmsetting Ltd, Manchester
Printed and bound in Great Britain by
The University Press, Cambridge

FICTIONS *and* LIES

Chapter One

THE WRITER PAVEL Pulin was strolling along the street one day, not hurrying, but also not dawdling. He had almost reached the boulevard. Just here, many years ago, on walks with his nurse, he would whine and complain, out of laziness, and his nurse would croon gently but inexorably: 'We'll just go as far as the Clear Pond and say hello to the little ducklings. Then we'll go home and make you some nice porridge.'

Nurse Klava was long gone, and the pond would be covered with ice right now. He walked along at an even pace, his breath misting in the frosty air. Fine, everything's fine. The most important thing was to avoid anything that would mar the delicate fabric of a successful start to the day. And the beginning of a new life.

Yes, the tension had gone; he was breathing more easily. He had never allowed himself to be troubled by wandering gypsy women before, and as a result he'd got into a complete state for nothing. So much for pride – that besetting sin of the intelligentsia! Instead of falling prey to delusions, he should have taken to herbal remedies straightaway and got his nerves in order. It's your nerves, Lida had said over and over again, but he'd got on his high horse. Old prisoners don't have nerves, he'd say. So he'd gone and let his imagination run away with him instead of acknowledging his own mental state.

At this point, Pulin had the unpleasant feeling that he was talking himself into something, persuading himself that he had been ill and now was not. He forced himself to cheer up at once:

he *was* well! Completely well, just as the old woman had promised! He had stopped hallucinating after all, and slept like a baby at night. The fears that had dogged him for so long now seemed ridiculous. Certainly, in psychiatric hospitals They could do what they liked with people, but to think that They could do it from a distance without one knowing – no, that was nonsense. Pulin shook off his gloom and ventured to take pleasure in the light snow, in a passing pair of nice legs in tight boots, his own lightness of heart. But then he made a mistake: he looked back over his shoulder. Immediately he started to sway and gasp for breath.

He knew those two: they were figures from his nightmares. They had appeared on ordinary Moscow streets as well, over the past two months, on buses and subway trains, in public places, always following him. There they were, dressed in their usual mackintoshes: one with a face like a chest of drawers, the other with a face like nothing at all, just a flesh-coloured oval. Clearly, the old gypsy woman had not helped after all.

A young man in a mackintosh, but with an ordinary square jaw, leapt towards the writer, lifted his head off the icy asphalt, looking concerned. All the blood drained out of Pulin's face, his eyes filled with dread, and he seemed to take leave of himself, yet knowing at the same time that the back of his head was held fast. As those who have had the experience say, the whole of his life flashed before his eyes. In that brief moment, he rejoiced at love, shuddered with fear and squirmed with shame so many times that there was really no need to rush him to intensive care. However, rules are rules, and that was where he was delivered.

Thirty-two minutes later Filipp Savich, head of the Fifth Directorate of the KGB, phoned one of his trusted subordinates.

'Andrei Mikhalych? Listen, I need you to go over to Pavel Pulin's widow – '

'*What?*'

'OK, calm down! She's not a widow yet, but apparently he's not expected to live. A massive heart attack. You writers are a nervy lot. Use your own judgement when you get there, but make sure that when she gets the news, you're really support-ive. The main thing is to see that nothing gets taken out of the apartment. Drop a hint about the State Literary Archive, the importance of preserving our literary heritage, that kind of thing. It seems that he's got a manuscript "in the bottom drawer". I want that manuscript on my desk tomorrow.'

'I'm on my way, Filipp Savich.'

'Good luck.'

Andrei Mikhalych, now forty-nine, was like a child when it came to riding in taxis, even though this was already 1970 and one would think he had had ample time to get used to it. But he never had, and still got a thrill from being driven in a saloon car. You tell the driver where to take you, and he takes you. This, comrades, is a far cry from some grubby train carriage, or a military transport, or a rickety truck requisitioned for wartime use from some collective farm and smelling of pigs. Andrei Mikhalych now had his own Pobeda which he stubbornly refused to part with even though it was an old model, bought with his Stalin Award. However, it would be unwise to drive himself today, he needed to concentrate on the task in hand. He never used official cars on jobs like this, so there would be less gossip. Let the taxi driver watch the traffic lights. Meanwhile, he could lean back and relax, not thinking, so that he would be sure to do the right thing by instinct.

When Pulin's widow-to-be opened the door, Andrei Mikhalych radiated sincerity and restrained elation.

'Lidochka Petrovna, I'm so sorry to come by without warning, but I've just left the meeting, and couldn't resist coming here, to be the first one to . . . But maybe Pavlik already knows? Is he at home?'

Despite this jovial tone, Lidochka Petrovna's first reaction was a stab of dread. Her face fell and she stared mutely at him with eyes full of frightened inquiry. She was too surprised to take in the fact that her guest, not just anybody but Andrei Mikhalych Belokon himself, had called her husband 'Pavlik', entirely naturally. Had she been capable of connected thought she would have recalled that her not so fortunate husband had called Belokon a high-ranking son-of-a-bitch. But Pavlik had been acting very strangely lately, anyway, seemed terribly withdrawn and said all sorts of wild things which he refused to explain. He just frowned when she questioned him, so she had stopped asking.

'He's gone out . . . I'm not sure when he'll be back . . .'

'Well, there's justice in that, too: who should be the first to hear the good news but "the dear companion of my darkest days"?' He felt that he had to quote from Pushkin to show that his business was pure literature. 'However, I won't keep you in suspense: there was a meeting up there,' Andrei Mikhalych pointed upward meaningfully, 'and I was there too, for my sins. You know we're getting ready for the Lenin anniversary. And as there's no bypassing our best and most talented people for that, Pavlik's name naturally came up. I know that we writers aren't favourites with those higher up, they're afraid to give us too much leeway . . . Especially those of us who've retained our integrity but who aren't too well adapted to everyday life. But talent – ah, talent will always come through! Better late than never, eh?'

This was Lidochka Petrovna's cue to respond, and she nodded, trying to gather her wits.

'In any case, it has already been decided to award Pavlik the Order of Distinction for the centenary. We'll try to push through the Workers' Red Banner for him as well, but that's not up to me, alas. Then there's the matter of issuing his work in three volumes – to publish, or not to publish? I'm all for publication, naturally, but what do you think the Soviet Writer editorial board thinks?'

4

'What?' breathed the still stunned Lidochka Petrovna. She was trying to rein in her imagination, but already it was leaping up towards the peeling paint of the ceiling.

'They've included it in their publication schedule,' announced Belokon triumphantly. He was honestly pleased by the wife's delight: let the poor woman enjoy a few minutes of hitherto undreamt-of bliss. Hope always makes life easier, doesn't it, comrades? It would be very fleeting, true, but surely it was better than nothing?

'Well, that's about it, except', continued Belokon delicately, 'in May we're sending a delegation to Paris, for a meeting with progressive writers. They should be there for Victory Day, just as a reminder, so to speak . . . After all, Pavlik fought in the war, he was decorated. So we conferred and decided . . . He's never been abroad, has he?'

'He was, in '45,' replied Lidochka Petrovna with dignity.

How little it takes for a person to start putting on airs! Already, she was holding her head higher. Amazing! However, Andrei Mikhalych did not take offence.

'Lidochka Petrovna, we were all there in '45! Except for the ones who were evacuated to Tashkent . . . Well, they'll be staying at home this time, too.'

'Are you in this delegation?' she managed to ask. This was not a casual or empty question: it was plain that if Pavlik were to go, then someone would be sent to keep an eye on him – and on all the others. This would at least explain why Belokon had condescended to pay this visit. But Andrei Mikhalych continued to radiate benevolence.

'I don't need to tell you how our delegations are composed: one front line war veteran, one woman, one representative of a national minority, one youth representative, and so forth. Pavlik and I are the same age, we both fought in the war, so what would be the sense of sending the two of us? I'll go later to the film festival in Poland.'

Lidia Petrovna felt ashamed of her cynical suspicions. It

looked as though Belokon had voluntarily stepped aside so that Pavlik could go to Paris, while it would have been easy for him to go himself. Heavens, what kind of a hostess was she – here the man had come with the best of intentions, and she was cross-questioning him instead of at least offering him a cup of tea. Belokon graciously took up the offer of tea, and Lidia Petrovna, remembering to smile, emerged from her earlier confusion, set out a dull glass sugar-basin and brewed the tea Moscow-style, with care and expertise.

Conversation over the tea became warm and friendly, and all that was needed for Lidia Petrovna's cup of joy to overflow was for Pavlik to walk in right now and hear the news. While she wondered whether to get out the bottle of cherry liqueur or wait for her husband's return, Lidia Petrovna listened to Andrei Mikhalych's tale of how the chestnuts bloom in Paris in May, his recollections of '45, and his insistence that her talented husband should look over all his manuscripts without loss of time since he was on such a lucky streak. There ought to be a chance of periodical publication for a good many things. He, Belokon, ventured to hope that his journal would be allowed first refusal.

'What do they call it? *Droit de seigneur!*' he laughed. 'Old friends, and all that – we get first pick, then all those other foreign friendly magazines or whatever can scramble for what's left.'

He told Lidia Petrovna a great many interesting details about how he and her husband had met while being treated for their first war wounds, two greenhorns. How, because they were absolutely dying for a smoke, they managed to steal some tobacco from . . . but Lidia Petrovna was not destined to learn whose tobacco they stole, because the phone rang, and almost immediately she gave a long and unnatural gasp of despair.

There was no knowing what she would have done if Belokon had not been there, but since he was he immediately took everything into his own hands. He made up a dose of valerian to calm her down, even though his hands shook and he dropped the glass at his first attempt. He yelled at someone over the phone, demanding that something be done and without any of the usual delays. Tactfully, he asked the widow whether she wanted him to call anyone to come in and help her. When she said she wanted nobody, he stayed with her, not like some casual acquaintance who would have left her to her own devices. No, he was not one to shirk another's grief – that's what wartime comradeship meant. She even cried on his shoulder later, when the tears finally came. His nondescript jacket smelled slightly of tobacco. He smoked the same cigarettes as Pavlik.

It is a well-known fact that Soviet writers are given first class funerals. Or a notch lower, depending on their rating. Those whose duty it is to organize these funerals never make a mistake. The widows do not need to do anything, so Lidia Petrovna did not even try. Nor did she have to be involved with deciding what to do with Pavel's writings. That would have been terrible: going through his papers, reading his recent annotations, seeing his uneven handwriting, or the tiny devils in their little houses that he doodled in the margins. She could not have coped, she would have gone out of her mind. Yet she knew she must not delay. The last thing she could do for Pavlik was to ensure that a collection of his works was published soon. It was what he too would have wanted. Belokon came to the rescue again. She need only say 'Do what you think best' in an exhausted voice for him to organize everything.

Her recollections of the funeral itself were hazy, but anyone there would have said that everything went as it should. The literati present noted who came and who stayed away and who ignored whom. For a few days there was a certain amount of talk, but as nothing out of the ordinary happened the gossip quickly died down. Filipp Savich, however, had his mind on something else. Very soon, he had to have a serious discussion with Belokon.

Filipp Savich never invited people he trusted to his office. There were other places for this purpose. Nor did he invite many of them to his own home. Andrei Mikhalych was one of the lucky few. Meetings like these were good for the ego and terrible for the liver. For one thing, Filipp Savich had a great deal of power, something Belokon admired and responded to keenly. Just as gravity, they say, can distort space and time, so power changes the character and physiology of those who come within its orbit. There is no shame in this, nor is there any resisting it: yes, it brings a rush of adrenalin, yes, it makes the pulse race faster . . . yet how much more intense life seems in those moments, how spectacularly one can soar or fall! Actually, Belokon had had very few falls.

Everything was so modest and harmonious: fine leather arm-chairs, a low roughly polished table, a white bearskin (evidence of the host's skill as a hunter) thrown carelessly on the floor. Coffee, cognac, lemon – nothing sloppy, everything austere and unadorned. Yet how different was this simplicity from that simplicity which had overwhelmed Belokon so long ago, and gripped his imagination even now. On that occasion he had taken in nothing: not the greatcoat, nor the pipe – had they existed at all? Maybe they were something invented by film makers. There seemed to be nothing else present in that place of muted echoes from dimensions inaccessible to man. Only He was there with the still young Belokon, whose whole being was alive with the sense that he stood before a father, a master, a judge.

The current regime was different, for all that it purported to be the same. Belokon sensed a depressing divergence, unin-spiring by comparison. Nevertheless, he knew how to deal with the current powers too.

'You're sure that she doesn't know?'

'I'd stake my head on it, Filipp Savich. There's another way to check, though.'

'No, there's no need. I'll rely on you in this. If the manuscript's not in the apartment and the widow doesn't know anything, let's figure out who might have it. He couldn't have buried it, could he? What do you think?'

'The thing is, Filipp Savich, he was very much of a recluse. After he got involved in signing that protest back in '66, his nerves went to pieces. He hasn't had many friends since. Then there was that business when they all quarrelled.'

Filipp Savich remembered that well.

'Yes, yes, go on.'

'He's got one or two friends, that's all. Nikolin is probably the closest to him, or used to be. I don't know whether he still was at the end.'

'Who's this Nikolin? Remind me.'

'Writes children's books, but he's not one of the best. He's been a member of the Union of Writers since –'

'Oh, yes!'

'He didn't come to the funeral. Phoned the wife to apologize, said he had flu and was running a high temperature. A little strange, I thought.'

'You think he might be our man?'

'It won't hurt to check.'

Thus Anton Semyonovich Nikolin, now code-named 'Storyteller', was included in the investigation launched by the Fifth Directorate of the KGB. For the time being, the investigation was listed as 'checking out a signal'.

Chapter Two

Since the storyteller claimed he had been sick, this was a fairly easy matter to confirm. Naturally, the doctor was not summoned to report to the KGB, but was tactfully approached at work in the district clinic – the Storyteller did not rate registration in a special clinic. So – the doctor was asked – did so-and-so request a house visit? Yes. It's noted on his card. Was he sick? We-e-ll, probably. What do you mean by 'probably'? What that means, comrades, is that we're in the middle of a flu epidemic, which we are calling isolated cases of respiratory tract infection, RTI, because we don't have such things as epidemics.

And doctors get sick, too. This means their workload falls on those who haven't yet succumbed. When does a doctor have to be extra vigilant? When the patient wants a certificate to get off work. There's a limit on the number of such certificates. Sometimes when a person is genuinely ill, he can't be given a certificate because the limit has been reached: so what do you do? Claim that he's malingering? In any case, you can't give him a certificate . . .

The doctor was young, not broken in yet, and seemed ready to expound at length on the injustice of the situation. Politely but firmly he was steered back to the point at issue. All right, he said, writers don't need medical certificates because they work at home. All they need is a prescription. Yes, something was prescribed, it's all here on the card. Antibiotics. No, he didn't check his temperature, the patient was not a child, after all, and he didn't need a certificate . . . Yes, yes, we've got that. So what

10

else do you want? The diagnosis is registered right here: RTI. If that's what it says, then that's what he had. Is that certain? Co-o-mrades, just look at this list of house calls for that day – do you really think it's possible to remember each one?

The doctor was disappointingly formal, shuffling his papers as if to say: the documentation is in order, so leave me alone. Either he knew more than he was saying, or he was plain scared. The attempt at a heart-to-heart talk fell flat. Pity. District doctors can frequently be of great help to the Directorate.

Well, there's more than one way to skin a cat. How old is the Storyteller? Forty. A good age. Let's take a look at his associates . . . Hmm, not much there, hardly anyone. That's no good. A Soviet writer should maintain creative contacts with his colleagues. Who else is on the file who would be younger than the Storyteller, but higher in rank? A good boss knows all his agents, of course, but it doesn't hurt to go through the files from time to time, to jog the memory. Every so often this leads to fresh ideas.

So, what do we have? . . . Hmm . . . This one won't do – he's become a bit introspective lately . . . and this one's hitting the bottle . . . Time to weed out the agents who are no longer up to scratch. Ah, here's the man we want! Usmanov. Kirill Sergeich. Shortened his name to Kir in a burst of artistic affectation, and publishes under that name. Code-named agent Arseni.

Sociable, charming, talented. Member of the Union of Writers. Yes, travelled abroad. Four times. Twice to capitalist countries. Recruited after his first trip overseas. Resisted and tried to wriggle out at first, but has settled down and is doing good work, keen as mustard.

So let's start an operational check on the signal. We'll put Arseni to work first. And take the plan to Filipp Savich for approval.

Filipp Savich approved.

Anton Nikolin, totally unaware that he had been cast as the Storyteller – and even less, by whom – really had been down with the flu. For several nights, huge pale horses appeared from the corners of his room, trotted up to his bed and snorted in his face. He was so unsteady on his legs that he could barely manage to reach the toilet or the phone. The antibiotics made his stomach ache, and Auntie Xenia, who lived across the landing, felt sorry for him and plied him with home-made yoghurt.

But every bad patch eventually comes to an end. Luckily for him, the sun was shining and the frost was not too penetrating when he set out for Vagankovskoye cemetery to pay his respects to Pavel. He knew, of course, that Pavel was not there, and that all he would be doing would be staring meaninglessly at the little mound of earth covered with frozen wreaths and bouquets. However, he believed that there was life only where there was a dearth of meaning. Wherever meaning reared its head – especially great meaning – it usually threatened life. He punched his ticket on the bus, and sat there, his neck swathed in a well-worn scarf. In truth, he preferred to say his goodbyes to Pavel alone. He would go and see Lidia Petrovna later. He would listen to what she had to say, trying not to show his unease, and mutter something inadequate, knowing that he would never find the right words. He didn't have the gift. For some reason, Lidia Petrovna was so silly he found it hard to respect her. Now with Auntie Xenia it was quite different; her he even admired.

Nikolin did not consider himself a practical person. Vague, uncertain-looking, he had no reason to do so. However, he had sufficient wit to slip the cemetery watchman three roubles. The old man escorted him kindly to the grave of Pavel Pulin, and just as kindly disappeared about his business without a word.

But it was cold, so cold! Just as well the marble slab had not been put in place yet, that would have made it even colder. The earth, for all it was frozen solid, seemed somehow cosier. Nikolin felt no grief, nor did he try to force himself to do so. He took a handful of seeds from his pocket, and threw them on the snowy mound for the robins or the other birds around. He did not know what he thought about or how long he stood there. Time moves differently in a cemetery. For that reason, he did not notice at first that he was no longer alone.

Kir Usmanov, in a suede coat and beaver fur collar, fussed around, pulling off his gloves. His mouth twisted in a childish grimace, he tried not to blink. Not wishing to stare, Nikolin turned his gaze back to the wreaths. Usmanov had not brought seeds, but stood there crumbling an ordinary small greyish baker's loaf. The cold nipped his fingers, as he rolled the soft substance of the loaf between his hands. Nikolin was not pleased to have his solitude interrupted; it was not as though this was a public bar, after all.

'That's the way it goes, eh?' muttered Kir, looking guilty and helpless. Nikolin felt ashamed of himself: here was someone grieving, and he was probably in the way. Still, who would have guessed . . .

'You have no idea how much I owe him,' gulped Kir, as if in answer to Nikolin's thought.

Hurriedly, stumbling over his own words, he began to relate how as a provincial student, he had come to see the recently rehabilitated writer. Fool that he was, he had taken his poetry to show him – and him a prose writer, would you believe it! He wanted advice on his future, not from a writer of influence but from one he could respect; and who was more to be respected than yesterday's internee? He went on to describe how Pulin, still showing traces of his stint in the Kolyma camps, still unfamiliar with the new times and new ways, did exactly what was needed: received the youngster warmly, gave him his blessing, and boosted his self-confidence.

'I left his home a new man . . . He lived in some filthy communal flat at the time, because his wife was registered there – he had no rights at all then, hadn't even received permission to register for residence in Moscow. It scared me, the way he spoke: short words, barely moving his lips. I thought that it must be a habit from prison: you know, so that you wouldn't know someone was talking. Then he smiled, and I saw that he hadn't had time to have any false teeth made. When I came in, I walked straight into someone's long-johns, hanging in the corridor to dry. Yes, long-johns, pegged to a washing-line. Slap, right in my face, and I thought – he has to put up with this every day. Still, when I was leaving we laughed together about that forest of washing. He walked me to the door, and you can't imagine how reluctant I was to go, he had to give me a little shove to get me moving, as if to say, come on, off you go! I ran down the stairs happy as a ten year old, and just as full of myself. I felt so happy I bought an ice-cream on the corner and dripped it all over my trousers . . . I was a child of the war, you know, no father . . .'

Nikolin understood what it was to be a fatherless child. Pavel came so alive in Kir's outpourings that Nikolin felt a stab of pain and had to reproach himself for a flash of stupid jealousy. Usmanov finished crumbling the bread, and stood there awkwardly, shifting from foot to foot. This would have been the moment for them to part, but somehow they moved off together. When they passed through the cemetery gates, Kir was horrified to learn that Nikolin had come by public transport, on such a cold day and so soon after being ill. He insisted on giving him a lift in his Moskvich to the Writers' Club where they could warm up in the cosy lower hall and each in his own way raise a glass to the memory of their friend.

Soon Usmanov was calling Nikolin 'old man', while Nikolin marvelled silently at what an agreeable fellow this Kir had turned out to be. Why had he avoided him? What was there to dislike about him, once you got to know him? Yes, there had been some unpleasant gossip, but in literary circles, who doesn't become the subject of gossip at one time or another? So what about that idiotic poem Kir had published somewhat rashly in the journal *October*? One look into Kir's tortured eyes was enough to show that he was not the shameless opportunist Nikolin had imagined him to be.

'Yes, old man, it made me sick just to shave – couldn't look myself in the face. But what could I do? The poem I wrote was completely different. I felt inspired when I wrote it, as if I was hearing an echo. And then it started: take this out, add some optimism here. They – you know what? They completely dispossessed me! They appropriated my intellectual property! As for me, I was flailing around like an unwilling virgin, and maybe would have got away with it if my brother hadn't got into trouble with the law.'

'Brother?'

'Well, yes. That is – no. Not by blood, I mean. A brother from the orphanage. I spent three and a half years there before my mother took me back. Nobody came for him though, so he grew up at the mercy of the state. He worked as a driver in the army, then took to long-distance trucking. Sometime later, he clipped a small car – some Zaporozhets – and was charged with causing grievous bodily harm while under the influence. My poor Mishka! One winter we had just the one coat between us, we took turns wearing it. Naturally, I ran around trying to do something for him. In that situation, I couldn't go on struggling, I agreed to everything They wanted, and would have agreed to more. Thank God I didn't have to. If anyone thinks the worse of me for that – let them.'

'Did you get him off?'

'He was given a twelve-month suspended sentence. So I suppose you could say yes. The thing is, I have a huge family. Forty-two, all brothers, not a single girl, the girls were kept in a different institution. They all know that I've made good, and think that there's nothing I can't do. Now you – you're a man of conscience, everyone respects you. So now you tell me, tell me about conscience. What should you do when you have a real live person on one hand, and your principles on the other?'

15

There is no saying what Nikolin would have answered, but he didn't have to, because at that moment they were approached by the humorist Mulin, red-cheeked from the cold outside, who asked them to sign in some friends of his. It was a rule that not just anybody could come into the Writers' Club restaurant, but only those who were entitled. Every person so entitled could bring in one guest, for cultural and creative relaxation. Mulin had brought along three people, who were waiting outside until Mulin could rustle up some help.

Mulin's guests were cinema people, a lively trio with the lack of inhibition typical of actors. They ordered mushrooms and other titbits. Nikolin felt warm and relaxed in their company. White tablecloths, the bearded actor puffing on a pipe, both girls good-looking, wearing the latest in modern boots, but without any airs or graces. It turned out that Kir knew them all, and the discussion, for some reason, centred on the Novgorod school of icon painting, the fifteenth century, and, as far as Nikolin could judge, the girls were as knowledgeable as any specialist on icons. If indeed there were any such specialists left nowadays.

Either because Nikolin had finally got his hands on some tobacco (he always smoked one cigarette after another when he was drinking), or because some errant viruses were still cruising round his body, he fell into a violent and embarrassing coughing fit.

'You're still far from well, old man,' sympathized Kir. 'All these tablets and powders we swallow ruin our health even if they do get rid of the bugs at the same time. Our grandfathers knew better. Tell you what – why don't I pick you up tomorrow and we'll go to the Sanduny for a good old-fashioned steam bath? An old fellow in Yelovichi showed me a rub-down that will get rid of anything. You just have to know the right pressure points. But it has to be done after a steam bath, the old boy said, or it won't work. If you're not as spry as a spring chicken after that, I'll shave my hair off! Now, Nastenka, wouldn't you say that's a fair bet?'

16

He bent his head towards her lap, so that she could appreciate his abundant, liberally waved light brown hair.

Nastenka – delightful creature! – ran her hand over his head as if appraising a mink pelt.

'Little scalp-hunter!' Mulin laughed. Nikolin and Kir grasped hands, and Nastenka struck them smartly apart to make the bet official.

Anton Nikolin, like most solitary people, would have been surprised to hear himself described as such. He was not a native Muscovite, but had managed by sheer luck to stay in Moscow after graduating from teachers' training college. He had none of those ties which most people have (or are cursed with) such as relatives, family connections, neighbours, childhood friends – they all remained back in Lipetsk, and faded away after his mother's death.

He became used to the capital by fits and starts, as he found himself hustled from one Moscow world to another. For some reason, his recollections of the grim and sinister Moscow of 1948 were all evening ones. Lights shining through rain, cars whizzing by, glaring headlights and indecipherable street signs. He was far too shy to ask passers-by for directions. Half of his fellow-students were army veterans, so the men in the class were divided into those who had fought in the war, and those who had not seen action. The eighteen-year-old Nikolin was still growing, but he had a quick tongue and could handle himself well in a fight, a young man in the army reserve, dressed in a tattered pair of trousers of which he was painfully ashamed. All the girls ignored him, even though there were never enough men to go round at dances. And the ones who did dance with him, behaved as though they were dancing with someone else. He knew only too well that they were pretending they were dancing with the Ringo Kid, or some other son-of-a-bitch from a foreign movie, whoever was the current idol. It was him they were seeing as they stared through Nikolin. Nikolin himself was a mere sop to their vanity, to save them from the ultimate humiliation of being a wallflower at the dance. Occasionally, a sense of fair play would prompt one of them to bestow on him a smile or a languorous sigh – here's a sop to your pride, too.

Then came the Moscow of 1953, with the momentous funeral which dwarfed any other events of that year. He recalled the Moscow of that time as a morning city, with tram wheels striking sparks from the tracks on a clear, white day. Everyone seemed to be waiting for something, while pretending to be busy with everyday affairs. Nikolin was relieved to see the end of standing ovations: only then did he allow himself to admit how painful and degrading he had found them in his student years. At every meeting – and what week passed without one meeting at least? – it had taken only one mention of the beloved Leader's name for a couple of bastards in the front row to leap to their feet, as if by command. Then, like it or not, the whole auditorium would rise to its feet and clap until blue in the face. Nikolin stood up and applauded, too, glancing sideways at his neighbours to make sure that he wasn't the first to stop clapping. In that unlucky event, chances were that someone would notice it and report you. But the beloved Leader died, and the vogue for standing ovations fizzled out. Moreover, it emerged that Nikolin wasn't the only one to feel relief, and there was added relief in the fact that people actually began to say so in as many words. By this time, Nikolin was teaching mathematics in a highly respected boarding school. He liked to organize hikes outside the city, and was adored equally by his pupils, their parents and the unmarried women teachers. However, he felt sure that the most important part of his life lay ahead, that his energies were up to more than looking after the school parquet flooring, organizing Christmas trees for New Year and supervising the school news-sheet.

There was also the Moscow of blazing rows in communal

apartments, of government departments with mind-boggling acronyms, of endless hours spent queuing in corridors outside big doors covered with fake leather, of endless pilgrimages through slushy streets for yet another official violet stamp. That was later, though, after he had married Lucia. And always at the last moment the precious residence permit seemed to elude him; the last moment followed by yet another last moment, over and over again. By the time he finally became a legal resident of the city, Nikolin had no strength left for rejoicing.

The Moscow of 1956 was like a whirlwind. Hundreds of thousands back from the camps, as though from beyond the grave, daring new publications, the Thaw, science fiction in the bookshops. A promise is always better than reality, and there was a promise then – freedom! Looking back at the newspapers of the time now, it all seems like a dream. But Nikolin remembered. It was there, it was! Why else were they all swept up in that wave of intoxication?

Then it emerged that he, a young and promising writer, welcomed to the staff of a youth magazine, knew next to nothing of the literary world. He mixed up editors' names, had no clear idea of the function of Glavlit, the main censorship administration, was ignorant of the structure of the Writers' Union – like an alien from outer space. At his first literary dinner, where he found himself almost at the very centre of affairs, he happened to ask naïvely who Lesyuchevsky was. His remark was followed by an awkward silence around the table. Later he was told that many people admired him for asking such a question, and that everyone remembered him for it.

Nikolin never stopped feeling himself an outsider in writers' circles, as though he were a charlatan or a student preparing to sit an examination for which he was unprepared. There were many things in conversation he did not understand, and many silences he was even less adept at interpreting. He feared making blunders, and so avoided asking questions. Afterwards, when understanding came, he shied away from it out of fear of contamination: what if I should become like that?

Everything that followed was so tied up with Lucia and Dasha that he tried not to remember.

Sadly, life had not made him a regular visitor at the Sanduny Bath House, as he realized the next day.

Kir plied the bunch of birch twigs with dexterity and confidence. Then they switched, took a plunge in the cold pool and now lay 'flapping their gills' as Kir put it, on marble slabs, resting before the next round in the steam room. This is where their conversation took a philosophical turn.

'You know what your problem is, old fellow? I read about it once in an American journal – it's called "mid-life crisis". God knows how that translates into Russian, but the idea's a sound one. Something happens to you at that age. The more talented you are, the worse it will be. Ailments of all sorts, depression, a feeling that everything's in the past, and there's nothing to look forward to. What would you call that?'

'The devil messing you around.'

'Perfect!' exclaimed Kir. 'You're a genius, my friend. Can I use that expression?'

'I didn't make it up – it's been around for ever.'

'No, I mean, can I borrow it?'

'Be my guest . . . How about a glass of beer?'

'Uh-uh! Another round of steam, then I'll give you that rub-down I told you about, and then we'll have some beer. But not a drop until we're through.'

The old man's rub-down exhausted them both. When Nikolin could feel his legs again, he tried to get up and felt as though he were floating. The sensation was incredible: he felt weightless and could move with no effort. Kir, naked and laughing, stood by, his wet hair falling over his eyes.

'Well, how do you feel? Like a new-born babe, eh?'

'Oh, yes. But how will you manage to drive the car? Won't we take off?'

However, the drive home was uneventful, and Kir gladly accepted Nikolin's invitation to come in. They brewed a pot of ferociously strong tea and whiled away a pleasant hour or two together.

On the second Tuesday of every month, agent Arseni had to arrive at a certain street crossing at a specific time. Here, he would flag down a 'private' car for which he never had to wait. He would get in, leave a written report, receive further instructions or orders, answer questions. He also had to sign for sums of money issued for operational expenses. They need not humiliate him to that extent, Kir felt, but humiliate him They did, all the way along the line. On the whole, Kir had become accustomed to the situation, but every now and then he would be shaken by a real, boiling hatred. Sometimes this hatred was directed at Those to whom he reported; at other times, at those about whom he was collecting information. Occasionally his hatred had no particular object. For instance, look at that crowd of people waiting for the lights to change. Standing there, just standing there like a flock of sheep, the stupid bastards . . .

Chapter Three

ANDREI MIKHALYCH BELOKON prepared to get down to some work. He liked both the process and the ritual of preparation. Pleasurably and without haste, he put his study and especially his desk in order. Then he switched on his heavy, green-shaded desk lamp. They don't make lamps like that any more, now it's all contemporary chic! Damned modernists. He checked the points of his pencils, both the ordinary ones, and the red and blue ones with the word 'Kremlin' in gold on the sides: these were deputies' pencils, which he treasured from the last Congress. Finally, he moved his typewriter to the middle of the desk, put a stack of clean paper on the right, and the manuscript on the left. Just as well the desk was large, a writer should have a large desk. Our factories these days don't turn out desks like this any longer – Belokon had had his made to order back in '48.

He settled himself comfortably in his chair, and cast a satisfied look around the room. Everything was just as it should be. It jarred a little that the portrait was not in its proper place. These days, the portrait hung in his bedroom. A bedroom is a private place, and you can keep whatever you like there. As for the study – well, the study is the front line of the ideological struggle. Anyone and everyone can come in here, messengers from the editorial offices, colleagues, favour-seekers and journalists. If today's rules meant that the portrait should not be in the study, there was no more to be said. Belokon knew all about discipline.

That was the reason he was working this evening: a manuscript had been forwarded urgently from the Central Committee for appraisal. Belokon began to read, then paused in dismay at the deplorable reluctance of today's editors to assume responsibility. If this had been submitted to his journal, he would never have dreamed of bothering the Central Committee with it, but handed it straight to Filipp Savich. On the other hand, the author was far from being an unknown. That's what happens, thought Belokon sourly, when we let people like this rise to prominence, and then have to rack our brains about what to do with them in order to avoid a scandal of international proportions. What shall we do, oh what shall we do? Send them to the mines, that's what: the old tsar was right in that, at least.

Belokon carefully marked all the ideologically unacceptable places and inserted a sheet of paper in his typewriter.

The plot of the story supposedly centres round the great turning point in the life of the village . . .

I make no mention of the prosody and style of the work, as it is my opinion that if the very ideological basis of the work is unsound, it cannot be justified by stylistic or poetic inevitability . . .

Minor problems are presented as supposedly major ones, the entire effect is contrived . . .

Damn, that was twice he'd used 'supposedly' on the same page. Never mind, he would substitute a suitable synonym later, no sense losing track now.

The story contains numerous statements offensive to the regime, which are not rebutted later. See pages 14, 32, 65, 115, 274 . . .

Expressions of hostility towards the state and the Party, frequently presented in veiled terms, are left to stand. Under the guise of criticism, the author introduces unacceptable, and at times demoralizing anti-socialist propaganda . . .

Now, let's move on to the author himself, and send off the appraisal tomorrow morning by courier to the Cultural Section.

Belokon went on to mention the author's contribution to the *Tarusa Pages*, his signature under collective anti-Soviet petitions to the government, and his outspoken behaviour at the Writers' Congress.

His task completed, Belokon leaned back and stretched his protesting spine. Half-past nine already, fancy that! Olga must be getting ready to put Denis to bed. Belokon rose hurriedly. Suddenly, he wanted nothing more than to play with his grandson. It's good to have your daughter living across the landing. He had been right to organize this when he got the flat. Probably the only good thing to come from her marriage. That and Denis, of course. Nothing gets silly ideas out of girls' heads as quickly as night-time feeds, tummy upsets and the attendant joys of motherhood.

Denis was watching the last minutes of *Goodnight, Children* on television and squealed with pleasure at the sight of his grandfather.

'Grandpa! Hooray! Let's play Red cavalry!'

He swarmed up on to his grandfather's shoulders. The boy was growing, no longer a feather weight. Belokon neighed loudly, tossed his head, and the game was on. Puffing and happy, they proceeded to demolish the enemy – the blinds, divan cushions and the coat-stand in the hallway, after which Olga dragged Denis off for his bath. She was clearly upset about something.

'I don't want you to bath me, I want Grandpa!' yelled Denis, and Belokon, grinning broadly, stuck his head around the bathroom door.

'Comrade commander-in-chief, permission to speak, please! Allow me to commence bathing of the conscript and to ensure enforcement of the command "lights out!"'

Olga smiled slightly, pushing a strand of hair back from her face.

'Permission granted, comrade volunteer. Your selfless valour will be rewarded with crab salad.'

For the next half hour, Belokon duly displayed selfless valour, despite the changing fortunes of war. Olga pottered around in the kitchen to the accompaniment of shouts and laughter from the bedroom.

A complex man, her father. He's become a bit heavier, but still looks marvellous for his age. Full head of grey hair, no sagging chin. How many women must have wanted to step into her late mother's shoes since '52? Olga had been only fifteen, but had understood this well enough. She had waited, prepared to reject any stepmother who appeared in their home. But this had never occurred. Father and daughter continued to live together, with a cleaning woman coming in to keep the apartment in order. They grew increasingly close but quarrelled violently, neither able to word an apology, but merely pretending that nothing had happened once the storm had blown over. There was a time when she had hated and been ashamed of him: for his reputation as a bully-boy in literary circles, for the smirks on the faces of just about everyone she met, who would say: 'Are you related to *that* Belokon?' For the way he lied and believed his own lies with indecent sincerity. For the way he idolized Stalin, he and his circle of old friends, filled with the same passion and with the eyes of killers. His eyes would become like that, too, whenever he drank with them, and she would be afraid of him in those moments. There was a time when she would shout accusingly:

'You'd walk over corpses if you had to!'

Eventually she had left home, but when he collapsed with what the doctors called a 'hypertensive crisis', she had come to the hospital every day with bunches of his favourite carnations. She knew the cause of his illness: that very same 'walking over corpses', but this time by her.

'Where is my big army belt?' came a mock-ferocious roar from the bedroom.

Olga snorted with laughter. By the time she was six she had realized this threat had no substance. Denis had not been fooled for a moment since he was born.

Belokon wrinkled his nose at the sight of cognac glasses on the table, and Olga reacted immediately.

'I'll tell the doctor on you! You should be grateful that he gave you permission to drink cognac!'

'Madame is in a bad mood, I see. Something wrong?'

'Oh, they've put back publication of the book. Five hundred and twenty-eight pages plus the cover, all in colour. Now you tell me, what reason can there be to put off publication of a children's book?'

'Who's the author?'

'Nikolin. Remember, I told you last autumn? And the illustrations were really good . . .'

'Always my modest child,' grinned Belokon affectionately. He remembered how much trouble Olga had taken over those illustrations: ran around museums, went to Kolomenskoye for some reason . . . She was certainly conscientious, thank goodness. Still, she could have done a lot better than illustrating books for all and sundry. Why, she could have become a portrait painter, or done landscapes . . . After all, she had an excellent education. He would have pulled some strings to help her along, she could have had an album of her work published by now, held exhibitions. But no, she dug in her heels and refused any offer of assistance.

Olga swallowed the 'modest' without comment, but a raised brow indicated a change from 'variable conditions' to 'storm warning'. Belokon had always loved watching that mobile brow. Lisa used to do that, and nobody else. He tried to calm her down.

'Just because they've put off publication doesn't mean they've axed the book. All the publishing houses are in a frenzy now, what with the anniversary celebrations. When did you say they planned to publish?'

'In February, but now they're saying not before August.'

'In that case, it could be a simple delay. Nobody had any objections to your illustrations?'

'They vetoed one that had a church in it. Parasites. I didn't even bother arguing with them.'

'Maybe they've got something against this Nikolin of yours?' suggested Belokon carefully.

'You'd be the first to know if that was so, wouldn't you?'

Olga looked searchingly at her father. He appeared quite unruffled; she felt a prick of annoyance.

'You do know something, don't you? I can tell. Come on, stop stalling!'

'Will you get down off your high horse? I don't know anything. Stop being so paranoid, for pity's sake! What am I, Nikolin's nursemaid or something? There's nothing unusual in deferred publication. Lenin-related subjects have priority right now, that's all. And you jump in immediately with your "why?"'

Olga's eyes narrowed, and she hugged her thin shoulders. He realized that she hadn't believed a word of what he said. He rested his elbows on the table, propped his chin on his hands and played his trump card.

'Would you like me to make a few phone calls tomorrow, see what I can do? Who are the publishers?'

'No thanks,' she cut him off. 'You promised not to interfere in my business.'

'All right then, no. So pull yourself together. Were you counting on that money so much?'

'Well, it doesn't lie around in the street, that's for sure. What gets me most is that this was my best work. Now it's all going down the drain – I know what that "deferred" means. Just because some –'

'Olga!' he interrupted harshly. 'Stop that!'

Belokon knew his daughter, but at times he couldn't help himself: the blood would rush to his head when she came out with her blasphemies. The last thing they needed now was a quarrel. Everything had started out so well . . . A lonely man comes over to have a cup of tea with his daughter, and then this happens . . .

'All right, all right. I'll say no more.'

She added water to the kettle and put it on the stove, standing there in her form-hugging slacks. Belokon saw that she had grown thinner – no bottom to speak of. She'd do herself in if she didn't start eating properly.

'That Kir of yours giving you any money for Denis, at least?'

'To hell with him . . . we'll manage.'

'So what do you imagine you're going to achieve by that?'

'Let's not talk about it, all right?'

'All right, tigress. Now just let me tell you something: you're being stupid. I don't give a damn about Kir – your relations with him are your own business. But there's no need for you to take it out on me. No – don't interrupt! I know you don't need anything. You're an artist, you're free. A bird without a care. You get through the day on a cup of yoghurt. But you've got a child, and I'm that child's grandfather. Don't I have the right to make sure that he doesn't go short of anything?' demanded Belokon, his voice rising.

In earlier times they would quarrel and shout at each other, but somehow it was easier to recover in those days. Now, when he started to lose his temper and she would hold hers in check, the offence caused was greater. It was like a clear demonstration of contempt: go on, old man, shout yourself hoarse, lose your self-control, you still can't reach me. The ungrateful whelp.

'Denis has all he needs. Dad, we've been through all this before. Do you want to have a row?'

'No, I don't want to have a row,' retorted Belokon, making an effort to keep his voice down. He would be restrained and ironical, if that was the best way to get through to her.

'A row is the last thing I want. I've simply seen that his leggings are darned from top to toe. Of course, it's very heroic – a single mother, and one who's such a genius that she's out of work half the time, darning holes in the knees of her child's leggings in the dead of night. As for admitting that with her talent for adapting to society she can't assure a regular income for her kid – no, her Christian humility won't let her! The heroine doesn't want a bean from the child's father. All right. But she rejects her own father as well. Our heroine tramples her father into the mire. You know what that's called in your church language? Pride. And if I remember right, that's the greatest sin of all.'

'Oh my, such knowledge!'

'I know that as far as you're concerned I'm not an authority. So ask any one of those Bible-bashers you're always running to. Let one of them explain it all to you – about pride, and about the need to respect your parents! You've got no manners,' he ended wearily and fell silent.

Olga flashed him a look of concern. Well, they'd done it again. There was her father sitting there looking deflated and grey around the mouth, trying hard to breathe evenly. Now he'd have one of his attacks. She jumped up and flung open a cupboard, fumbling for a large jar which had stuck to the shelf.

'Come on, Dad, calm down. I'll make you a rowan blossom tisane, it'll bring your blood pressure down.'

'You know I hate that stuff, it smells of old socks,' complained Belokon fractiously.

Finally, though, he let Olga coax him into swallowing a cup of her witch's brew. He couldn't help feeling touched by the worried look on her face. She loves her old man after all, the hell-cat. Settling down, he realized that he had gone too far: he shouldn't have touched on that sore spot. That was always the trouble: every time he got fired up, he needed to trample on someone, bring them down. After every fight with Olga, he would promise himself that he would be more tolerant in future.

But how was it possible not to blow up at her, she would try the patience of a saint. Some daughter he had!

'Now, Olga, don't take it to heart. You're talented, you know that. There'll be better times ahead for you, believe your old man. You're young, you've still got plenty of time. As Denis gets older, things will be easier. But for the time being, be sensible and don't take it out on the child. You've given me a marvellous grandson, he's a real eagle! So as your father I'm asking you: do what you want, but not at his expense.'

He slapped her playfully on the bottom and smiled, just as he had when she was small and there were no differences between them; when he was the best Dad in the world, and they would go together to the zoo, to the circus, and even to football matches.

As he was leaving, he laid a previously prepared envelope firmly on the telephone table. Olga opened her mouth to protest, then looked at her father and shut it again. That's more like it, my girl!

Filipp Savich did not go into each and every case personally. However, this was a special situation. The last thing anyone needed before the centenary celebrations was to have some new anti-Soviet concoction published in the West.

Filipp Savich's feet began to itch again, and he drew a heavy breath through tightly compressed lips. There is no reliable cure for nervous eczema. You just have to put up with it: sometimes the itch affects the groin, then moves on to the thighs. Just as well the rash rarely spread to his hands, and even when it did, it was scarcely noticeable: nobody had spotted it yet. Hands are an important matter in our business. Our business involves a lot of hand-shaking. This isn't the army, you know, comrades.

He had once seen an army colonel, a regular Adonis, whose heroic looks would have been a boon to any film producer. This colonel never removed his gloves, even at the dinner table, because his hands were covered all over obscenely with eczema. The colonel's lips were tightly pursed, making his mouth a little lop-sided, which added an almost unbearable glamour to his aristocratic features. The poor man had been suffering all his life, and grown accustomed to it. Still, he carried out his duties in an exemplary manner, and it was clear that the ever-present gloves would be no obstacle to his future career. For a moment, Filipp Savich had experienced a feeling of kinship with that colonel, even though the latter could know nothing of Filipp Savich's hidden agony – as very few people did. The two of them had got along very well, and Filipp Savich remembered the colonel with warmth. The recollection would perk him up in such difficult moments.

Filipp Savich flung open the window: the heating was working full blast, never mind the waste of energy. Heat always aggravates eczema. A pleasant, cool breeze stirred the papers on the desk, and Filipp Savich returned to them.

Arseni was doing good work with the Storyteller. They had been seen together . . . here was a list of dates and places from other sources. Arseni had brought in agents of influence: introduced them to the Storyteller, revived old acquaintances, organized a party. The agents of influence were doing very well, especially Kuzma and Snow White. These two were particularly valuable because they did not realize they were being used; freethinking intellectuals they considered themselves.

Throwing a writer in prison is far too crude a solution. Under the current thinking, such methods are to be avoided. Our preferred strategy is educational. We create a proper milieu for the writer. A representative sample, as psychologists say. Social gatherings in Moscow kitchens have much to recommend them to this end.

In fact all was going well except for the fact that Pulin's manuscript had not been located. Time was pressing. Filipp Savich turned his attention to the results of a secret search of the Storyteller's apartment in his absence. Interesting. It looked as

though the Storyteller had no new manuscripts in his possession, not even of his own. No notes, no diaries, no letters from
friends, if you didn't count New Year's greeting cards. There
were some letters from readers, but these were mainly written
by children. Manuscripts of published works were stashed in
boxes on shelves under the ceiling, and all covered with undis-
turbed dust. But what work was he engaged on? What did he
do, this Storyteller? Publication of his latest book had been
deferred, so he should be hard at work on another one – everyone has to eat, after all. The only useful thing yielded by the
search was his telephone and address book.

Maybe Arseni had scared him off by pushing too hard?

'Hello, Viktor Stepanych? Would you come to my room,
please?'

Viktor Stepanych, a young man in a neat grey suit, entered
and tried not to shiver. He had heard accounts of Filipp Savich's
legendary stamina from his earliest days with the Committee –
back in the days when he was still learning that in the circles into
which he had been so generously admitted, it was not the done
thing to speak of the KGB, but to refer to it simply as 'the
Committee'. The chain of association in his head was clear and
simple: first came the Committee, within the Committee came
the Fifth Directorate, the head of the Directorate was Filipp
Savich and they were his crew. Filipp Savich always had his
window – or at least the small ventilation window – wide open
no matter how cold it might be outside. He seemed impervious
to the cold – amazing man that he was. All the staff of the Fifth
Directorate knew Filipp Savich's love of fresh air, and would
make sure that their rooms were sufficiently cold if they had
reason to expect that he would call in.

Viktor Stepanych managed to hold his superior's eyes
without fidgeting. He was properly respectful and attentive. A
good worker, he could go far.

'Things are not looking good, Viktor Stepanych. Not good at
all. A lot of effort has been expended, we've got a mountain of

documentation, but where are the results? Do you think you're working in a hospital? Or a secondary school?'

Viktor Stepanych, being a good worker and knowing Filipp Savich's little ways, prudently refrained from answering.

'Let's hear your latest plans.'

'Filipp Savich, we'll hold Arseni back for a while. He can be ill, or go away somewhere – say, for ten days. His latest instructions were not to try to offer the Storyteller any money. He's got this bad habit of trying to help the needy.'

'Has he already tried to give him money?'

'He says he hasn't.'

'Right. Go on.'

'We're tapping the Storyteller's phone, and also the widow's and Arseni's. Of course, we're looking at the mail, too.'

'Do you have any new ideas?'

'The Swings, Filipp Savich.'

'That's better! Only don't overdo it.'

'Nothing physical, of course, Filipp Savich!'

'No more heart-attacks. You answer for his well-being with your head. At this stage.'

The 'Swings' plan was worked out, amended and approved the same day. The Storyteller's case had now entered another category: operational procedures.

Chapter Four

NIKOLIN SUFFERED FROM an annoying tendency to wake between three and four o'clock in the morning. Not necessarily as a result of bad dreams, although he had his share of those. These awakenings in the dead of night were particularly unpleasant in his youth, when he was living in a hostel. At that time he had set it down to chance circumstances and felt ready to strangle whoever was snoring – as at least one person invariably was. It seemed to him that were it not for that pest wheezing like a chainsaw, he would have had no trouble dropping back off to sleep. Instead of which, Nikolin would catch himself unconsciously breathing in time with those infuriating snores, and lie there seething with impotent rage.

Only later did it emerge that the hostel had nothing to do with his problem. Still, it was a long time before Nikolin, being free to get up and switch on the light without bothering anyone, began to think of doing so. And so it went on. Once, some six months after they were married, he complained about it to Lucia. Instead of offering the expected sympathy, she burst out laughing in what Nikolin felt was a very heartless way. Seeing that she had offended him, Lucia hugged his head to her breast.

'My poor samurai,' she crooned.

'Let go, you madwoman, you'll break my neck!'

'Rubbish, I'll only twist it a little, and nobody will know the difference.'

She stretched unerringly to a top shelf and pulled down a book, which she thrust at Nikolin, already open at the right page. She had an uncanny knack for locating whatever she wanted in their huge mountain of books just as easily as if she were pulling a lipstick out of her purse.

From what he read it appeared that Japanese samurai frequently rose at three o'clock in the morning and devoted an hour or so to practising such arts as swordsmanship, calligraphy and even music. Nikolin found the last hard to believe.

'For heaven's sake, they have paper walls in their houses!'

However, after giving the matter some thought, he concluded that while making music in the small hours was a question for the samurai's own conscience, this was indeed a special time. Lucia herself immediately launched into an enthusiastic monologue about unity with the cosmos, the hour of the bull, this being the time when monks got up to pray for mankind, when geniuses throughout history did their best work – with a further aside on the nocturnal rituals of the Melanesian islanders.

The monks would not be too thrilled to be mixed up with that lot, thought Nikolin, watching her fondly. He had not yet become fully accustomed to the idea that she was his wife. When she got worked up about something, and this happened very often, even her hair seemed to crackle with energy, like a cat's: touch it, and sparks would fly.

Primitive tribesmen, monks, Tibetan lamas and samurai warriors fitted into her world as comfortably as furry toys under a child's blanket.

He said as much, and she flashed back a quick question.

'What did you take to bed with you when you were small?'

Nikolin gave the matter some thought.

'There was this celluloid crocodile which I dragged around everywhere.'

'There, you see!'

She immediately made up a cheeky little rhyme about a crocodile who swallowed a Young Pioneer, and snorted when Nikolin pulled a face.

'Di-i-isgusting!'

'Absolutely! But you're the aesthetic one, so it's divine retribution that you should be up and working during the night. You'll write an earth-shaking novel, and I'll sleep so as not to be in your way. You've got a lamp on your desk, haven't you?'

So this became their routine. Nikolin did not have the courage to start on an earth-shaking novel, but continued writing as he had begun: children's stories, which found favour among adults, too, and adventure stories for boys, full of sails, home-made bows and arrows and deadly harpoons. The children's stories were published more frequently than the others, which were rather too far removed from the realities of the Young Pioneers. One story, which centred around underwater diving and hunting, was vetoed on the grounds that children might decide to try it for themselves, and someone would be injured by a 'spear gun' – a stick launched with the help of a stout piece of elastic.

However, Nikolin noted that even writing stories for young children was easier and better when there was nobody around: when the world consisted of the table lamp, with its lowered shade, a yellowish stack of paper and a pencil, and the surrounding darkness from which all sorts of fantasies could be conjured up. He disliked using a typewriter, and resorted to it only for typing up the completed piece of work, editing it as he went along and keeping in mind the demands of the censor. He had no trouble 'coursing a hare' in front of the typewriter, silly lump of metal that it was.

When he first explained to Lucia what 'coursing a hare' meant, thinking that she would find it funny, she burst into unaccountable tears. For several days after that she felt sorry for Nikolin and, unpredictable creature that she was, even started serving him coffee in bed.

Nikolin rubbed a tired hand across his face and rocked back in his chair. It was getting light, and the slight feverishness which always accompanied the completion of a task well done had passed. He felt as though he were emerging from under an anaesthetic – slight nausea, a racking sensation in the joints and the feeling of imminent pain creeping up from nearby.

Time to make coffee. Lucia would not be bringing it. Lucia doesn't make coffee any more. Ever. The pain had lessened after five years, as was to be expected. Nikolin no longer thought 'there she goes!' in the street, as had happened so often in those first terrible months. The same coat, the same hair, just about to turn the corner. He would start running after her, then pull up in sudden realization of the truth, and feel a terrible, twisting pain somewhere near his heart: no, she's no longer here. Not at all. That can't be her walking along the street.

It was different now, but even the dull pain that remained was exhausting. An exhaustion that had to be carefully hidden, so that nobody should graze the sore spot with a careless touch.

He sipped his coffee with pleasure. A cup of coffee and a morning cigarette were a sacred ritual. His head spun slightly, but everything inside seemed to perk up and resume its normal position. He pulled out a screwdriver and felt for the head of the bolt with practised ease. Now, we'll just put all the papers into a file. Nice little file, that, made out of thin plastic. Someone had brought it from Poland. The file slipped into its place, and Nikolin screwed back the bolt.

Next – the wastepaper basket. The good thing about writing with a pencil is that there are fewer sheets to throw away. You want to change something – you erase it, and carry on. Nikolin pulled the two discarded sheets out of the basket and tore them into tiny pieces, just as Pavel had taught him, and flushed them down the toilet. Long live the domestic conveniences of the big city. Another hour, and Auntie Xenia would be around to clean. He shaved and dressed unhurriedly, then opened the balcony door. It was snowing lightly, the flakes fine and dry. How about that – and to think it had started to thaw yesterday. Nikolin breathed the frosty air, deeply and with pleasure, driving out the residue of nicotine from his lungs. A nice morning. Just the ticket. Grey with white flecks.

He wandered back to the table and tore open a thick envelope of letters from readers. He had dropped round to the editorial office of the children's journal *Salute* yesterday, and they had given him his mail. Grateful readers send the writer letters care of the editorial office, where else? There was only one envelope addressed in an adult hand. Nikolin opened it first, leaving the children's letters for later. Children's letters are always a joy to read, even the silliest.

Tatyana Kuzina . . . wait a moment, that rings a bell. Heavens, of course, Tanechka, they were in the same class at school in Lipetsk! Yes, he remembered her, she had a fringe, and had shown him how to dance at a school social at which he had cringed from shyness. He hadn't seen her since leaving school.

Tanya wrote that she was now living in Moscow, on Kachalov street, with her twelve-year-old daughter . . . Lord, how time flies! The daughter had been to a Pioneers' camp that summer, where there had been three issues of *Salute* containing his story about a boy who went to get a dog from a deserted dacha. The girl had been entranced by this story, told her mother about it, and when the author's name came up, Tanya couldn't help wondering whether it might not be the same Anton who used to be able to stand on one hand and who made an inkwell explode in geography class, or simply someone with the same name – in which case she apologized for bothering him. She added her phone number.

Amazing! Kachalov street was a mere two blocks away from the Writers' Club! Just think, they could have passed in the street any number of times without recognizing each other. He'd give her a call. Or maybe even drop in, to give the young girl the thrill of meeting a real live writer.

The next four letters aimed straight for the jugular: why hadn't there been any more in the last two numbers of the journal about the boy who managed to tag along with a geologists' expedition? The story had stopped at the most interesting point, so how about the rest? And what happened to the bear?

One insistent youngster from Aktyubinsk even begged Nikolin to send him the whole manuscript to read and promised faithfully to return it as soon as he was through. Nikolin sighed. He already knew that there would be no continuation of that story which the children's magazine *Bonfire* had published. In fact, they had received a severe reprimand from the relevant quarters for the uneducational nature of the story, and another for not seeing this for themselves and allowing the story into print in the first place.

The next letter ran as follows:

Dear A.S. Nikolin,

    I know why your books aren't published any more. You're a good and honest man, and they're all bastards so they hate you. I hate them too – you know who I mean. My dad says that people like you would have been shot under Stalin, and that they'll soon be shooting you again, and so they should. I hate my dad, too, because he hits me with his belt and kicks me. I have decided to run away and come and live with you, so I've already formed an organization, there's six of us, and you'll be our leader. We'll show them who's going to do the shooting. Please send me your address because I don't know where you live.

    Goodbye for now.

Efim Motovilov

Nikolin emitted a low whistle. Strange letter, that. Unpleasant. He could just imagine a departmental meeting at the Writers' Union. Or how he would be hauled up on the carpet by the administration. And how the letter would be waved in the air and read out publicly.

You see where we are, comrades? Some influence our Soviet writer Nikolin is exercising over the rising generation! No, no – this is not a coincidence. For instance, Maria Ivanovna here doesn't get letters like this, does she? Maria Ivanovna, have you ever, in twenty years of working in children's literature, received anything like this from a child? You see, comrades? Membership of anti-Soviet organizations isn't offered to just anybody. This, comrades, is a political matter, and we must react to it as vigilant Bolsheviks . . .

Nikolin groaned and twisted the letter around in his hands. The flap was firmly glued down, and the writer had made strokes along the join. The strokes all matched up . . . but that didn't mean a thing. A child's ploy, and one which would only attract attention: what secrets could the letter contain? He wondered whether they had unsealed and read the letter in the office. On one hand, this was unlikely: the girls who were supposed to deal with correspondence were all lazy and careless, and would hardly manufacture work for themselves. They had enough to do with their own letters, they felt. It was an open secret that any number of letters were quietly thrown away without being opened. They'd put aside the ones addressed by name, and pass them on to the writer himself to handle. On the other hand – those strokes . . . They could arouse feminine curiosity or even a rare urge to act conscientiously, in which case the next thing would be: 'Here, Josif Sanych, look at this strange envelope that has arrived for Nikolin!'

Then again, this was not the first letter that used this childish ruse to ensure confidentiality. What about that teenager who had already written twice, saying that she had her passport and wanted to find out if her favourite writer was married? She'd put strokes on the envelope flap, too. If one reckoned up how many young women sent letters to writers . . . Anyway, these strokes were of no importance. Children drew rabbits and heavens knows what else on envelopes.

But the question refused to go away, and Nikolin read the letter again. He found it hard to estimate the writer's age. The handwriting was that of an eight or nine year old at most, but the contents suggested someone older. And wasn't the writing a bit too artistically scrawled? Children usually try very hard when they write, copying and recopying their letter to make it look good.

The more he thought about it, the less Nikolin liked the whole business. He pulled himself up sharply. If he went on like this, God knows what else he'd dream up. There was no end to his imaginings. He screwed up the letter and the envelope, put them in the ashtray and set a match to them. He'd received no such letter, and that was that. The smell of burnt paper dissipated quickly, and then Auntie Xenia rapped on the door.

'You'll catch your death of cold in there doing your exercises, Anton Semyonych! And you so sick not long ago! You seen what they've written about the Americans today? Damn parasites, they are, with their bases. You wouldn't like a kitten, by any chance? There's been one on the first-floor landing since yesterday, crying like a baby. I'd take it myself, but my Cleopatra would tear it to shreds – terrible tempers these Persians have, that's for sure. And mine's worse than most. She wouldn't put up with him for a moment, fiend that she is. You going to go out today? I thought I'd clean the top cupboards. Look, you've thrown your socks around all over the place again. Are these to go in the wash, or what? My legs are that swollen today, you wouldn't believe. Must be the weather . . .'

Auntie Xenia didn't stand on any ceremony with Nikolin: she berated him for smoking, for not eating proper meals and for not dressing in a manner befitting his position. She did as she liked in his flat, treating it much as her own. She had been on good terms with Lucia and they had often performed little neighbourly services for each other. After Lucia's death, she looked after Nikolin as though he were a small child. It had somehow been decided automatically that she would do his cleaning and ironing for a small sum. Nikolin was not annoyed by her tirades, in fact he rather enjoyed them. Auntie Xenia had knocked out two German tanks near Moscow while still a young girl, and had a medal to prove it. Since then, her character had gone from strength to strength. Nowadays, she could be sent to tackle tanks bare-handed. Nikolin listened obediently as she ordered him to go out and buy food – his fridge was empty, and she, Auntie Xenia, needed a packet of vermicelli, four hundred grams of sausages and a packet of cottage cheese. Because her legs were swollen.

The lift was under repair, so Nikolin took the stairs. He limped slightly: either it was the weather making his knee ache, or the troublesome joint was playing up in sympathy with the lift. He'd wrenched that knee badly in his young days, imagining that he was a skiing champion as he hurtled down a steep hillside. Since then, the knee would remind him of its existence from time to time, for no obvious reason. Not too often, thank heaven. Who knows, it might stop playing up altogether by the time he turned eighty.

The kitten was still on the first-floor landing, and began mewing pathetically at the sight of a human being. Nikolin looked away and skirted the little animal. Really, you'd think one of the neighbours would take it in. Nikolin felt disturbed. Something nagged at him. For no reason.

The Swings had moved smoothly into first position.

Chapter Five

FILIPP SAVICH STUDIED the little tin with keen interest, turning it around in his hands as if that would help him decipher the Chinese characters embossed on its surface. The tin was from Hong Kong, gilded, and decorated with a red tiger. The tiger looked highly aroused.

Many and varied are the materials needed for the Committee's operations. The government supplies these materials on a reasonable if not unduly generous basis. Sufficient, but not too much over. Getting supplies is a straightforward matter: you write up a requisition, stating your reasons and the quantity. The requisition is then forwarded to the relevant authorities. They, naturally, will cut down the quantity, so the request should be for more than is really needed. Sometimes this would annoy Filipp Savich: damned bureaucracy, damned nuisance. But he knew that it was the government's job to practise economy. They couldn't not decrease the quantities requisitioned. That was the way the System functioned, and it was too risky to change things. There had been only one man in the history of the System who occasionally brooked no cuts. Indeed, sometimes he even went the other way.

'You need two hundred tanks for this operation? Have two thousand, but make sure that the city gets taken. It's your head on the block if you fail.'

'Yes, comrade Stalin!'

Filipp Savich sighed. Yes, that was magnificent. But for all that, it belonged to history, to revolutionary romanticism. Not the sort of thing we need today. What we need now is stability. Then there would be fewer heads to roll in the Committee. No amount of romanticism, from Filipp Savich's point of view, was worth being woken up at three o'clock in the morning to be dragged off to a tile-walled room equipped with a drain and hose-pipe, where – a whack across the teeth with an iron bar, then lower down, and then even lower . . . No, better requisition more, and let those higher up practise economy.

The tin in Filipp Savich's hand was something he had not ordered before. Other methods existed, had indeed been used, but their effectiveness left something to be desired. This particular panacea had been recommended to him by an old friend, who was a big noise in the merchant navy. This friend had once had to sort out a very tricky situation at sea, having to get to the bottom of some nonsense that had got into the heads of an entire shipload of upstanding Soviet seamen. A real nightmare that had been: an emergency situation outside Soviet waters!

The tin contained a hundred tablets, and the requisition had stated that these were needed for operations connected with the Storyteller. Filipp Savich unscrewed the lid. The tablets were cream-coloured, very small and completely odourless. A whole hundred was a bit too much for the Storyteller. Now, if he were over fifty years of age . . . but no, even that would be a bit rich. Filipp Savich counted out twenty, and hefted the gilt box in his hands for a moment. Nice little box, pity to waste it. As for the operation, what difference did the packaging make? He opened a desk drawer and pulled out a small white plastic container, emptied the twenty tablets into it, and tucked the gilt box with the tiger away in his safe. Might be an idea to finish work early today.

There was a time when Filipp Savich had been hideously embarrassed by his eczema, and had avoided women in his youth: it would be downright humiliating to undress with such a complaint. Later on he realized that he had been silly. He hadn't understood the nature of feminine love. But at the very start of his career, when order was being reimposed on the army after the war – a task naturally entrusted to the Committee, though it went by another name in those days – a report came in concerning rampant immorality in one of the assault regiments, with the colonel named as the main offender. According to the report, no woman, and especially no young woman, was safe from the colonel's importuning – whether in camp, in the neighbouring villages or out on manoeuvres. It was here that Filipp Savich made the acquaintance of that remarkable colonel whom we have already met, and whose eczema was no secret. Filipp Savich was deeply impressed. How about that! It was patently obvious that the colonel had no inhibitions about caressing women with his gloved hands, and that women had no hesitation in responding.

So much was clear that Filipp Savich did not even bother to clarify the facts. Very ably, he managed to extricate the colonel from his predicament, even though at that time it involved him in considerable risk. He acted out of solidarity: what draws people closer together than mutual suffering? He was also sincerely grateful for the lesson he had learned. Instead of the colonel, he put the informer behind bars, which in those days was easy as winking. They say that not a single good deed goes unpunished. However, everything went off without a hitch, and he accepted his own and the colonel's good luck as a benign stroke of fate. From that time on he shed his ridiculous complex, and women welcomed his advances. On top of that, his nerves settled down, so the outbreaks of eczema became fewer and milder, bothering him only during the central-heating season. Not surprisingly, he ached to make up for lost time, but for that he had the rest of his life before him. At that time, indeed, almost the whole of it.

After putting away the little tin, he reached for the phone.

'Viktor Stepanych? Come in, would you?' Filipp Savich had big plans for Viktor Stepanych. The young man showed signs of turning out to be a good analyst, he was not going to be stuck in these trifling jobs for long. Moreover, as he went up the ladder he would be indebted to Filipp Savich for every promotion, remembering who it was who had raised him from nothing . . .

Viktor Stepanych had not been idle. As a promising young officer, he had been trusted to devise an operation independently for the first time. And he had excelled himself: what plans he'd brought for Filipp Savich's approval! Brilliant plans! He sat still as a statue, trying to conceal his anxiety, betrayed only by the flush on his face. He forced himself not to stare at Filipp Savich, just giving the occasional quick glance out of the corner of his eye, trying to guess which page Filipp Savich was reading now. And now?

Filipp Savich finished reading, pushed back the files and sighed loudly.

'That's some imagination you've got there, I must say. Enough for the whole Writers' Union. How come you haven't considered an alien encounter?'

Viktor Stepanych was so dazzled by the sheer magnificence of this idea, that he missed the increased affability in Filipp Savich's voice.

'I say, that would *really* be something, Filipp Savich! We could have this strange light appearing in his windows for about a week – he never shuts his blinds. Then, a mysterious phone call: be ready, we'll explain everything when we meet. Then – at night, of course – an alien from who knows where on his balcony. He wouldn't even have to be a little green man. An ordinary sort of person, dressed a bit strangely and with unusual gestures – just a little out of the ordinary, no overdoing it. The whole thing could be very finely orchestrated. This alien could say something to the effect that we're pushed for time, and we haven't had the opportunity to find out everything about your civilization. It might be worth haggling about a memory-wipe after the encounter. I tell you, Filipp Savich, the Storyteller will sing like a canary! And he'll hand over the manuscript for sure: I mean, it's a sight better than just sending it abroad! After that – we put him to sleep. Not bad, don't you think?'

Filipp Savich burst out laughing, and continued chuckling to himself like an indulgent grandfather. A bit hot-headed, this young son of a bitch, but he'd definitely go far! Then the laughter stopped abruptly.

'Maybe you'd like to bring Hollywood in on this? Get them to make a remote-controlled robot or something? And out of pure gold, for special effect? But you tell me, how will the Committee pay for all that, eh? And just for a routine operation with an errant writer!'

The light went out on Viktor Stepanych's face, as though someone inside him had flipped a switch.

'Now, don't get downhearted,' continued Filipp Savich. 'We train you young ones to make sure you succeed. You have to think economically, Vitya. Crisply, imaginatively, but without frills. And act economically. Aim for minimal action with maximum results. As for the dramatic effects – well, your subject will provide those for himself. He's the Storyteller, after all. You've not done badly. I particularly like this bit, and this, and this too. The rest is elaborate nonsense. However, there's one aspect you've completely overlooked, and that's something I find disappointing. Come on, I'll give you one guess, what did you miss?'

However, try as he might, Viktor Stepanych failed to spot the omission, and had to be prompted by his mentor.

'Have you ever heard of a monk being a member of the Writers' Union? Or a member of the Writers' Union being a monk?'

Viktor Stepanych's face lit up like that of a schoolboy who had finally found the answer to a particularly difficult problem.

'Of course, Filipp Savich! A woman! No, two would be better, so the only question would be which one he'll choose.'

'Not which one – both,' corrected Filipp Savich testily. 'Play on the difference. You like stereo sound, don't you? Better than mono, isn't it? Look through the birds we've got on file, choose some good ones, call them out and give them their instructions. I'd suggest you consider Forget-me-not. The lady's not in her first youth, but she could wipe the floor with our younger agents. And she's as clever as a snake. She's never failed us once.'

Viktor Stepanych nodded keenly, but suddenly blushed crimson.

'Filipp Savich, these birds – I've . . . er . . . never had to instruct them before. Perhaps you'd give me a few pointers . . . I mean, I get the general drift, but specifically . . . Well, what kind of expressions do I use?'

Filipp Savich erupted.

'Damn it, what have they been teaching you? Do I have to chew everything over and put it into your mouth? What expressions, indeed! He doesn't know the expressions, if you please! You ask Forget-me-not, she'll teach you! Go on, get out of my sight, and get cracking. A waste of time, messing around with you all . . .'

He flung up his hands, but switched to a milder tone: who was to teach these tyros, if not an older, experienced comrade?

'For the future, remember this: if you don't want to tackle a subject head on, make use of examples. Like, there was once a bad man, who engaged in undesirable activities, and who had to be stopped. So a valiant woman, one of our agents, distracted him from what he was doing. And she did it in a way that gave our operatives enough time to get the situation under control. As a reward for her work, the agent received a 600-rouble bonus for New Year, as well as an imported sheepskin coat and improved living conditions. And so on . . . got it? Oh, one other thing: take these and give them to the bird. It's something quite new. One tablet in any drink – tea, alcohol, doesn't matter – and it'll arouse a man like a bull-moose at mating time. At least, that's what the scientists claim.'

He handed Viktor Stepanych the little white plastic box.

Viktor Stepanych sat in a comfortable, tapestry-upholstered armchair and thought about the forthcoming meeting. The dacha was warm, its walls faced with oak panels, and the carpet under his feet was the thick variety once favoured by prosperous merchants. There are a number of such dachas in the Moscow region, unremarkable from the outside, but extremely well-equipped inside. No naughty schoolboys ever sneak into their grounds to steal apples, and couldn't even if they tried. Nor are they ever burgled by the Moscow riff-raff; their windows are never smashed, nor are their bath-houses set on fire. There is no access for the riff-raff, and there won't be. No children are ever to be found at these dachas, there are no pensioners, no cats and dogs, no strawberry beds laid out around them, no sign of chickens. Not even birds build their nests in the vicinity, though that is really very strange, considering the surrounding peace and quiet. But the fact remains that they don't build nests and raise fledglings. Science has not turned its attention to this phenomenon yet, so it remains unexplained.

Forget-me-not should be arriving any moment now, but could be a bit late as she had to make her way over from Akulova Hill. Viktor Stepanych had completed all his preparations. All the necessary materials had been conscientiously assembled. He allowed himself a tot of Stolichnaya just to loosen up a bit. He opened the pill-box and counted the tablets, then lapsed into thought. It's all very well to say 'hand them over', but how many should he give? Filipp Savich's precepts about economy and minimal action had taken strong hold of his mind. He dropped three tablets into a tiny glass bottle. That should be more than enough. Especially if this Forget-me-not was such hot stuff. The others would come in useful elsewhere. They'd make a terrific gift, and it would be interesting to know just how a bull-moose feels in rut. He'd thought everything through, the only thing he hadn't settled on was the tone of the forthcoming conversation. Should it be brisk and businesslike? Or slightly playful and casual? Or –

And here she was: a fringe peeping out from under a grey fur hat, high boots, a glimpse of knees clad in fishnet stockings. She was certainly a stunner, and it was impossible to guess her age.

'Viktor Stepanych? Why, you're so young! I'd imagined you quite differently.'

He took a few slow, deep breaths through his nose to stop himself from blushing, and hurried forward to take her coat.

'How do you do, Forget-me-not. Please take a seat.'

'Goodness, aren't you polite! Now tell me all about it.'

Viktor Stepanych didn't know what to do with his hands. When you're sitting behind a desk, there's no problem. But when you're in a dacha, with two armchairs, a low coffee table – he could hardly put his hands on that. He picked up the stack of files and began flipping through them.

'We've got an assignment for you, Forget-me-not. The subject is a very withdrawn type of person. A writer. His wife had a mental breakdown in 1962 after the death of their three-year-old daughter. She tried to commit suicide. He stuck by her, though. She was given psychiatric treatment, and seemed cured. He took her down to the Crimea to convalesce. That was in the summer of '64. She drowned. Since then he's retreated into himself, and that's no good. We're going to have our hands full working on him. Mind you, we once had a similar case. The fellow was a world-class musician who took a whole lot of nonsense into his head. However, a lovely woman, a true patriot, brought him back to normal. We worked with him a bit more later, and he became just like everyone else, our Soviet man. He's got any number of international awards. That contact worked really well.'

She gave Viktor Stepanych a long, sparkling look.

'How far should I go with this contact?'

Viktor Stepanych choked, battling to keep his composure.

'We don't limit our operatives' initiative.'

'Fine. Who do I have to get him away from?'

'He's got no permanent attachments.'

'Is he impotent?'

'No. His file shows that he's physically normal.'

'Just buttoned up, then. Can I have a look at his file?'

'Yes, of course. And here's his photo.'

'Say, he's not bad-looking! I like grey eyes.'

She settled herself comfortably, tucking her legs under herself, and began leafing through the file.

Viktor Stepanych tore his own grey eyes away from her knees and began to study the pale yellow roses on the carpet. Forget-me-not knew exactly which pages to consult in the bulky files and scanned them quickly, murmuring the occasional comment.

'Ah-ha . . . what a sweetie-pie . . . so that's the way you like to do it . . . and you don't mind the French way, either, no shyness there . . . how about from the back? . . . and with a little candle . . . Hates rows . . . doesn't like partings, just walks away . . . hasn't been spotted with males . . . He's not a weirdo, is he, Viktor Stepanych?'

'What do you mean?'

'I mean, he's not likely to want to have a go at me with a belt, or tie me to the bed, or anything like that?'

'We've nothing to indicate that.'

'All right, we'll manage. Now then, what do we like by way of clothes? Mmm, nice . . . and undies with a bit of black showing from under red . . . Lovely man . . . Can I take some notes?'

'Yes, only –'

'Don't worry, I know the drill. Anyone finds it, they'll think I've been to a fortune teller: a king of clubs type, likes stockings, hates tights, prefers sherry to vodka, leaves his condoms at home . . . Do I work on him at my own discretion, or is there a cover?'

'There is. You're his classmate.'

'But he's forty!'

'We-e-ll, women are always better preserved than men. And kids sometimes start school a year early . . .'

'In other words, I have to be at least thirty-nine? Tell me, Viktor Stepanych, was this your idea?'

'But you're –' he started to expostulate, then hurriedly bit off the rest.

Who would believe that this furious predator had been purring like a kitten a few moments ago? The pupils of Forget-me-not's eyes slowly dilated and narrowed. Viktor Stepanych tensed involuntarily and braced his legs. However, she made no movement, even her face remained perfectly still. The look she gave Viktor Stepanych was like a bullet between the eyes, but then she smiled slightly.

'All right, all right. Now, I'm going to need special clothes for this job.'

'What special clothes?'

'For a start – French knickers from De la Roche, a dozen pairs at least. More would be fine, but not a pair less. Make a note of it. Bras – here, let me write down the make, or you'll make a cock-up of it. I can see you don't know anything about these things. Stockings . . . Look, it'll be easier if I write out the list myself.'

She leaned forward for the sheet of paper, then flopped back in her chair and began to write quickly. When she asked for a second sheet, Viktor Stepanych felt moved to utter a faint protest.

'Isn't that a bit much?'

'Not at all! Otherwise, what do we have? A Soviet agent going out on a job wearing East German crap like this?'

Before he could blink, she was out of her chair and had whipped up her skirt; her knickers were exactly at Viktor Stepanych's eye-level. They looked all right to him: a snug fit with bits of lace here and there. Forget-me-not twirled around, to give Viktor Stepanych every chance to assure himself of the dire quality of East German workmanship.

'You say you don't limit your operatives' initiative, but yet you can't supply your agents with proper special clothes. Aren't you ashamed of yourself? Honestly, I feel embarrassed on behalf of our country. Knickers like this aren't good for anything but seducing snotty-nosed twenty year olds!'

'Forget-me-not, this is intolerable,' spluttered Viktor Stepanych, faint but persistent.

'Why don't you complain to Filipp Savich, then? Tell him you find me impossible to work with. Surprise him.'

No, there was nothing to be done about the wretched woman. Moreover, judging by the length of time she had been an agent, it was quite possible that she had worked closely with Filipp Savich in the past. After all, he hadn't always been head of the Fifth Directorate. Forget-me-not, meanwhile, continued pressing her point.

'And another thing – sorry to interrupt! – that case you mentioned earlier on. You didn't get round to telling me what reward this patriotic woman got for her efforts. An Austrian sheepskin coat, or some Romanian piece of junk? And what about living conditions? I'm a married woman, so I find these things important.'

To give Viktor Stepanych his due, he surrendered graciously.

'Come now, why so modest about the reward? You're a highly valued operator! A better apartment, a sheepskin coat . . . all that goes without saying! Nowadays, the prospects are much greater. The Committee's expanding, there's a lot of work abroad – for those who have proved themselves capable, naturally. Let's be friends! As for the special clothing – well, I was simply thinking of the poor sap on our payroll who is going to have to spend half a day digging through women's underwear making up the requisition.'

Forget-me-not giggled.

'Yes, and everyone staring at him and thinking he's a queer!

53

There he'll be, buying knickers by the ton, because our request will be reduced, but the guys higher up will make the figure larger to get a cut for themselves! Can't you just see him, staggering home, dog-tired, and then his wife takes a peek, to see what he's brought home . . .'

This time they both had a good laugh, and settled the remaining details of the operation quite amicably. She accepted the tablets with good-natured interest.

Chapter Six

'NO, IT'S NOT that I'm against getting it, it's just that I'm sick and tired of hearing nothing but "get me this, get me that" all the time! First it's jeans, then it's trainers, now it's a cassette player ... And what does this all lead to? How does it affect your intellect, your soul? Your entire outlook on life starts and ends with jeans! In other words – all your interests are below the belt!' stormed Koretsky senior. In his agitation, he had slammed a cup of coffee down on the polished table, and was now furiously scrubbing with a paper napkin at the stain which remained from the spills.

Koretsky junior, being a shrewd young man, made no attempt to interrupt his father. He knew that these outbursts of righteous indignation about the shortcomings of modern youth were perfectly normal and restored his parent's equilibrium. Father was an intellectual, after all. Moreover, he would soon run out of steam and be back to his old self. The son could afford to listen to the father attentively, even sympathetically. After a while, he chose the right moment to say the right thing.

'Dad, nobody's saying that matters of the soul shouldn't come first.'

'Well, and where do they come with you young people? What do you want from life, you tell me that!'

'I can't,' admitted Dima readily. 'Can you tell me what your generation wanted from life?'

'Our generation, our generation! We wanted the war to end, that's what! And to win.'

'No, but before the war? And after? You can't blame us that
there's no war now to justify your generalization. Do I have any
right to lump all the people of your generation together and ask,
what do you want? You, and, say, a tractor driver from Irkutsk,
and some bastard of a bureaucrat? Do you have common spir-
itual needs?'

'That, my dear son, is chopping logic. And changing the
subject.'

'Then, Dad, I've got nothing to say on the subject. I think all
those declarations "in the name of Soviet youth" are downright
unethical. Who are these "young people" you want to identify
me with?'

Dima's shafts were well aimed. He was a late and only child.
Where did his contemporaries come into the equation – why
should his father worry about them? No, this was simply a case
of parental anxiety.

Koretsky senior ran a hand over his chin, the way he always
did when he was worried.

'All right, you're a unique personality, and I'm not lumping
you in with anyone. I'm just concerned that you should be
heading in the right direction. All that materialism . . .'

'But Dad, don't you see? I don't ask you to get me tickets to
the Taganka theatre, do I? No, I get them myself in my own way.
I don't ask you to get me tapes of Vysotsky's songs, because I
know how to get them better than you would. Everything I read
– from the Bible through to hatha yoga – I get myself. And not
from the library, obviously. It's not my fault that I have to find
ways to get these things myself. Do I burden you with my spir-
itual requirements? And for that matter, do you think a double
cassette-player is a purely material matter? Mightn't it have a
higher purpose? How do you rate music?'

'Well, I know what music you're talking about! I listened to
what you were playing once, and it's nothing but wails and
grunts.'

'That's because of the quality of the recording. And that's why

I want a proper player – it'll make all the difference. Anyway, what would you like me to listen to? Tell you what – let's switch on the radio. Our very own platform of Soviet culture.'

He twiddled the knobs sardonically, skipping over a survey of international news and a talk about the evils of alcohol.

'. . . And now – we begin our programme of popular songs with "My love, far away",' came the dulcet tones of the announcer. 'The music by Komitevich, the words by Belokon.'

Koretsky senior perked up immediately.

'So, what do you have against that? Back in '43 we wrote down the words of that song and learned them by heart. Wounded soldiers used to cry, just listening to it. And not just the wounded, for that matter. You're so demanding when it comes to poetry. You know and understand it. So listen to this song, and then tell me what you object to in it. Does it sound false? Or written to order?'

They listened in silence until the song ended. It was a good song. And the music straightforward, yet not too banal. Just the kind of thing a soldier could hum to himself. Before battle, when every sense is heightened, but underlying all is that deep peace that comes from being at one with one's fate.

It was only when the rousing bravado of the next song – 'Oh, the fields of my collective farm / Oh, blue skies up above' – filled the air-waves that Dima glanced at his father with a conciliatory smile.

'See, Dad? One good song – but how much rubbish alongside? D'you know, I had no idea that that time-serving old hack had ever written poetry. I'm not saying a word against the song, it's got power and was written by a poet. Maybe it's just someone with the same name? I've heard it before, of course, but never made any connection . . . Can it really be by the same guy who's on the *October* magazine?'

Dima's father was pleased by his son's objectivity, but in response to this question could only spread his hands in agreement.

'"There are more things in heaven and earth, Horatio . . ."'

Naturally, he agreed to get the cassette player. After all, it would be Dima's twentieth birthday in a month's time. So Dima did not have to resort to the usual argument that clinched matters, when it came to higher issues: 'It's not as if I'm asking you to get me something by Solzhenitsyn!' He loved his father and tried to spare his nerves whenever possible.

Dima and Petya had arranged to meet on the Arbat near the metro. Petya was supposed to bring a new batch of stuff. It could all have been managed more easily: samizdat in Moscow was no big deal. Why, samizdat was practically being read openly on the trams. But, it had to be remembered, there was samizdat, and samizdat. For instance, they didn't put you away for reading Gumilev these days, but you could expect the full whack for the *Chronicle of Current Events*. Secondly, they both enjoyed the conspiracy. It was simultaneously fun and rather frightening.

Petya was already there: you could see him a mile off, the great beanstalk that he was. His jacket, too, was instantly recognizable. Dima derived a genuine aesthetic pleasure just from looking at that jacket: a fur-lined flyer's jacket of World War II vintage. It had belonged to Petya's uncle, and his mother had stored it away carefully until Petya was old enough to wear it. The jacket was practically indestructible: worn but sturdy leather and firm straps, despite a multitude of minute cracks. A real bomber jacket, in other words. The aesthetics of minimalism. And Petya wore it with style, as if quite unconscious of it.

In fact, like most tall men, Petya paid scant attention to his clothes. He was one of the lucky ones, when all around him were youngsters having to grit their teeth at wearing sweaters knitted by their mothers. You couldn't refuse to wear these sweaters, but at the same time were ashamed to appear in public in them. You could tell at a glance that the poor women had taken to their knitting needles as an exercise in calming their nerves. However, Petya's mother was an exception: her work was great, and she clearly enjoyed doing it. Dima's favourite sweater had been a present from her: made out of undyed Estonian wool, it sported a large letter 'Y' on the stomach – interpret it as you will.

The young men greeted each other with a nod, and fell into step. Dima had a spool of tape in his bag with songs by Galich, copied for Petya, and another of Okudzhava – poor quality – which he was returning. Petya was carrying a selection of Akhmatova's poems, retyped in five copies on onion-skin paper: his biologist mother, among her many virtues, possessed a typewriter. She had no idea, though, that her son could type. There are some things mothers don't need to know.

Actually, Petya had not used that typewriter to reproduce Sakharov's 'Thoughts on Progress'. He had access to another one, on which he hammered out the faculty news-sheet. He put in a lot of effort as a member of the news-sheet's editorial team in order to obtain use of that typewriter. There was a fair chance that the Sakharov material could be subjected to expert scrutiny, which would determine the machine on which it had been typed. Petya was also returning a borrowed copy of *Moscow-Petushki*, which meant that after their meeting Dima would have to race around to Stella's place: she had let him borrow it for two days, and rather unwillingly, at that. The work was new, and hardly anyone had read it yet.

They went into a café, had a cup of coffee, and reached for their bags. This time, each took the other's. Smart lads, they had bought identical bags, so that they could be switched without anyone noticing. They were very proud of themselves for think-ing up such a cunning move.

Then they swapped stories about their exams, had a few laughs. They studied in different institutes, but winter exams were held at the same time for everyone, and inevitably gave rise to a good few amusing tales. Especially concerning girls from out of town. Jumpy lot. Both Dima and Petya had sat through their finals, qualified for student stipends, and had a week free before lectures resumed. They agreed to go to Dima's dacha the day after next and do a bit of cross-country skiing. No girls, though, just the two of them, OK? There were matters to be discussed.

Stella lived quite close by. Dima had never been to her place during the day. Just in the evening, one among many. Be proud, young man, to be admitted into the circle of the elect. But remember your place! Kir, bringing him here for the first time, had introduced him as 'my sidekick'. And this title had stuck – sidekick. He was served lemonade – or wine when everyone else had it. They patted him on the head, praised his poetry. Condescendingly. Heavens, Dima, how you've grown, and I didn't even notice. Let's measure how much. Just a moment, I'm on high heels. People, look, he's taller than me now! Bravo! Here, let me kiss your cheek: grow up to be big and clever. It was only this New Year that Stella had allowed him to switch to the personal form of address. And about time, too!

She knew who she was dealing with now. This time she hadn't relied on that weirdo Natalia, or Petrovich, the little god of the crowd, with his oh so piercingly analytical stare. He'd have to be severe with her if she started that 'sidekick' business again. But no, she wouldn't, thought Dima triumphantly.

But – whoa! What was he doing, travelling on public transport and thinking about her? What should a real artist do in a trolley-bus? Study people. Note and file away different types in his memory. There was any number to be seen. So look at them and remember. Remember odours, too. Listen to people's speech patterns. Now, there's that old woman coughing – what does her cough sound like? And what did that young fellow by the door just say? 'Hey, pal, bite the ticket for me, would you?' That's not a Moscow expression – 'bite' instead of 'punch', much more colourful. Wonder where they say that? Murmansk? Yalta? Ryazan?

He began to make his way to the exit.

'Be careful with that bag of yours, boy. Stop pushing,' reproved a fat woman at his back.

No need to guess where she came from – Moscow, and no mistake.

As he neared Stella's house, Dima remembered that she had said she was off work sick when he'd phoned. That's why she was at home during the day. What an ass he was, he should have remembered to buy her a few lemons, at least. Maybe he should pop into a nearby food shop? But no, he had come on business, not to observe the social niceties. He could always go out to the shop later, if need be. He expected to find her wearing a sweet little dressing-gown, pink most likely.

However, when the door swung open, Stella greeted him with sparkling eyes, fully made-up, and with carefully disordered hair. So much for being sick.

'Hi, Dimka! You're as punctual as a German. Br-r-r! You've brought the cold in with you. Put on the kettle, will you?'

She had already opened his bag and was fishing around inside.

'Are these tapes for me, too?'

'No, leave those. They're for poverty-stricken students.'

'And does this poverty-stricken student want a bite to eat?'

Once they were in the kitchen, she wrote something quickly on a scrap of paper, and handed it to Dima. 'Date changed. Earliest – begin. April. Keep, or –?'

Dima underlined 'keep', then burnt the paper. It was unlikely that Stella's flat was bugged, but it was still safer not to discuss such matters out loud.

Stella eyed him covertly. A heroic kid, this. Fresh-faced, with serious eyes. Obviously thirsting for a challenge. If someone didn't rein him in, he would end up a hero for five years at least. That's why Stella always distanced herself from all those human rights activists, and intended to keep it that way. They feel no compunction towards young kids like this, don't worry about their safety. Nor do they want to acknowledge that they, with their experience, contacts and world celebrity, have much, much more room for manoeuvre than these youngsters.

She had always known her limits. Once, just once, she had overstepped them, back in '66. It was a mistake she never repeated. Stella did not overrate her own importance. Yet even within her limits she could allow herself considerable leeway. Quite sufficient to maintain her self-respect. So what right did she have to push this kid further? If anything were to happen to him . . . She could see it clearly. How they'd shave his head, for instance. How the blunt blades of the cutter would plough through his hair, how they'd trample through the locks on the floor with their boots . . .

'Dimka. If something happened to you, I'd never forgive myself.'

He looked at her scornfully.

'Are you my nursemaid, or what?'

'Stupid. You've got a lot of talent, though I shouldn't say it. Those who know it often don't look after it . . .'

Stella believed what she said. At that moment, at least. What had she done? Maybe this as yet unformed young man was destined to write something that would turn out to be greater than anything the late Pavel had written. And she, bitch that she was, had used the kid, knowing that he was in love with her . . .

'Look, Stella, either you quit talking rubbish, or I'm off. Making tragedies out of nothing!'

He made as if to rise. That was the way to treat her. Act like a man.

'No, no. I'm not letting you go anywhere.'

She seized him by the shoulders, breathing into his brightening face.

'I won't let you go. Don't even think of it.'

His hands proved unexpectedly strong. And she enjoyed surrendering herself to them. She had always known that this would happen eventually. Careful, now, that's no way to remove a lady's tights! What do they teach you in that institute of yours?

The apartment of Stella Yanovna Krol, listed in the files of the Fifth Directorate under the code-name 'Snow White', was not bugged round the clock. The tapes were switched on only when one of her soirées was attended by someone of interest to the Committee. That evening an aspiring young singer was due to perform her songs in front of Stella's guests. The Department was keeping an eye on the singer. Stella spent a good two hours on the phone, ensuring a good audience. Among others, she phoned the Storyteller.

So the tapes were running from 5 p.m. onwards. From the sentence about a lady's tights. For one hour fifty minutes and twenty seconds, a decent, upstanding Soviet woman seethed in outrage at her monitoring post. Damned bohemians, it was disgusting to have to listen to their goings-on! So much for the moral level of the intellectual élite! Finally, the oohs, aahs, laughter and squeaks came to an end. Clearly and sadly, a disembodied voice said: 'Time for you to go, sweetie. There'll be a huge crowd here anytime now, I'd forgotten all about it. Give me another kiss, and on your way.' And then, an added whisper: 'Be careful!'

This 'be careful' was recorded, and aroused Viktor Stepanych's interest.

Dima went out into the snow, trying not to sway, like a sailor back on firm ground after a lengthy period at sea. What a woman, what an unbelievably fantastic woman! It was already dark. There were neat rings of light at the base of every street lamp, and a dark oblique line through each circle of light. Winter whispered down from the sky, all at once, saving nothing for tomorrow. It fell at his feet, and he trod on it pleasurably, sensing his strength.

Chapter Seven

NIKOLIN WAS HALF a block away from the food shop when his sleeve was suddenly seized by a cheeky-faced gypsy woman, who seemed to spring up out of nowhere. Her brightly coloured skirts swept the snow, and her grip was like a vice.

'Let me tell your fortune, light of my life! I'll tell you the whole truth, keep nothing back! Don't grudge a penny for your fate, your whole life's about to change.'

Nikolin was clearly unwilling to stand in the middle of the street and have his fortune told. And he didn't have the money to get involved with this gypsy. He pulled out a three rouble note, and thrust it at her, shaking his head.

'Another time, thank you.'

Nikolin regretted the three roubles, and despised himself a little for not being able to send the gypsy packing as he would have liked. Still, that was a skill he was never likely to master. Why, oh why was it so fatally easy for just about anyone to take advantage of him? The fact that he grudged giving the gypsy those three roubles made him feel even more annoyed with himself.

Meanwhile, the gypsy had released him, and informed his disappearing back and the entire block in a ringing contralto:

'Beware of a tall woman with chestnut hair. She wants to ruin you! Think I'm lying? It's as true as your name's Anton, and that you're a good man!'

Nikolin shuddered, and forced himself not to turn back.

Once in the shop, he decided to make up for the loss of the three roubles by economizing on sausages.

'For a kitten, eh?' sniffed the saleswoman, cutting a sausage in half to bring the weight to exactly two hundred grams.

Returning home with a cloth shopping bag in one hand and a string bag in the other, all Nikolin wanted was to get through the rest of this crazy day without anything else peculiar happening. Now, when there was so little left to do on his story, it was as if the devil had suddenly decided to make sport of him and upset his inner equilibrium.

The kitten was still on the first-floor landing, and greeted Nikolin like an old and valued friend. It would make a nice picture for his young readers, he thought: their beloved author, who wrote so lovingly about abandoned animals, steps carefully over this pitiful ball of fluff. And leaves it to die on the staircase. Or, better still, in the snow, should some devotee of domestic hygiene chuck the kitten out into the yard.

Nikolin swore under his breath, and put the kitten into his pocket. The little so-and-so immediately began to purr at full volume, considering its future to be assured.

Auntie Xenia was still poking around the upper shelves of the cupboard, and greeted the kitten's appearance with vociferous approval.

'That's what I admire most about you, Anton Semyonych, you're so kind! You ever had a cat before?'

'Never in my life,' admitted Nikolin. 'I had a dog in Lipetsk when I was a boy, but I've no idea how to handle this creature. How am I going to take him outside, living here on the fourth floor?'

'Now, don't worry. I'll tell you everything you need to know. He'll bring you luck – see, his fur's three colours.'

She lifted the kitten by the scruff of the neck and peered under its tail with the air of an expert.

'Still impossible to tell if it's a he or a she, poor mite. Lots of fluff, but no substance. Where's your substance, eh?' she asked the kitten, giving it a little shake.

The kitten replied with an uncertain squeak.

'Well, never mind, Anton Semyonych. If it turns out to be a she, I'll drown the kittens for you. I'm always glad to do a nice person a good turn. As for its toilet – just hang on a minute.'

She went off to her own apartment, leaving Nikolin to glum contemplation of his dilemma. To cap it all, the kitten may well turn out to be a female. And he was stuck with it.

Auntie Xenia returned, carrying a rusty tray, congratulating herself on her foresight in not throwing it away – just as if she knew it would come in handy one day. She covered the bottom of the tray with finely shredded newspaper, and put it on the floor in the lavatory.

'Bring him here every time after you've fed him, he'll soon get the hang of it. My Cleopatra does her business into the bowl, but you'd need a wooden seat for that. Mind you, she's unusually smart. Still, even ordinary cats can be very clever sometimes. He won't try to wander before next March, so you've got more than a year of peace ahead of you.'

She unpacked the shopping, and put the halved sausage into a saucer. The kitten flung itself noisily at the food, and Auntie Xenia spent the next twenty minutes instructing Nikolin on the differences between cats and dogs. Alone at last, Nikolin looked at the kitten with a degree of perplexity.

'Wicked little beast!'

The wicked little beast tried to climb up Nikolin's trouser-leg, but its tiny claws were not strong enough, and it flopped to the floor. Nikolin sighed, picked it up and began scratching behind its ears.

Possibly, three-coloured kittens really do bring luck. What else could explain the fact that by nine o'clock the following morning Nikolin, happy and exhausted, wrote THE END on the final sheet.

He hesitated, knowing that it was useless rereading it now: he had to give his mind a rest. Nevertheless, the temptation was irresistible, and he started reading, quickly and excitedly. Yes, yes, this was it! Hardly had the branches closed behind Stepan, his hero – who despite the author's every intention refused to give up and die in that mosquito-infested forest – than he could hear the brazen trumpet of success sounding at his back and infusing his heart with its sweet strains. Don't be a coward – admit you've done it, at least to yourself!

He'd let the work lie for a week or two, no harm in that. But before you let any alien eye look at it afresh, allow yourself a little pleasure. Today. Now. You know, you know that it's the goods! Stepan, already half-turning away, seemed to pause a moment and grin back over his shoulder: so, you've made it, eh! And then Nikolin was alone in the whole wide world. Sitting before a silent stack of poor quality paper, so the manuscript would be as thin as possible. Sound, trumpet, sound! In an empty heart, like a deserted house.

Feeling drained and weightless, he pulled out the screwdriver and removed the screw. It was not as though his hands couldn't feel anything; they did what they had to, but no more. They showed no initiative, no instinct, the way they had half an hour earlier. They did not forge ahead of their master's thoughts, nor try to guess them in advance. They simply worked from A to B: returning to their original function, they promised nothing beyond ordinary fitness to the task. It was this that somehow caught his attention. Nikolin studied his hands with interest, but saw nothing unusual. The fingers were knotty, the end almost square. The fingers of artistically inclined people are supposed to taper elegantly towards the tips. He had read or heard that somewhere, but couldn't remember exactly where and when, but it was a long time ago. His stubby fingers had been a disappointment to him even when he was growing up.

Now he grinned at them affectionately, and hammered out 'Frère Jacques' on the table with his wrists, as if playing the piano. In the line of encouragement. Then, slowly and carefully, he packed up all he had written and put it back in the place of concealment. Next, he dealt with the contents of the wastepaper basket. Finally, he snapped his pencil in half. For some reason, he always did this when he completed a piece of work. Superstition, maybe? Then he dropped down on his sofa-bed, like a puppet with the strings cut. The kitten, who had been sternly instructed, once and for all, to keep off the bed, crawled along the pillow and settled itself under its master's chin. And so they slept for almost a whole day, and did not open the door when the bell rang.

It was the phone that woke Nikolin, and he hesitated, wondering if it was worth while answering. But whoever was on the other end was very persistent. Damn it, they were not going to leave him in peace. Doing his best to sound wide awake, he picked up the receiver. It was Olga, the illustrator.

'Well, Anton Semyonych, did you get it?'

'Get what?'

'Your presentation copy,' rejoiced the voice at the other end. 'You mean, you haven't got it yet? The publishers sent me my copy today, with a nice note from the Big Boss. The cover's excellent, and the colours are fine, too. They managed to make some change in the publishing schedule . . . Yes, the print run is the same as in the contract! Anton Semyonych, three cheers?'

'Three cheers, Olya, congratulations! Without your illustrations –'

'Yes, let's smother each other with praise! You're very good at doing that! So you start, while I gather my thoughts.'

'Olya, my dear, I have never, ever, had so much luck with

anyone, such compatibi – Oh, wait a moment, will you? There's someone at the door.'

'That's all right, I'll call you back later. Hip-hip –!'

In the doorway stood Auntie Xenia, holding a package.

'This came round from the publishers, a courier brought it,' she reported, her voice tinged with respect. 'You weren't there, so I signed for it.'

'Thanks a million, Auntie Xenia!'

Nikolin tore the package open, and turned the book lovingly over in his hands.

'You wrote that, didn't you? All these years we've been neighbours, and I still can't get used to it, how clever some people are! Can I have a look at it? Oooh, aren't the pictures lovely! You could spend hours looking at them. Well, I must be running along, I've got dinner on the stove.'

Nikolin scanned the appended note from the Big Boss, then scooped up the kitten.

'Well, Brysik, we're rich! Come on, you wretched animal, tell me how you'd like to celebrate? Champagne? A gypsy orchestra? I'll buy you ten cans of crab meat, if you want. You haven't tried that yet.'

But Brysik showed no interest in anything, and headed back for the bed. Nikolin, however, felt it was impossible to remain at home. He glanced at the clock, and realized that it was no longer Wednesday, but Thursday. And on Thursday he was invited to Stella's to hear some brilliant guitar player. Fine. Stella was a wonderful person; carefree, impetuous. Her home was always full of people like her, naturally talented and gifted. So there'd be music, clouds of cigarette smoke, and plenty of drink, and they could talk their hearts out about matters eternal.

The atmosphere at Stella's was exactly as Nikolin expected. The hostess, looking young and happy, and already slightly tipsy, dragged Nikolin into the kitchen.

'Good, you made it! for some reason, you look fresh as a daisy today.' Stella used the familiar form of address with everyone. 'You've brought a bottle? Good man! Put those nuts into that other dish, would you? Help me get the snacks into the big room, then I'll introduce you to anyone you don't know.'

She moved closer, and lowered her voice in warning.

'There's a balding guy over there. Arkadi Kirin. Watch yourself around him. He's the informer in our house.'

'Then why . . .?'

'What can I do? He phoned and wangled an invitation. Anyway, he's tame. And I've warned everyone about him. Don't look at me like that! D'you expect me to throw him out? Forbid him the house? Say to his face: "You're an informer, get the hell out of here!" I don't have any actual proof, just my own suspicions. In any case, if I get rid of him, they'll just send another one, and it will take time to figure him out . . .'

Nikolin snorted. As far as he knew, computer programming required disciplined thinking, and Stella was a programmer by profession. Even had a master's degree. On the other hand, the only programme Nikolin knew was not distinguished by its logic. Yet the whole country lived in accordance with it. So why shouldn't machines tolerate an absence of logic? Just change their chips, or whatever it is they stuff into computers.

The brilliant guitarist was already tuning her instrument. Two young men were pottering around in a corner, setting up recording equipment. Nikolin had met just about everyone present at one time or another, but would have been hard put to name half of them. The man Stella had mentioned looked familiar, too. And that pleasant couple of geologists in identical sweaters, showing some healing stones or other from the Gobi Desert. The bearded ESP buff Mitri, whom Nikolin had met through Kir, began blathering on again about Nikolin's supposedly incredible aura. Does he always smell of onions, wondered Nikolin, or is it just coincidence? But Mitri soon switched his attention to the young musician.

'Wait, wait! There are bad vibrations where you're sitting.'

He waved his hand around in the air behind the girl's back.

'No, you shouldn't be sitting there. And you ought to move that icon away from here, Stella: the vibes are bad. From the corner as far as that stool. And don't put any food here. Hang on, I'll find a place where the vibes are good.'

Wide-eyed, the musician shifted to the spot indicated by Mitri. The young men began shifting their recording equipment and muttering oaths.

'I wouldn't mention *those*, if I were you,' adjured Mitri severely. 'Because, every time you mention *that one* by name, a new one is born.'

The young men snickered uncertainly.

'And I wouldn't advise you to laugh, either. They'll gobble you up.'

As if on cue, the microphone started emitting unhealthy noises, and Mitri spread his hands deprecatingly.

While the young men fussed around repeating 'testing, testing, one-two-three . . .' Nikolin ran an eye around the room, looking for somewhere to sit as far away as possible from the tame informer. The room was large, with plaster figuring around the high ceiling. It was painted in pistachio and various shades of cream. Standard lamps in the corners shed a soft glow, creating an intimate atmosphere. Stella's father was an official figure in the world of the arts. One of those who received first class funerals with all the trimmings at Novodevichi cemetery.

Familiar faces were clustered around the glass coffee table, engaged in a heated discussion.

'I tell you, that's it. They finally wore him down, the bastards. He's handed in his resignation.'

'Rubbish, I saw him the day before yesterday. He's done nothing of the kind.'

'In strictest confidence . . . Stella, pass me a pencil, would you?'

Stella, who was perched on the arm of a chair, nodded her

head towards the phone. A pencil was already stuck in the dial. Nikolin knew the received wisdom that if you put a pencil where the zero is on the dial, then turn the dial, the pencil gets stuck, and bugging through the phone becomes impossible. He himself had never resorted to this method. Pavel maintained that this was a deliberately circulated rumour, and that the trick with the pencil actually gave a signal to those concerned that they should activate their bugs.

'They won't touch him directly. They'll simply fire his staff and leave him with nothing . . .'

The discussion concerned the journal *New World*, and its chief editor. The editor had managed to keep his journal afloat for thirteen years, and Nikolin had come to think of them both as unsinkable. Three of those involved in the discussion had submitted manuscripts to the journal, and the argument was not whether it would survive, but whether they should demand their work back when the blow fell. The general feeling was that the manuscripts should be reclaimed. It would be the decent thing to do. On the other hand, where could they take them later? Maybe the noble thing to do would be to burn them?

'If only,' began Stella, pressing her hands to her collar-bones, 'If only I had it in me to write something, real literature, the way you all can . . . You're ingrates, you have no appreciation of your talents – I wouldn't even mind publishing it in a porn magazine! Because it's not yours, not at all, it's a gift from above. And you've got no right to throw it away.'

Viktor Stepanych, listening to the recording, nodded approvingly. He would make a note of that sentiment, and have it spread around. She was a gem, this Snow White! They'd have to take good care of her. She'd probably kill herself if she realized that she was an agent of influence, with a number and pseudonym. Yes, she'd hang herself, for sure. In fact, she'd already made one attempt, when there was all that business about signing the appeal. And potential suicides don't change their methods. Their views sometimes – their methods, never.

Although Nikolin had no manuscripts with *New World*, he couldn't help being saddened. He felt sorry for the editor, who was bound to drink himself to death. Or die from the injustice of it all. A complex man. A good man. And good men can be mortally offended. Maybe, if one never took offence, one would live for ever.

Stella bustled about, lighting candles. The lights were switched off, and the girl began to sing. She sang well, and her voice was surprisingly beautiful; it seemed to resonate with sadness. As for the melody – it was as though it had not been made up, but had a life of its own. It was like witnessing the first day of creation. Or the first evening. Maybe it would have been better if she had not interspersed her own songs with those set to the poems of García Lorca or Marina Tsvetayeva. Or maybe not. There had to be some respite, or you'd find yourself float-ing off into some – what did Mitri call it? – astral plane.

Nikolin sat smoking quietly on a small divan. He liked watch-ing candles melt. Nastenka, sitting beside him, put her head on his shoulder. Her long curls, obedient to the laws of static electricity, stuck to his synthetic-mix jacket. Nastenka was sad, too, silent tears running down her face. Her mascara didn't run, though. Must be French.

The gathering broke up after midnight, and Nikolin and Nastenka found themselves leaving together. Nikolin asked her why she was upset: in the light of the hallway and then the lift he could see that her tears were not just the result of the music.

'Oh, I'm so tired. It took us all of today to film just one episode. And I was acting better than I've ever done. Then I heard them say: this will probably be cut, anyway. That was just the scriptwriters coursing a hare. You know what that means?'

Nikolin nodded. So they call it that, too. And why not? The two professions were very close. They have mobs of censors milling around, and not a single one of them could let the simplest thing pass without sinking in a claw. So their masters wouldn't get the idea that the cat's not doing its job of catching mice. For that reason, the cinema people, naturally, put in pieces for the sole purpose of supplying material to end up on the cutting room floor: here's a titbit for you, choke on it! These pieces are carefully devised and lightly tacked to the plot. So the censors' scissors wouldn't damage the main fabric. Yet occasionally these doomed pieces turn out so well, it's a pity to have to sacrifice them.

Nastenka, finding a sympathetic listener, began to cry in earnest, choking on big, child-like sobs, smearing lipstick all over her face. The poor lamb, thrown to the pack of censors by her master: there you go, eat her!

Nikolin sighed, and offered to see her home. It was far too late for her to try to catch a passing car. Nastenka beamed gratefully, and stayed pressed to his arm all the way. Her disarming trust warmed Nikolin's heart. Pleasurably, he drew her closer to his shoulder. As was to be expected, he stayed at her place for the night.

Chapter Eight

I_T_ W_AS_ S_ATURDAY_, and Petya's mother was at home. It was she who opened the door to admit Dima, her hair still damp from the shower and a frivolous apron tied over a training-suit. Something was bubbling in the kitchen, obviously requiring her attention. So all Dima received was a fleeting smile and a wave to indicate where his friend was to be found.

Petya was doing a hand-stand on a couple of old flat-irons, and wriggled a welcoming foot.

'Greetings, loonies,' said Dima, settling down on the couch to watch. Without taking his hands off the irons, Petya stamped them up and down on the seagrass mat, then tried to raise one hand off the floor, still holding the iron, and transfer his weight and balance on to the remaining hand. However, he began to teeter, and immediately abandoned the attempt. He dropped his feet to the floor and sprang up, waving the irons in the air like a pair of boxing gloves, skipping in Dima's direction. Dima nodded amiably at this familiar joke.

Petya's fascination with irons had begun in the sixth grade, when they were all forced to forage for scrap metal. Petya found an old flat-iron: it was unbelievably heavy, decorated with a gargoyle head on top, with an inscription in Old Slavonic: its weight and size were truly Herculean. Petya couldn't bring himself to surrender such a find to the Pioneer leader, and spent a week cleaning and oiling his treasure. The iron emerged as a thing of beauty, and the inscription could now be easily deciphered: 'Kalashnikov and Sons'. This may not have been the

75

fabled merchant Kalashnikov who was buried at the crossing of three roads, and certainly not the creator of the famous machine-gun. It must have been some intermediate relative, who was likewise not without some poetry in him.

Petya was captivated, and had remained so ever since. The whole apartment was full of old irons, big and small. They were used as paper-weights, door-stops, nutcrackers and hammers. Petya's entire fitness routine was devised around irons, and he even learned to juggle three tiny ones used for ironing lace, with delicately curved high handles. Petya's hobby put an end to the problem of birthday presents: you always knew what gift would please. Provided you could find it, of course.

Petya's mother served them a pan of fried eggs sprinkled with cheese, and expressed the hope that they wouldn't show up before tomorrow night. She had some urgent work to finish, and could do it better without anyone under her feet and the cassette player roaring at full volume. Their food was in that bag over there. Heave ho, and off you go!

The bag was heavy, and there were Petya's skis to lug, too. Once they had clambered aboard the train, Dima wondered aloud whether Petya's mother hadn't sneaked an iron into the bag. Petya shook his head decisively.

'No, she's already done that once. Never repeats herself.'

The weight proved to be not an iron, but three cans of stew. This came to light when they reached the dacha, which was icy cold and magnificently empty. Some ten years ago, Dima's parents still came here with friends in winter, but they were all a bit too old for skiing now. So from one summer to the next, this was Dima's refuge. It was always possible to come here for a day or two. Snow. Silence. Like the end of the world. The dacha did not retain heat very well, but the stove was a beauty, so long as you kept it going. There was plenty of wood on the pile, and an axe in the shed. Great!

This was their first task. They cleared the snow off the stoop, got the stove going, and then set off on their skis. However,

Dima managed to snatch a moment and went to the old pear tree to check that everything was in order. The package was where it should be, in the hollow in the trunk. It was wrapped in several layers of polythene, then oilcloth, and had not been disturbed. It was a pity that he couldn't tell even Petya about it. This bent old pear tree had been Dima's private hiding place since early childhood for all those things that were none of his parents' business. At various times, the hollow had housed catapults, maps of imaginary countries, live bullets, first poems, imported condoms, practical guides to hatha yoga, and the first retypings of other people's works, emanating secrecy and risk. Dima had left clear tracks in the snow, but Petya wouldn't ask anything: they had this rule between them – no questions. As for neighbours – there weren't any: they were all huddling in their Moscow apartments and wouldn't appear before May.

They shushed off on their skis. Around them the day was ideally bright and empty: there were just the two of them, and the snow which lay over the whole of Russia, her waters and forests. The sky was low and friendly: you could almost reach it with your ski stick! Light grey: clean but well washed. Like it or lump it, you won't get another. When the light began to fail, the sky became more daring, and started throwing out stripes of fantastic hue. But they, too, faded eventually, to be replaced by a frighteningly deep void, full of whirling constellations with ancient names. Time to settle by the warm stove in the yellow light of a 60-watt lamp. Away from the reaching paws of moving shadows and indeterminate sounds. Who the hell knew what they were? It was no time to be out and about in the forest, freezing your ears off.

Viktor Stepanych had, naturally, ordered surveillance to be mounted on Dima, although he did not nurture any great hopes that this would yield anything. That whispered 'be careful' probably had nothing behind it: just playing at conspiracy. The

Storyteller, now, was another matter altogether: Viktor Stepanych felt it in his bones. Everything else was just a question of going through the motions.

Suddenly, the phone rang: it was the surveillance officer, reporting in on his mobile phone. For your information, Viktor Stepanych, the suspect checked out something in the hollow of an old tree in the garden of the dacha. No, he hadn't removed anything, and went there empty-handed. Yes, he was certain, there was a clear view from here in the neighbours' loft. No, the other young fellow hadn't gone anywhere near the tree, he had stayed inside.

Viktor Stepanych's heart missed a beat: could this be it?

'Maintain surveillance. Don't do anything. Keep your eyes peeled. If he takes out anything, report to me immediately. No matter when.'

Viktor Stepanych liked the sound of the surveillance officer: alert and interested. After six hours of sitting in someone's freezing loft, with the prospect of spending the night there, the officer had not yielded to boredom and sulks. The worst of such an assignment was having to wait, with nothing happening. That's when you start cursing your beloved superiors in a poisonous whisper, and if you can't whisper, then just moving your lips. To keep your spirits up. But as soon as something happens, the watcher's instinct comes awake in a flash. Like that of a good hunting dog. Then he's ready to freeze into immobility, filled with the passion of the chase.

Viktor Stepanych hurried to advise his chief. A brief report. Request to authorize an operative group.

'If he takes anything out of that hollow, Filipp Savich, I think the best thing would be an attack by hooligans on their way home. Give them some bumps and bruises, and seize all their stuff.'

'Good idea. Who's the other fellow?'

'Doesn't look as if he's got anything to do with it, Filipp Savich. It's a former classmate. A student. Name of Nizov.'

Filipp Savich sat in silence for a few minutes, thinking.

'All right. Keep watching the main suspect for the time being, don't disperse forces unnecessarily. And careful with the bumps and bruises, just enough and no more.'

'Just enough to make it look convincing, Filipp Savich.'

'Right, right. And what if he doesn't remove anything?'

'Then a covert extraction, once they're gone. After that – depending on results.'

'Good man. Get moving. And be a bit more independent, I've got more serious matters to deal with than a couple of students. Maybe he's hiding a copy of *Playboy* there from Mummy and Daddy. You can call up operative groups yourself in future, I'll authorize it. But don't let it go to your head – I'll judge you by results. Off you go.'

Filipp Savich felt tired. There were indeed far more important matters on his plate. Oh, if it were only possible to arrest all these 'more important matters'. Lock them up, and throw away the key.

Too straightforward for our times, but a man could dream. Especially when it concerned his main bugbear – the man who had already caused Filipp Savich a great deal of trouble, and whom he now loathed not only professionally but personally. Solzhenitsyn. The camps brought you inspiration – well, stay in them. We'd make you keep your head down there. And we wouldn't have to treat the rest of your entourage with kid gloves, either. Damn it, it's not an entourage, it's a whole network, and cunningly woven, like a spider's web. Threads have reached abroad, and are growing there, too: it's impossible to keep track of it, let alone control it. Information passes along it soundlessly, and information, as is known, tends to flow with exceptional speed. And he sits in the centre, like a spider. That's why the Committee gave him that code-name in its files: Spider. Filipp Savich thought that up himself. It sounded hostile and offensive. And why not? Is he friendly towards the Committee? Does he do anything but insult us?

Some paradox: here we are getting set to mark the centenary, and trying to suppress any scandals. So as not to cast a shadow over the celebrations. And *they* were becoming increasingly bold. Would the Deceased, whose centenary was at hand, hesitate to deal with them? No, he wouldn't even waste prison skilly on them, but have them up against the wall. However, that was out. For now, at least. And you, Filipp Savich, make sure you keep all the reins in your hands, and don't you dare miss a thing. You'll be judged by results, too.

Nizov. Petya Nizov. So that's the way of it, eh? That was all he needed. Still, no sense in worrying before time.

Dima and Petya sat by the stove, faces flushed from the heat. They'd downed the stew with great chunks of bread, brewed up some mulled wine and sat drinking it out of large, heavy mugs.

'You're just trying to soft-pedal! He's a bastard, and that's all there is to it,' seethed Dima.

'Oh, come on, he's just a hack, one of many. What do you care?'

'Well, I do. I hate him.'

'Because you liked him once?'

'So what, was I the only one he fooled? OK, so mine was a special case. But how many kids believed in him? How talented he is, they thought, how daring!'

'So blame yourself. You idolized him – a clinical case. Chuck me an apple, will you?'

Petya bit deeply into his apple with a succulent crunch.

'And why did he set himself up as an idol?'

'Was he the only one? There were any number who went a lot further than he did. Admit it – you're just being personal.'

Dima could not deny this: everything in his relations with Kir had been personal from the very first moment. That time by the

Mayakovsky monument. Dima had been only a kid when he happened to be there, listening. In his imagination, he had seen himself, not at the edge of the crowd, but there, on the podium, reciting his own poems. An honest-to-goodness rebel poet. The only hitch was that at eleven years of age he hadn't written all that many poems. But Kir had, and someone had recited his works. And Dima held his breath: this is it. The real thing.

Then came the end of 1965, and Dima was among the crowd on Pushkin Square. The crowd was gaining confidence, streaming towards the statue. Dima, his heart hammering, squeezed his way forward. He saw placards being unfurled and just had time to read the words: 'We demand a public hearing for . . .' before the operative groups rushed forward, scattering the crowd indiscriminately and tearing the placards to shreds. Some people were being dragged to waiting militia wagons, others were being beaten to the ground. Someone's hand fell heavily on Dima's shoulder, he cried out in fright and tried frantically to wriggle out of that iron grip. And at that moment, cold, hard fingers closed on his ear.

'Damn you, Mishka, where the hell have you been? You have to shove your nose into everything . . . just wait till we get home!'

And then, in a conciliatory tone:

'Comrade, this lad is mine.'

The gorilla in the padded jacket had already realized that he had grabbed the wrong quarry, released Dima and surged forward to join the fray. But the fingers holding Dima's ears stayed where they were until they had left the square. Only on the other side of the road, near the street light, did they unclench. Dima did not realize, at first, who he was looking at.

'So why the hell did you poke your nose in there?' asked the man whom he now recognized as Kir.

Dima had seen his photograph any number of times, but his wits were temporarily scattered.

'What about you?' was all he could think to retort.

'Me? Pure chance – I was just passing by. When I saw the

crowd, I thought there might be someone selling oranges,' explained Kir, cunning devils dancing in his eyes.

'Then I saw a kid being grabbed. Well, I thought, if there aren't any oranges to be had, I'll take a kid instead! What's your name, anyway?'

Inevitably, from then on Kir had become the most important person in Dima's life. He analysed Dima's poems kindly but mercilessly. Taught him to control his flights of fancy, to go easy on the metaphors. Introduced him to his circle and into adult life generally. At the same time, he repeated over and over again that fifteen, indeed sixteen years of age was not old enough for the fray. The real battles were still ahead, and there was no need to expend energy on trifles. One should keep one's head for the real, major tasks in the future, but for the present – keep working. So Dima kept working, although he found it hard to satisfy the dictum of 'not a day without a line'. However, he read voraciously: everything from Faulkner to Kafka. And waited for Kir to say: it's time!

The call never came.

In 1968, he cried when he saw Kir's signature among those of other Soviet intellectuals appending their 'unanimous approval' in *Pravda*. Bit his nails. Pointedly ignored Kir in company. But it still hurt, even now.

As for Petya – Petya didn't understand. All he was interested in was his beloved emperor Paul I. Petya's one complaint was that he couldn't gain access to the Special Archive. He may have had more luck if he'd been doing history, but a student of electronics didn't stand a chance. So Petya was a fine one to talk about idols. On the other hand, why shouldn't he imagine a favourite emperor for himself?

Dima rose, mug in hand, and stuck out his elbow.

'A toast to an unfairly maligned emperor!'

Ah, that was better. That went down well. In fact, they'd had a good time. Their backs and legs were pleasantly tired, but they sat there talking about Paul and the Heir to the Throne, and agreed that the end of Alexander was not really an end, but a retreat. Then they read aloud for a while – each one his own poems. They'd taken no papers with them, so read from memory. That's the good thing about a technical education – it trains the memory and keeps it in trim.

When all the apples were eaten, they went to bed. Tomorrow promised to be just as snowy and good for skiing, and towards evening they'd head home. The twisted old pear tree dreamed quietly in the yard. Dima had plugged the hollow with rags, so no snow could penetrate. Nothing would happen to the bundle until April.

There was no need to order the operative group posing as hooligans into action: Dima did not go anywhere near the tree again. Viktor Stepanych's intuition urged him to go to the scene himself, so he went. He waited the usual forty minutes after the young men left the dacha, according to regulations: after all, what if they had forgotten something and came back? Such lapses had occurred a number of times in the past, so the Department had laid down hard and fast rules concerning clandestine extractions of evidence.

Viktor Stepanych did not worry overmuch. He persuaded himself that he was prepared to find nothing but a copy of *Playboy* or a favourite teddy bear. His fingers, sheathed in thin gloves, unpacked the layers of polythene without undue haste. A document should be exposed as carefully as a lady's legs, and give pleasure in the process.

He allowed himself to savour his triumph only when the object lay before him in all its glory. Viktor Stepanych's apprehensions were finally allayed when he saw the first page, which carried the title: 'An Apple In the Well'. And, in slightly smaller letters: 'A Novel in Three Parts'. It was Pavel Pulin's manuscript. At long last.

Chapter Nine

RESTRAINING HIS ELATION, he phoned Filipp Savich.

'Filipp Savich, may I see you?'

'Give me six minutes, Vitya, then I'll be free.'

Oh well, he could survive those six minutes. Take a triumphant look at himself in the mirror, for instance: congratulations on the success of your first independent operation, comrade! Pity his cheeks were so round, it made him look less imposing.

Filipp Savich, however, didn't give him a chance to open his mouth, but sprang a question on him at once, catching him off guard.

'What the hell do you think you're playing at with that gypsy-woman business?'

'But, Filipp Savich –'

'Didn't I tell you to keep the fancy stuff down to a minimum? Well, didn't I? How's Forget-me-not supposed to work on him now?'

Viktor Stepanych had to contain himself in silence while the thunderbolts flew around his head. When the storm passed, he attempted a careful explanation.

'There was no gypsy woman, Filipp Savich. At least, there may have been, because he told the story himself, twice: to Buttercup and to some of his colleagues in the hallway of the Writers' Club. But that was pure chance. She wasn't one of ours.'

'And I suppose it was by chance that she happened to know his name, and to caution him against a woman with chestnut hair?'

'Well . . . she may have guessed, Filipp Savich! Gypsies can be like that.'

'Are you allowing superstition to creep into your work? You find that gypsy and sort her out!'

'Yes, sir,' responded Viktor Stepanych obediently, though he knew that this would be impossible. There were hundreds of gypsy fortune-tellers plying their trade in Moscow, not to mention the ones just passing through . . .

Having received the correct answer, Filipp Savich became genial.

'All right, then. Now, what was it you wanted to see me about?'

On cue, Viktor Stepanych laid the much-sought stack of papers on the desk.

Filipp Savich leaned back in his chair, squinting approvingly.

'Good work. Tell me the whole story.'

While Viktor Stepanych related the details, Filipp Savich watched him and wondered whether he had done enough to bring his junior down to earth. Maybe he should deflate him a bit more? As soon as he had heard Viktor Stepanych's voice, full of suppressed triumph, like a schoolboy who had won a maths contest, he guessed correctly why Vitya was so keen to see him. He also knew that paternal strictness was called for. The first success is a dangerous thing, and can go to a man's head. Before you know it, today's winner is tomorrow's loser. Still, it didn't look as though Viktor Stepanych's head had swelled too much, so Filipp Savich permitted himself a smile, at which Vitya shone like a polished brass knocker.

'What do you plan to do next?'

'I thought, Filipp Savich, that I'd keep up surveillance on this student, Koretsky, for a while longer. To see if I can trace the link by which he got that manuscript.'

'And do you know what I'd do, Vitya, in your place? I'd arrest him.'

Viktor Stepanych's mouth formed a silent 'Oh', and he sat

there, looking like a landed fish, while Filipp Savich expounded his opinion further.

'See how neatly everything falls into place? People have become slack, we need to bring them back to heel. We can't arrest the main enemies at the moment, because it would cause too much of a rumpus. On the international level. But this is just a student, who's done nothing and who's unknown in the West. On the other hand, he hangs out at those literary get-togethers. At Snow White's, for instance. People in those circles will notice, the word'll get round Moscow and a whole lot of anti-Soviet stuff will be burned.'

Viktor Stepanych recognized the familiar pattern: minimum effort, maximum results! Filipp Savich continued, stressing the 'we', which added to the pleasure.

'As a matter of fact, I'm certain he got this manuscript from Snow White. She had known Pulin for a long time. But we won't touch her – she knows too many people, including foreigners. You could find yourself with a real can of worms on your hands. One "friendly" film producer even invited her to come to Italy and take part in a film, stupid fool. No – we'll leave her strictly alone. Let the kid carry the can for it. He can play the knight in shining armour to protect his lady-love. A house search first thing tomorrow morning is bound to turn up some more stuff. After that – a quick investigation, because there's nothing more to be had from him. Let him stew in the lock-up until the celebrations are over, and then off to the camps for three years on a charge of harbouring hostile materials with intent to disseminate them. His father's a gynaecologist, quite well known in medical circles, but not enough to cause us any problems. There won't be any fuss, and the intelligentsia can sit back and bite their nails: oh dear, oh dear, look what being in possession of samizdat did to the poor boy! They'll start trying to pin the blame on someone, and quarrel among themselves. That'll keep them busy. As for the surveillance squads – we'll give them a break: they've done enough tramping through the snow.'

Viktor Stepanych fairly sizzled with zeal.

'We'll do the search tomorrow morning, Filipp Savich. Should we turn over both apartments?'

'Why bother with the other kid? Give you a free hand, Vitya, and you'd turn half of Moscow upside-down! Let's say you find something to incriminate every single person. So what? You couldn't lock them all away. No, the one we need is the one who had the manuscript. Concentrate on him. If the other one should surface in the course of the investigation, then we'll consider what to do about it. Get all the necessary documents ready concerning Koretsky, and once the search is over, straight into the car with him. Open a separate file on him, and get it to the Procuracy. And close the file on the Storyteller.'

Viktor Stepanych couldn't believe his ears.

'What do you mean – close it?'

'Why not? We've got the manuscript, thanks to you. The Storyteller wasn't concealing it, as was shown by the search of his flat. Either Pulin didn't trust him enough, or he was smart enough to refuse. There's no reason to continue his investigation and waste departmental resources. That was a false trail, so let it go.'

Viktor Stepanych was genuinely agitated.

'Filipp Savich! I just *know* that we shouldn't let the Storyteller off the hook! There could be other material involved.'

'Maybe, maybe . . . But where is it? You've been after him for how long, and what's to show for it? Suspicions, nothing more. Me, I suspect them *all*, but does that mean we have to waste *two* birds on each and every one of them? To say nothing of other costs.'

'I . . . insist!'

No sooner were the words out of his mouth than Viktor Stepanych froze with horror at his own impertinence. He sat as if glued to his chair, hardly daring to believe that he had spoken thus to Filipp Savich. What would happen to him now?

Yet Filipp Savich acted as though nothing unusual had been said, and merely nodded benignly.

'Well, if you insist – go ahead. I'm giving you two days. Work at it. You'll only have yourself to blame if it doesn't turn out as you expect.'

Andrei Mikhalych Belokon was celebrating. He'd finally nailed the bastard! He'd proved he was right! He'd demolished the myth of indestructibility! Sound the trumpets, beat the drums! Of course, there were others, even higher up than Andrei Mikhalych, who had been working in the same direction. But nobody had nurtured such burning, personal hatred towards *New World* and its chief editor as Belokon – and he knew it.

All the groundwork had been done, all that remained now was to lean back and hear what happened as the bastard was dragged upstairs and dealt with. How he would try to justify himself, write rebuttals and protests. Fat lot of good that would do him! He'd be made to grovel in the shit, like a naughty schoolboy. Publishing his work in a hostile émigré journal was beyond a joke. Let him try and prove that he didn't know how the manuscript got there. If you didn't send it, then who did? Pushkin? Even assuming that Belokon knew very well who'd sent it, we'll hold our peace. There are some secrets one doesn't share even with one's friends.

And friends there were, seated all around him, flushed with cognac, looking younger than their years. Their favourite record was playing on the gramophone, quietly and soothingly. They always put it on after the first toast. The first toast was always to Stalin, and drunk standing. When it got to the fourth song on their favourite record, someone would always give Belokon a pat on the shoulder: you're a genius, my lad! That was something that could never be destroyed, even if the Mausoleum were to be closed down.

Yes, early deaths had thinned their ranks, and the years left

88

their traces, but they were all still strong men. Unbroken by grief, and not yet reduced by life – even in today's situation – to obscurity. Belokon looked them over with affection: Mishka – a Central Committee instructor, Tolik – a district prosecutor; even the lowest-ranking, Sashok, was the Party organizer of the *Cinema Journal*. Among themselves, they still used the polite patronymic form of address. It had started as a joke, but after a while they'd realized the rightness of it: it showed respect for the One who had made them what they were.

How and why this had happened to each of them, in their separate ways, had been told and retold on innumerable occasions, but they never tired of the retelling, and every time some new and precious detail would come to light. How many still remained loyal to Him out of all those millions who had lived and been guided by His name – who had retained enough fortitude not to recant, not to denounce the dead lion? Maybe there were more than one would think, taking the country as a whole. It was hardly something to shout from the rooftops. But they recognized each other without words, even perfect strangers – just as on that first day, near the deserted Mausoleum when His body was removed. Mortified, but not prepared to accept betrayal.

Ah, a rousing artillery chorus. Their hearts lifted as they picked up the tune.

> *For the Motherland, for Stalin –*
> *Fire on the enemy, fire!*

They poured another round. Belokon had called this convivial gathering since there was plenty to furnish the table. It is a mistake to think that Party officials eat nothing but black caviare. There were spring onions, and pickled cucumbers, and grey bread, sliced the way soldiers do. All this brought the past that much closer.

'. . . Thought that at last I'd get a chance to sleep: I'd been two days under fire, and even before that, I'd only cat-napped. We hadn't even had a chance to hang up our puttees to dry when I got the message – report to the senior political officer, quick smart! And he says to me: get your stuff together, you're going to Moscow. Not a hope of getting packed with the car already there, waiting. So off I went, wet puttees and all . . .'

The friends listened with warm attention, each one recalling his youth. Belokon continued, as though he were treading the Kremlin passageways all over again.

He had not been told Who wanted to see him. And they were right not to tell him. If they had, he would have surely cut himself to shreds while shaving. But the urgency of the escort, the brand new uniform he had been issued, with instructions to clean himself up in ten minutes, the fact that he was driven through Moscow not in an ordinary car (it didn't stop so much as once) – all made him suspicious, not daring yet longing to believe. It was those two poems which brought him to the Kremlin via *Combat Sheet* and the *Front Line* newspaper. He did not know, then, that they had been published by *Front Line* and attracted the attention of the Leader. Such a thing was beyond his wildest dreams.

With fluttering heart Belokon recalled Who had smiled at him as he stood frozen on the threshold of the study. And whom in turn did *He* see? What was in that youthful, round-faced lieutenant whose stomach felt as though it were frozen to his spine?

Apparently, something more than just those two poems, Belokon believed to this day. The poems were just a happy coincidence. And Lyonka wouldn't have minded. No, he would have been only too glad. They shared the same cigarette, the same spoon to eat out of the same canteen – so why quibble at poems? They both wrote, both appeared periodically in *Combat Sheet*. And was it only chance that Lyonka's cartridge case with its maps and personal papers should have fallen at Belokon's feet when that shell exploded and Lyonka was no more?

Petted, made famous overnight and raised to dizzy heights,

had Belokon ever failed to justify the faith placed in him? Two Stalin Awards for prose – now that was no coincidence, that was all due to Belokon's own work, his own sweat and talent.

Naturally, there were ill-wishers, and snide remarks: where are his new poems, why has he suddenly switched to prose? But he always had a ready reply to that: I'll never write anything better than I did about the Father. That was the peak of the genre. That shut everyone up, leaving them with nothing more to say. They shut up until 1953. By that time, though, it was better to leave Belokon alone: his position was unassailable. If anyone was foolhardy enough to squeak – well, Belokon remembered them by name, and never lost a chance to get his revenge. Anyway, those who dared raise their voices against him in public were always lower down the ladder than he – never higher. Just once, Filipp Savich had mentioned Lyonka's surname, which had been forgotten by everyone else. Casually, in passing.

'They say he was a very promising young fellow. Pity he didn't live long enough to prove it. Did you ever chance to meet him when you were at the front?' Then without waiting for a reply, he switched the conversation to another topic.

Got the message? But what was Belokon supposed to get? Not to try to slip the leash? He never did, anyway.

Belokon sank back into his thoughts, while the talk around the table moved on to another subject: everyone was complaining about their children. They're good for nothing. They have no appreciation of the care they've had. This is a universal trait, no doubt: complaining about one's children, and boasting about one's grandchildren. Those who have grandchildren can never see any wrong in them. Take Olga, for example: could Belokon have called her over to share his triumph tonight? Hardly. Most likely she was among the literary crowd mourning the demise of *New World*. He'd heard that the whole office was swamped with all sorts of people. Sympathizers. So let them mourn, in their damp coats smelling like the fur of wet dogs – but one would like to think that one's daughter was not among them, right?

Belokon pushed these thoughts aside, so as not to spoil his moment of success. He passed around Denis's photo. All the children on the photos produced by their grandfathers were cute, but Denis outshone them all.

What, had the record finished playing already? Ah, Mikhail Sanych was putting on the other side.

Let us, comrades, sing a festive song . . .

Damn, the needle had jumped straight to the second verse . . . Never mind, they picked up from there.

Let us drink to our free Motherland,
Let us drink, and pour again!

That's good. That's the way we like it.

Dima's mother didn't cry, just stared in bemused silence, as though waiting to emerge from a bad dream. When they started on the kitchen, the fair-haired one, the one checking out the top shelves, held up his dust-covered hand and said: 'Hey, look at this dirt! Call yourself a housewife?' And wiped the hand against the wall. It was only then that she started to cry.

Dima's father protested indignantly at first, insisting that there had been some misunderstanding, and tried to call somebody up. But they barked an order at him. Nobody was to use the phone while the search was in progress. He subsided, seeming to age in the space of a few seconds, and now sat hunched up, trying not to look at what was going on around him. The searchers spared no effort: every book was taken down and shaken, one of them lay flat on the floor and checked under the bath with a flashlight, the beds were turned upside-down.

They even went through his mother's underwear drawer, sniggering suggestively all the while.

Dima was ordered to sit between two witnesses, where everything was brought and dumped.

'Here, take a look at this. Filthy anti-Soviet muck!'

The witnesses, seemingly, could recognize anti-Soviet muck at half a glance. They exhibited no desire to study it any closer, but just nodded obediently. Dima didn't have a copy of the latest issue of the *Chronicle*, but a few old issues came to light. There was one copy of Turchin's *The Inertia of Fear* and assorted retypings of bits and pieces of samizdat. Even the exercise books with Dima's own poetry were added to the heap of confiscated goods and noted in the inventory: time to sort it all out later. In the end, there was a considerable pile, and an operative sat at Dima's desk, listing things item by item: one typewritten text . . . beginning with the words . . . ending with the words . . . total of three pages . . . handwritten text . . . beginning with the words . . .

Dima's thoughts skittered around in confusion: was Stella's flat being searched? How could he let her know where he'd hidden the manuscript? Should he head for the dacha as soon as they left? What might they find at Petya's? Should he say something to his mother? Or would it be better to say nothing in front of *them*, and explain later?

After three hours he needed to go to the toilet, but a tall, broad-chested fellow accompanied him and squeezed in too, preventing Dima from shutting the door. And watched. Dima found he couldn't do anything, and decided to wait until the search was over. When all the confiscated items had been sealed into a couple of large canvas bags, Dima heard a quiet command from the corridor.

'Call the car.'

It was then that he realized that they were going to take him away.

Wordlessly, he embraced his mother. What could he say?

Chapter Ten

NIKOLIN'S FIRST CONCERN now was to type up his manuscript. He knew there was no point in taking it anywhere. Nobody would or could type it. There was nothing Soviet about the novel. This was his first work written, as it were, 'for the bottom drawer'. This expression, of course, was a misnomer, because nobody in their right mind would dream of keeping something like that in their desk.

He noted with surprise that he felt practically no urge to show or read the work to anyone, no need to force himself to hold back. Lucia would have read it, and he would have held his breath, watching the expression on her face with each page. As it was – who was there to show? A hundred – maybe only fifty years hence, he firmly believed – this work would be acknowledged as part of the body of Russian literature. Good things don't age. His task, as the author, was to find a good hiding place, where the work could lie safe. And then wait. Times change, so do people. Even the climate was subject to change. So he would wait on events. Nikolin had no doubt that he would be able to keep his creation safe, both from anyone else's hands and his own folly. How many people had already slipped up through carelessness! Some had allowed their work to circulate, others placed too much trust in the Thaw and had done the rounds of editorial offices. Still others had plumped unreflectingly for publication in the West, and where were they and their works now?

Samizdat was rife with inaccuracies from numerous retypings, pages would go missing, inexplicable abbreviations would creep in (a tired typist could easily miss a paragraph). Yes, the reader would still savour the forbidden fruit, but whether this did literature no damage was questionable.

As for the West – that required very good contacts to keep matters under control. Otherwise it was tantamount to throwing your work down a well, with the chances that the publication (if it got that far) would be mutilated. It could even be that the KGB would fix up a pirate publication, in which case the mutilations would be even worse. The late Pavel had warned him about this. Before long, you'll find yourself sitting in your cell biting your nails and cursing your own negligence. In the meantime, while you can barely keep body and soul together on camp skilly, our glorious state organs will fish out the true text.

Pavel himself had furnished Nikolin with an object lesson on the difference between theory and practice. His own novel 'Apple' had been like a live ember in his hands, and Nikolin had been horrified to learn that Pavel had shown the manuscript to a number of people. As a result, when he'd asked Nikolin to take his work for safe-keeping, Nikolin had refused as gently as possible. Once the work was out of the bag – sorry, old friend, but it's no go. I don't have anywhere reliable to hide it.

Pavel had left, trying to conceal his chagrin. As for Nikolin, he felt so ashamed of himself that the palms of his hands burned. Yet what else could he do, if Pavel hadn't been able to control himself; if this ex-prisoner, who'd been through the mill, vacillated between fantastic hopes – of the Nobel Prize, for example – and equally fantastic fears: fears of the new neuroleptic drugs, now reportedly being used in psychiatric hospitals, of being spied on by his own wife, or even of being followed by aliens in the street?

It was not difficult therefore for Nikolin to overcome the temptation to type up several copies of his novel, even though his typewriter could take five sheets at a time. What would he do with them later? It would be like coping with a litter of kittens: you could find homes for one or two, and then be stuck with having to drown the rest. Or throw them out and let them fend for themselves. No thanks. Two copies on proper quality paper would be quite enough. One would be for concealment, at Grandpa Klim's. You could hide a machine-gun on his allotment, with Grandpa being none the wiser. The other could be secreted under the step in his apartment: he'd wait a month or two, read it again with a fresh eye, and then do a final edit, with pleasure and without haste. Meanwhile, he would live life to the full, so there would be no temptation to go rooting under the step before time.

Nikolin wrapped himself up well in warm clothes, asked Auntie Xenia to keep an eye on the cat, left her his keys and set off for Lipetsk. To visit Grandpa Klim. The old man did not live in the city itself, but on a collective farm, Red Something-or-other. When Nikolin had been a schoolboy, they used to have to go to this collective farm to help with the weeding. And it was here that he met Grandpa Klim. Actually, Klim had hardly qualified as a 'grandpa' at that time, but was a hale and hearty man, for all that his hair was grey. But early greyness can happen to anyone. Klim's foot had been sheared off when he was working on a fishing trawler, and in place of it he had a wooden block. Klim became a bee-keeper, an occupation favoured by many retired seamen.

As was to be expected, he lived with his hives at some distance from the other farm folk. From among the senior boys he had singled out two, and allowed them to hang around him. This was no small piece of luck. They would mend his roof, bring up firewood, do any of those chores which his injury made hard for him. In return, he would give them honey. On the quiet, of course. They understood the need for silence – survival on a collective farm was impossible without a few tricks up one's sleeve. And to be able to present one's mother with a two-litre jar of honey back in 1946 bordered on the miraculous. Nikolin could still remember the smell of that honey: fragrant to intoxication, to tears of happiness.

Nikolin had visited Klim on and off ever since. It was astounding, how long it took Klim really to age: there must be truth in the old adage about bee-keepers' longevity. But eventually, the wrinkles multiplied and the straight back began to bend. Klim was no longer to be seen leaping around on his wooden foot, but hobbled about slowly and carefully.

He was always honestly glad to see Nikolin, and would immediately start plying him with honey and cucumbers, just as he had in the early days. He would haul up some mead from the cellar – something that was always on hand. Then Nikolin would set about putting the old man's household to rights. It gave him pleasure to take up the axe and the spade, for all that his hands would still ache from it a week later.

The bees – God knows which generation by now – never bothered Nikolin. Grandpa Klim claimed that he knew the magic word for taming bees, and it certainly seemed so. Especially in view of the fact that his bees were the fierce, watch-dog type. During the honey-gathering season, even the local boys knew that it was wise to give the apiary a very wide berth. As for when the hives were wrapped up for the winter – what interest did the old man's domain have for anyone? No cucumbers to be pinched, no apples, nothing at all. Just herbs and grasses hanging up to dry.

The old man would lie on his bunk above the stove, while the wind howled outside and a cold new moon drew in its belly. There were times when Nikolin thought of this kind of life as a sound way of existence, and envisaged it for himself. Not now, of course, but at some time in the future. To retreat from everyone and everything, and never hurry again. Think, and tend the bees, nothing else. But what if you were to find something inside yourself that you didn't like? It would be too late to change anything.

His cogitations were interrupted by two tipsy young men, who were spoiling for mischief in the half-empty train. They moved down the carriage none too steadily, obviously not having consumed quite enough, and feeling the lack. Both of them swore profusely at nobody in particular, but in such a way that anyone could take it as a personal affront.

'Watch your tongues, there are children here,' protested one woman, which was just what they had been waiting for. Both hooted with laughter, then one of them struck her across the face with his open palm so that her hat flew off and rolled away across the ribbed floor of the carriage. Other women burst into indignant protest, though not leaving their place, bewailing the fact that there were no real men left these days to keep hooligans like these in line. A child somewhere began to bawl. Nikolin, unsure of whether he ought to despise himself or, on the contrary, be proud of his ability to keep his temper, sat without a sound. He was glad that he was by the window, and not by the aisle. He leant closer to the wall, staring out, feeling his precious manuscript against his side. Electricity posts and wires slid past, the odd bird flew disquietingly across the lowering sky.

Matters resolved themselves without his interference, as it happened. From somewhere at the back of the carriage came the only words which could distract the two men from their trouble-making.

'O-o-oy lads! Come 'n 'ave a drink!'

Three thirsty souls joined in perfect communion. They didn't trouble anyone any more: their talk was disjointed, but muted, and their singing heartfelt, though off-key. The offended woman, swallowing sobs, retrieved her hat and moved into the next carriage.

Nikolin completed his journey without any mishaps.

Petya, totally unaware of what had happened, phoned Dima after lunch: just to talk, nothing else. The receiver gave out a strange sound, something between a hiccup and a sob, and then a subdued voice said:

'Don't ever phone here again.'

Petya knew Dima's mother's voice, it couldn't be her. Or could it? It was enough to make anyone apprehensive, but it was clearly useless trying to redial. So what should he do? The thought of going over to Dima's place was a bit scary: obviously something had gone very wrong, and they didn't want him there. Maybe Dima had died? Run down by a car? No, that was nonsense. He'd have to go to Stella's, that's what. She might know. Dima had spent a lot of time there recently.

Petya thought Stella was an empty-headed nonentity, mutton trying to act as lamb. For the life of him, he couldn't understand what Dima saw in her. He'd gone there once or twice, but could tell that Stella wasn't too enamoured of him, either. Still, he had tried to remain objective. Admittedly, his objective opinion hadn't influenced Dima at all. Dima, for all that he was very bright, was always keen to meet new people, it didn't really matter who, and was very susceptible to flattery.

Stella was in tears, her face blotched and not at all attractive, hair hanging loose.

'He's been arrested, understand? They say his flat was searched. And now – piss off, I haven't got time for you.'

Petya drew himself up.

'But – I've got to do *something*!'

'Everything that needs to be done will be done without your help. You'd better watch out for yourself. Just listen to you – do something, indeed!'

She closed the door. Clearly, there was nothing more to be had from her.

Petya came to himself to find a dumpy woman with a red armband and a scarf over her beret in front of him demanding a fine. Damn, he'd forgotten to cancel his bus ticket. Silently, he pulled out the money and tried to ignore her lecture on cunning fare-dodgers.

He needed to collect his thoughts together calmly. First of all, check out his own home, it was possible that there would be a search there, too. Secondly, he had to find a way to get information about Dima's arrest to the *Chronicle*. Damn, he had no direct contacts for that. The *Chronicle* had an iron rule for such cases:

> *Anyone may pass on information to the* Chronicle of Current Events *by telling it to the person from whom they received their copy of the* Chronicle. *This person, in turn, will pass it on to the person who gave them their copy, and so on. Please do not try to work through the chain yourself, or you may be taken for an informer.*

When Petya read this for the first time, it had seemed very prudent. Now it seemed stupid. What if your information was highly urgent? How could you tell how long the information chain would be? And what did they mean by 'telling' it to someone? What if they got Dima's surname wrong? And the actual facts? What if someone in the chain had gone off skiing and wouldn't be back for a month?

Whoa! – he had to go home first. He dived into a phone booth on the way. For all that it was covered with ice, the phone was actually working. By way of encouragement, the mounting on which the phone was hung boasted the only word which hooligans of all ages and backgrounds can spell without so much as a single error. Petya called a few numbers he could remember by heart. The information had to be released along the grapevine as quickly as possible, it could herald the start of a new wave of house searches at many addresses. A few words over the phone don't take long. What should he do with all the papers he had at home – burn them? And what was he to say to his mother? It wasn't as though he had to dispose of a mere page or two.

As soon as he got home he went through all the samizdat he had accumulated. They were hardly likely to arrest him for having poetry by Voloshin, were they? That alone weighed a good half kilo. How about the song 'Comrade Stalin, you're a great man of science'? Was that sufficient cause for arrest? Who the hell could say? Petya rapidly extracted those materials which would undoubtedly be considered criminal: not that much, thank heaven, he could burn all that in half an hour. Pity, but needs must . . . And he'd better get the aluminium basin clean again before his mother showed up. It would have been better if they lived in an older house, that would at least have meant they'd have a solid-fuel stove.

He set the extractor fan in the kitchen to maximum, opened the window as wide as it would go, and put the basin on the ceramic tile which usually acted as a stand for the kettle.

Burning the papers made Petya feel a lot easier; his spirits began to lift and he even began to feel hungry. Carefully, he flushed the ashes and singed scraps of paper down the toilet, smeared the basin with cleaning paste and left it to stand. Next, he made himself a gargantuan sandwich with raspberry jam. Damn it, he thought, marvelling at himself, his friend was under arrest, yet here he was, enjoying a sandwich and savouring the taste of jam. Still, look at it whichever way you liked, that jam was absolutely delicious.

The next step was to go through stuff which was less incriminating, but which had been typed on his mother's typewriter. This pile turned out to be much larger than the first. He'd been in too much of a hurry with the basin. He burned the second pile, mentally cursing himself for not wiping the basin thoroughly. The papers burned more slowly this time. And chucking in whole stacks was counter-productive, better to burn one sheet at a time. Everything left unburned went into a rucksack, weighed down by one of his less valuable flat-irons. He scrubbed out the basin hurriedly, and put all the disturbed books back on the shelves. Then he dashed off a note to his mother, saying that he would be spending the night with friends. Luckily, she was an understanding sort, and wouldn't worry.

Petya had decided to visit two brothers outside the city limits, who were engaged in reprinting Bibles. He would warn them, and hide his own stuff out there. If he was unlucky, well – he'd throw the rucksack into the water, weighed down as it was with the iron. It would be a while before the ice melted, so all he'd need to do would be to make a hole in it. That wouldn't be a problem, the brothers' house was right by a small river. Great conspirator that he was, Petya left his address and phone book in his desk drawer, although he should long since have known that such items are regarded as the prize catch in any house search, even if they contain no more than the phone numbers of one's girl-friends.

Pioneers and Young Communist League members! Do not do as Petya did!

It was just as well that Petya wasn't at home when his mother came back with a load of frozen fruit imported from Yugoslavia. She had spent a long time queuing for it while her son was busily burning samizdat. It was all the more fortunate, because half an hour later Filipp Savich came round in person to see her, carrying a bunch of Crimean roses. And not for the reason one might think. But for a serious talk.

Chapter Eleven

FILIPP SAVICH HAD not always been the head of the Fifth Directorate. His rapid promotion began later, a little time after Stalin's death. But back in '49 Filipp Savich had been, if not exactly small fry, still not the largest fish in the pond. Maybe that's what had helped him survive all the purges and shake-ups. He had an instinctive understanding of the System from the war years, when he was a young political instructor in the sections which followed their own side's soldiers into battle, shooting down any who tried to turn back or run away. Under the System the rule was: if you wanted to live, maintain a low profile. Don't stand out in any way. Don't try to excel. Acquire the reputation of a useful nonentity – at least, for a while. Don't put yourself forward, let others do it for you. And bide your time, the golden opportunity always comes to those who wait. The way it came to Stalin – and that, how many years after the start of his career?

By 1949 Filipp Savich had perfected the art of saying 'the final decision is not mine' in such a way that one immediately knew the truth was quite the reverse. That everything depended on his decision.

When that young academic with haunted eyes came to see him, he gave her his stock response. There must have been hundreds of them running around office corridors at that time, at every level – no longer demanding justice by then, but broken by circumstances, and prepared to do anything.

The situation, at first glance, hardly seemed worth bothering about. It concerned a biologist who specialized in snake venom;

he had researched and devised a number of successful anti-venenes. He'd even received commendations for his work, bits of paper which she was poking across the table at Filipp Savich in the insane hope that they might somehow help. Snake venoms were used in medicine, his laboratory was trying to synthesize them in order to satisfy the demands of the domestic pharmaceutical industry. As if there were not enough snakes in the country to go around its millions of citizens . . .

There are any number of eccentrics manning the laboratories of our vast Motherland, if the truth be told. Some count the feelers or whatever they're called on beetles, others try to cross buckwheat and barley with the aim of increasing the grain harvest . . . And this one had devoted his life to researching cobras and similar undesirables. Probably couldn't appreciate his lovely wife because of all those reptiles around him.

And the lovely, haunted-looking wife herself was right here, across the table from Filipp Savich. She wasn't to know that the Committee was very interested in studying poisons just then, even taking whole laboratories under its wing. And some very unusual things happened to the staff: some rose meteorically, others fell just as spectacularly. Who would've thought there could be so many saboteurs among all those idealistic academics? Incredible! The public prosecutors could barely keep up with all the cases uncovered.

Probably that's just what has happened to this fellow, too. Or maybe he had suddenly realized what kind of uses these poisons would be put to by the Committee, and dug in his heels. People with ideals can be like that: they can easily spend ten years working on human extermination programmes without realizing what they're doing. They go on thinking that they're contributing to medical research. Then, in the course of developing antidotes, they simultaneously synthesize poisons for which science has found no cure. Then, if they suddenly see the light too late, like little children, they start to shed tears: we didn't mean any harm!

Then again, he may have made some very important discovery, and once such discoveries have been fully developed, it is not wise to leave the participants alive: they know too much. There had been government projects in various fields where all the participants were charged and shot as soon as the project was completed. To ensure one hundred per cent secrecy.

Another possibility was a straightforward intrigue in scientific circles, someone laying a trap for someone else. In order to achieve the desired results, political motives are introduced: our respected colleague, alas, is guilty of ideological errors. This was the means whereby genetics and cybernetics were excised from Soviet science. The government does not oppose this: whoever emerges on top in these internecine struggles is deemed to be the more politically aware. And political awareness is a Soviet scientist's most important attribute. In any case, whatever had happened, the husband of this long-legged beauty was a wrecker and a saboteur. It is true that in this instance, even if Filipp Savich had, for some strange reason, wanted to help, he would have been powerless.

Actually, in all fairness, he did warn her. Then asked an unexpected question: had she lived at such and such an address before she was married? She raised her head regally, as though to say: are you intending to arrest me, too? This was an unfounded suspicion. She and her husband worked in different fields. It was just that Filipp Savich had an excellent memory. He had lived once at that address himself, and he remembered a little girl, Natasha, who had been one of the children playing in the yard, a little kid in a Panama hat. He remembered her because she had once been bitten by someone's dog, and had yelled her head off. Later she began to develop into a long-legged creature with neatly bobbed hair, but this was just at the time when Filipp Savich moved elsewhere.

Strange how fate can bring two former neighbours together again. It emerged that she, too, recalled the incident with the dog and her chivalrous saviour. She just hadn't recognized him.

Hadn't expected to meet him here. In any case, Filipp Savich accepted her sacrificial passion. They met a few times. The staff of the Committee have their human weaknesses, too, and occasionally, despite instructions, do not tell their superiors about their casual amours. A little later Filipp Savich deemed it wise to disappear. Firstly, wives of persons under investigation were occasionally placed under surveillance. The last thing he needed was to be caught in a connection like that. Secondly, he genuinely liked her very, very much, and no good could come of that. He had to keep his head at all costs.

Filipp Savich married as he should and whom he should, a young woman without a stain on her record. She bore him three daughters, they had no luck with producing a son. Filipp Savich, for obscure reasons, wanted a son at all costs. And he kept waiting and hoping. But after the birth of three girls, his wife suffered one miscarriage after another, and the doctors advised against any further exercises in reproduction.

Shortly afterwards, Filipp Savich's golden opportunity finally arrived, and he began to rise rapidly through the ranks. This meant surrendering one lot of obligations, accepting new ones, assessing his staff in order to decide whom to take with him, and whom to ditch there and then. Moreover, a close colleague of his fell, and fell badly. There were great changes within the Committee, the entire body was being restructured. Many lost their places, along with their entire crews, making room at the top for their more fortunate colleagues. It was imperative to go through the records to determine whether any of those marked for the new seats of power had been connected in any way with this unfortunate colleague.

It was while he was engaged in leafing through an old, closed file concerning a surveillance operation that Filipp Savich saw a photo of that same Natasha, designated as the widow of a saboteur. She was holding a baby in her arms, one which wouldn't have been walking yet. Filipp Savich stopped in his tracks: how many files had he flipped through like this, mechanically, not reading the contents? He looked at it more closely, and emerged almost one hundred per cent convinced. The dates tallied. In fact, they couldn't do otherwise – the baby was the spitting image of the infant captured in photos of his own early childhood. Filipp Savich's visual memory was particularly good.

By the time Filipp Savich had this revelation, Petya was ten years old. He knew that his father had been a prominent scientist, who had been repressed and later rehabilitated. Many of Petya's contemporaries knew these words and could say them without a stammer. He had a wonderful mother: attractive, cheerful and a PhD. None of his classmates had a mother like that. For that reason, he tended to divide her friends into two groups: those who wanted to marry her, and normal folks. The normal ones he treated normally. The others he hated, and did his best to show it. In all honesty, this was not out of deference to the shade of his father, whom he only knew from photographs and who didn't seem out of the ordinary. He had worn glasses, and was not particularly handsome. It was just that he needed his mother for himself. So there was absolutely no need for her to waste any love on anyone else.

He rated Filipp Savich as a normal friend. If only because he talked to Mother about his daughters, telling her how they were getting on with learning ballet and English. Petya sympathized with their sufferings, but not unduly. Very likely they were stupid enough to be first-rate students. If you don't have enough sense to get only average marks, you have only yourself to blame when adults decide to foster your talents. That's when the going really starts to get tough.

In Petya's imagination, Filipp Savich was surrounded by a special aura: he never said directly where he worked, but once let slip that it was all top secret. Something to do with space. That was enough to set anyone's head spinning: space! Maybe Filipp Savich designed space-ships, or even trained cosmonauts!

Filipp Savich's visits were not very frequent. Several times he took Petya and his mother to the theatre. Sometimes, when

Petya had school holidays and his mother had to work, Filipp Savich would take him out for the whole day in his car, and they had a marvellous time. They ate ice-cream in cafés where there was music playing and went to the shooting range where Petya could shoot for as long as he liked. Petya even liked just driving around the city, especially when it was raining or snowing and the windscreen wipers squeaked against the glass, sitting beside Filipp Savich whose kind, thoughtful face wore a slightly tired look. At such times Petya would stop asking questions about the cosmos and whether there was any life on Mars, and they would just sit there in companionable silence. But outings like this were rare, too. Of course, he must have some kind of life of his own. But on Petya's birthdays there would always be presents, and what presents! For instance, what other boy could boast that he had a pair of real naval binoculars?

Petya understood, his mother had told him. Filipp Savich had once tried to save his father, and had got himself into considerable difficulties. His very life had been in the balance, he was lucky to be alive. True friends like this had been few and far between in those years. So, in a way, getting presents from Filipp Savich was like getting them from his father.

Another good thing about Filipp Savich was that he didn't try to interfere in any of Petya's business. A man of tact. It was only when Petya was preparing to go on to higher education that he asked which institute Petya was planning to enter. And he had approved: physics and electronics was a good choice. There were fifteen applicants for every vacancy? That was good, too, it meant studying would be interesting. Nor did he exhibit a shadow of doubt that Petya would be selected. It was true, Petya breezed through the exams without any problems: the money his mother had spent on coaches had been a good investment.

Despite his respect for Filipp Savich, Petya never uttered a word about his clandestine interests. It was not always the case that those who had been adults in Stalin's time were crippled by fear. But those who had children could not be unaffected. At least, Petya knew of no exceptions to this rule. So why try people's nerves further?

Petya reached his destination by the last train, and rapped on the window.

'Open up, sleepy-heads!'

The brothers Mikha and Lyokha, sandy hair on end, panicked when they heard Petya's news. Petya began to regret that he had overdone the rasping note in his voice, because the effect this produced was more than he had bargained for. They began to flap around the house, wasting time on useless activities. Destroy everything! Leave no traces! Is there enough time?

'My God, the dogs are barking! They must be here already,' cried Lyokha, clasping his bony hands to his face.

It took a considerable effort for Petya to calm them down. The dogs could be barking at any number of things. There was absolutely no need to rush off and sink all their photographic equipment in the river: they were artists, after all, so why shouldn't they have a magnifier and a dryer? However, they were adamant about the binding press.

Petya realized that this was no place to hide anything, and began feeding the contents of his rucksack into the burning stove. This was something not even the terrified brothers could object to, as the stove was burning anyway, and a stack of birch logs lay beside it.

But oh, oh, what *were* they to do? They'd been reprinting Bibles on photographic paper, and that burns so slowly. And then there were the Gospels which had already been bound with synthetic covers, which would stink the place out, but not burn.

Feverishly Lyokha ripped the covers off the thick volumes. Goose-pimples, covered with bristling hairs, showed through the strategically slashed holes in his jeans. Mikha dragged the master copy over to the fire: an excellent edition on thin rice paper. Petya jerked him by the shoulders.

'You'll be throwing the icons into the stove next! So what if they find a Bible in the house – you won't get punished for that!'

'Don't you understand anything? This Bible's *tamizdat* – published in the West! In America!'

'Well, that would give you a chance to suffer for the Lord,' remarked Petya mercilessly.

He had known the brothers for two years, and they had always treated him with condescension, offering lofty instruction. They rebuked him for not being versed in patristic literature, for the improper tone of his mind, for forgetting to cross himself when he entered a room with an icon. They were aghast to learn that Petya did not observe the fasts decreed by the Church. When they sat down to eat Mikha, as the senior, would invariably say grace and bless the table. He did this even in other people's houses if he felt the hosts were likely to neglect this duty. Petya didn't know whether this was the done thing or not, but it was better not to argue with the brothers, they had learned everything down to the finest detail. Of course, this was something one had to respect, but Petya could never feel quite at ease in their company. He knew that he was not firm in the faith and had doubts concerning his relationship to God. However, he felt that he lacked sufficient humility to fortify his faith under the tutelage of Mikha and Lyokha.

Now he felt that he was running short of human charity, too. All right, if they're so determined to sink the press – let them. He'd help them carry it. But he drew the line at throwing the Bibles into the river – let them do that themselves, if they were so set on it.

'I'm still a godless good-for-nothing I'm afraid,' he told them with heavy sarcasm. 'I can't bring myself to do it.'

Lyokha stared at him with frightened, pale blue eyes: what a time to be preaching at them!

They chipped away the thin ice at the spot where the brothers had plunged into the river on the feast of the Epiphany, in keeping with ancient tradition. The press sank with a deep gurgle and disappeared from view. After this, Petya went back to the house and didn't see what else the brothers did. Perhaps if he'd stayed he would have realized what happened to photographic paper under ice if it were just thrust under and not weighted down.

The brothers agreed to let Petya stay the night, since there was no way for him to get back. Nobody came to conduct any house search, everything was quiet. The dogs – yes, they yapped from time to time, but not enough to disturb the surrounding peace. The stars passed majestically across the surface of the river, peering at their own reflection in it or perhaps wondering what was hidden underneath.

Filipp Savich did not have much time to prepare what he had to say, nor did he know how to go about it. The art of managing people consists of two simple things: knowing what a person most wants and what he most fears. Then acting accordingly.

When Natasha was running around on her husband's behalf, everything was crystal clear. She wanted to gain her husband's release, and for everything to be the same as it was before. Nothing else. What she had feared was that her husband would be killed. Nothing else. Of course, her husband was shot. From then on, Natasha was not afraid of anything. Filipp Savich admired this, and was irritated by it at the same time: how did one deal with a woman like that? All his previous experience with women was no help to him here.

For instance, he had thought that women should be made to feel pain in bed: not too much, of course, but still . . . This aroused him, and it aroused them, too. They evidently enjoyed it. But the very first time, Natasha just sat up and stared at him in amazement as if not understanding what he was doing. Why on earth did you do that? Filipp Savich felt confused, and pretended it was an accident.

When he encountered her again as the mother of a ten-year-old son, he understood her even less. What did she want? Nothing, by the looks of it. As if she were serving a sentence decreed by fate: honourably, even gaily, but without any special hopes. Fate was clearly courting her, trying to arouse her interest. But she accepted life's gifts as a matter of course, with no particular emotions: a successful career which any man might envy, material well-being, a nice, self-contained apartment, her own beauty and the admiration of surrounding menfolk.

There were so many widows with small children – how many of them could boast such good fortune? Most of them were stuck in communal housing, clinging to their beggarly wages, their faces stamped with constant fear and humiliation. Their children were condemned to round-the-clock crèches. Driven by desperation some placed their offspring in children's homes – and felt shame before their children and the whole world.

Had Filipp Savich found her in such straits, everything would have been easy: he would have fixed her up, and she would have sobbed with gratitude and happiness. As it was, he had nothing to offer her. Natasha didn't value her luck. She wasn't even afraid for Petya, which shocked Filipp Savich to the core.

On his second visit, accompanied by a large, cellophane-wrapped bouquet, with a ceremonial partaking of fashionable coffee rather than tea beside a decorated Christmas tree, Petya burst in, his clothes frozen stiff, his lips blue with cold. He had been skating on the ice, and fallen through into the freezing waters of the pond. His friends had pulled him out, and he had run all the way back home in his wet clothes. It was the end of December, the temperature had plunged to minus twenty, and the most surprising thing was that that damned pond hadn't frozen through to the bottom. How would a normal mother react in such a situation? Why, she'd be expecting her child to come down with double pneumonia at the very least! On top of that, she'd have been immediately overwhelmed with the thought of what would have happened if nobody had been there to pull her son out, and started weeping and wailing over

him, and scolding him at the same time! Whenever Filipp
Savich's daughters so much as got their feet wet, his wife's face
would immediately crease into lines of worry and fear, eyebrows rising to a pathetic peak, mouth agape . . .

As for Natasha, she merely smiled and ordered:

'Quick march into the bath!'

Then she apologized casually to Filipp Savich, and disappeared into the bathroom after her son. He could hear a rush
of water, the struggle as they removed the rigid frozen clothing,
then Petya's yell, 'Mum, that's too hot!'

Then they were laughing. She first, then the boy. He didn't
know what they found so funny, the noise of the water was too
loud.

She left Petya in the bath and returned to Filipp Savich, calm
and slightly flushed. He tried to voice his concern:

'Maybe you should call a doctor? I know a good paediatri-
cian . . .'

'Nonsense, he won't get so much as a sniffle. He's a strong
child,' she said easily. 'Once he's warmed up, I'll give him a cup
of tea with raspberry jam and put him to bed. He'll be right as
rain tomorrow. No one gets sick during the school holidays.'

She was right: he learned that when he phoned the next day.
He even felt a little put out that she wasn't mistaken. But then,
the main thing was that the boy was all right. His boy. His son.
His only son.

If Natasha realized what a hold she had over Filipp Savich now,
she never gave any sign of it, nor tried to exploit it. She didn't
need to. It seemed she was convinced that Filipp Savich had
done everything he could to help her husband, but without
success. She continued to address him in the familiar fashion,
called him Fil, and was as easy with him as with an old friend.
She let him see Petya, take him out occasionally, and give him
presents – as if he were one of the family. As for him – he never

tried to cross the tacitly drawn line. He knew that this was best for Petya. Let his son grow up, and then they would see.

But now he had to talk to Natasha and gain her support, or nothing would work. No matter how well or how little they knew each other, they had to sit down and discuss what was likely to happen to Petya.

'Only don't ask me who told me. But the information's one hundred per cent certain. Half the city will know tomorrow. Petya hung around with this young fellow, didn't he? Possibly they both dabbled in samizdat, and the other one is now under investigation for it. He could take fright and babble all sorts of things, true or false.'

Now he saw fear enter Natasha. Just as it had done twenty years ago. It grew like a flood, from her hands to her eyes, filling them completely. This self-assured, ironic woman was folding up like a glove crumpled by a merciless hand, and with it went her confidence and irony, leaving her no refuge. Filipp Savich pitied her, but he couldn't help entertaining a certain satisfaction. How do you feel now, sweetheart? It wouldn't be long, though, before she got a grip on herself, so he must say what had to be said without loss of time. Now, when they were united by their common fear for Petya, and her fear was greater, they could come to an agreement.

Natasha wrung her hands.

'Oh God, this is terrible! What can I do, what can I do?' she cried distractedly. 'Fil, can't you suggest anything?'

'First of all, we have to make sure that Petya doesn't do anything stupid. Are you sure that he won't make any half-baked attempts to save his friend?'

'I don't know, I don't know . . .'

She was crying quietly, dabbing at her eyes with a paper napkin from the table. Suddenly Filipp Savich wanted to know the truth, right this minute. Generally speaking, he had always appreciated her silence on the subject, acknowledging tacitly that he had a family of his own. She had never attempted to pin him down with circumstances or by saying the fateful words. He was grateful for her reticence, and never posed the question himself. Why should he? The answer was clear enough without that. But now, he couldn't bear it any longer. He wanted her to tell him. Enough of this hide and seek.

'Natasha – whose son is Petya?'

She shuddered and began to sob uncontrollably. Jumping up, she strode over to a chest of drawers, yanked one open and tossed him a bundle of photographs in a rubber band.

'So you've decided to break me now, have you? All right, do your worst! God, what a fool I am, what an idiot! So we're going to go all noble, are we? Maybe you mean to tell Petya that his father isn't who he always thought? Oh, by the way, son, you'll have to change your patronymic. He might have still been alive when your mother behaved like a whore . . .'

She was edging towards hysteria. Filipp Savich brought a glass of water from the kitchen, made her drink it, wiped up what she spilled.

'Natasha, pull yourself together. You're behaving like a silly schoolgirl. How could you possibly think . . . That's not at all what I had in mind.'

'What, then?'

She looked at him angrily, accusingly.

'What I meant is that if he's my son, you should know you can rely on me. I want to save him just as much as you do. And the only thing to do is to get him out of Moscow as quickly as possible. Change his surroundings, give him a new purpose, until this whole thing blows over.'

'What about the Institute?'

'And what if he's kicked out of there on the basis of what this Koretsky has to say? Or something worse?'

She was listening intently now, prepared to join him in seeking a way out. Yes, Fil's right. He's got contacts, he'll arrange for Petya to get academic leave.

Only no psychiatric examinations, anything but that!

115

A scientific expedition? Won't that be dangerous? Will they take him? What would he be doing? Assist in gathering samples? A whole six months?

She had never been parted from Petya for as long as a month. Even when he went to Pioneer camp, she would visit him twice a week. But she agreed, of course she agreed! When was the ship sailing?

The chief question remaining was how to convince Petya himself. This was something Filipp Savich took upon himself. He would have a talk with him, man to man.

'Believe me, Natasha, this will be for the best. No, I'll swear by whatever you want that I won't say anything to him. That belongs to the past, and the past should be left alone: would it have been better if he hadn't been born? And nobody but the two of us needs to know the truth. There's no point in turning the boy's world upside-down.'

Filipp Savich was pleased that she was so sensible. He had no doubt that he could talk Petya around: a lad with parents like them could only be bright. The moment he'd entered the flat, Filipp Savich had caught and identified the faint smell of burnt paper.

Chapter Twelve

VIKTOR STEPANYCH WAS a man of considerable composure. His mind might be in turmoil, caught up in various schemes, his emotions could be in a state of ferment, the adrenalin coursing through him from head to toe, but you would never guess from his outward appearance. Sitting calmly at his desk, he tapped a blank piece of paper lightly with a pencil.

All very well to say two days! What could you do in two days? Especially when nothing practical suggested itself, just a lot of wildcat schemes. He felt like packing it all in, getting drunk, and finding himself a woman. But his well-trained mind immediately computed how many hours these pursuits were likely to take. Even now, he had much less than the initial forty-eight at his disposal.

He bitterly regretted having insisted. Did he need to go one better than anyone else? What had prompted him to pit his intuition against his master's? No, this was one mistake he'd never repeat. But at the moment, he had no way out: he must succeed, and within the deadline.

What he would have liked to do more than anything was to grab the Storyteller by the lapels, and beat the hell out of him until the bastard confessed. Spit it out, and don't waste other people's time. Then loop a guitar string round his throat, and tighten it until he was blue in the face, loosen it just enough to let him get a few gulps of air, and then tighten it again. And again. But we're not using such methods against the creative intelligentsia. At the moment.

He'd ordered the Storyteller to be followed to Lipetsk, but he doubted if this would result in anything. His file showed that he'd gone there before from time to time. All those damned writers took themselves off to the village every so often. They have this thing for crazy old men and women. Then they go around bragging about what some stupid old peasant has said to them about this or that. They want to commune with nature, you see: oh, look at that sunset! And look at that dear little pony cropping the daisies!

Dammit, they'd built special 'creative retreats' for them, where surveillance could be conducted easily, and where there was enough nature for them to choke on, but was that enough? No! They wanted more: the smell of harness leather, and out of the way places no sane person would want to go to, where you could burst a blood-vessel looking for a spot to hide an observer. While they enjoyed the rustic setting, if you please, fooling around with axes and hoes and hauling buckets of water from the well. Tolstoy or one of those started it all, and the fashion survived to this day: you have to walk around barefoot, poke around in the earth, shovel snow in winter. Just like kids. In any case, it would be a while before anything was likely to emerge from the Lipetsk visit, and Viktor Stepanych was already down to thirty-two hours!

He'll have to have a talk with the neighbour, that's what. She cleans for him, and might know something. The woman's proved her patriotism, has a medal. Why hadn't he thought of this sooner? Even if she doesn't know anything, she could be instructed to keep her eyes skinned . . . Oh time, time! Can't you slow down just a little, damn you! Of course she won't have time to keep a watch on the Storyteller. So what else could be done?

Auntie Xenia received a telephone call with a politely worded request to come round to the house administration office for a moment. Viktor Stepanych wasted forty whole minutes on that old bag, and if you count travel time – one and a half hours. As was to be expected, she didn't know anything and hadn't seen a thing. Patriots like that should be shot in droves. Even her eventual agreement to keep her eyes open had to be dragged out of her. Only the final argument seemed to make any impression on her: are you, or are you not, a sound Soviet citizen? This works almost every time: what possible answer can there be to such a question apart from the obvious affirmative? Who would claim to be anti-Soviet? Viktor Stepanych closed the interview by implying dire consequences if she didn't keep her mouth shut. The one good thing about old fools like her is that they're easily frightened.

What next? It was almost evening, and evening is invariably followed by night. One working day left. To make matters worse, a tooth started nagging under an old filling. Was it because he'd been out in the cold? Or was it nerves? Viktor Stepanych hoped devoutly that it was the latter.

He had been terrified of dentists since childhood. They treat you, sure. But isn't it equally true that they try to get some pleasure out of it for themselves by driving the drill down with full force on the tenderest spot? Some more, some less, but each and every one of them derives a sadistic thrill from the yells of pain issuing from the tipped-back chair. This was a thrill Viktor Stepanych understood very well, especially when one could indulge in it with complete impunity. There is less impunity in the specialized clinics than in those designated for the man in the street, the kind in which Viktor Stepanych had endured his first agonies, but even so . . .

He poured himself a shot of whisky, and downed it in solitude. This kind of drinking never enhanced anyone's image. His healthy young body hankered timidly for female company, but Viktor Stepanych told it to calm down: this was not the time. Maybe he should take a walk before going to bed?

One of the great things about the capital of our Motherland is that you can walk the streets in safety all night long if you feel like it. Nowhere is the militia more vigilant. All suspicious elements are whisked out beyond the 101st kilometre from the city, and rightly so. After all, there are foreign embassies dotted around the capital, and government officials, and foreign tourists. There's no place for undesirables here. Moscow isn't Konotop. Viktor Stepanych was from Konotop himself, and knew that one thing you didn't do there was to walk the streets after dark. In fact, all sorts of unpleasant things could happen in broad daylight. He would never forget how, when he was in the tenth grade, he'd been robbed of the prestigious fur hat his uncle had given him, the kind of hat worn by ranking Party members and regional Party secretaries. If Viktor Stepanych hadn't clawed his way up in the KGB with only his own talents to help him, he would have been stuck in Konotop for the rest of his life. And had no choice but to attend a dental clinic where some municipal Gorgon reigned supreme.

Viktor Stepanych strolled down the well-lit street, little puffs of vapour emerging rhythmically from his nostrils. Either it was the whisky or the general tension of the situation, but the injustice of that long-gone incident rankled with him all over again. Not only had they taken his hat, but added insult to injury by waving a screwdriver menacingly in front of his stomach: hand over the hat yourself! And he did.

It was the fashion among the roughs of Konotop to use screwdrivers as an offensive weapon. Carrying knives is forbidden by law, but screwdrivers are another matter – for all that a thrust from a screwdriver can be just as deadly as a knife. Still, one could hardly forbid the Soviet working class to own screwdrivers. Everybody has one. Even that wretched Storyteller, a weedy intellectual who probably doesn't know how to hammer a nail into a wall, has a few tools in his flat.

Some twinge of recollection surfaced at the back of Viktor Stepanych's mind: he'd been present at the second house search, and had seen those tools himself. A small selection typical of your average intellectual: PVC glue, a hammer, a pair of pliers, some nails and screws in an old coffee tin, a roll of insulating tape and a ball of string. The whole lot tucked into a kitchen drawer. There wasn't even a drill. Nauseatingly ordinary. There had, however, been two screwdrivers: one that was like any other, and one that was very short, half of its handle cut off. Now that was rather unusual.

Still, it wasn't the Storyteller's only unusual possession. That statuette of Buddha made out of some semi-precious stone or other, with a blue plasticine wolf beside it. Some combination! No, that wasn't it, there was nothing strange in that at all: someone had given him both items, he couldn't throw them away without giving offence, so they stood on a shelf side by side. Just the same as with children's drawings stuck up on kitchen walls.

But the unformed thought gnawed away at his subconscious, and he strove to bring it to light. The screwdriver, the screwdriver! He couldn't have shortened the handle himself, there was nothing to do that with. A present? But who'd give a present like that? Yet, if it's among his tools, that means he uses it. Even though it must be awkward with that short handle. Viktor Stepanych could make no sense of it, but since his intuition had started this, he would let it see him through. Let's concentrate on that screwdriver. What reason could there be for cutting off half the handle? In order to use it in some place where an ordinary screwdriver would be too long to serve the purpose . . . a secret hiding place? But they'd checked every possibility.

What if they'd underestimated the Storyteller? Maybe Viktor Stepanych had been too ready to think of the Storyteller as your typical four-eyed intellectual who was useless with his hands? The kind who can never hide anything properly, whose ingenuity doesn't extend beyond shoving things under a pile of dirty washing. And the Storyteller, if it came to that, didn't wear glasses. We'll have to look again. That was the only hope. It was only logical to assume that if the Storyteller was engaged in writing something clandestine, he wouldn't hide it in the middle of Izmailovo Park. It would have to be at home, close to hand.

They could search the place first thing in the morning, since the tenant was out of town. Or maybe he should call a search right now? No, that would be unwise: they'd have to switch on the lights, and the old bat next door knew that the flat was supposed to be empty. And speaking of the old bat, she had keys to the flat and could walk in on them at any moment to feed the cat or something.

No, he told himself, keep your cool, friend. We can neutralize the old bat if need be, but it was unlikely that she'd be up and about before eight o'clock in the morning. And she certainly wouldn't be waking at five or six to go out into the yard and check whether the lights were on in the neighbouring flat.

Viktor Stepanych did not sleep that night. He sat there, turning every possibility over in his mind: if he were the Storyteller, where would he choose for a hiding place? The balcony? Hardly: you could see everything from the street. The washing machine? But you wouldn't need a specially adapted screwdriver for that, an ordinary one would do. At 4 a.m., still with no solution in his head, he set off to supervise the search as eagerly as if it were his first date.

He switched on the light, and told his subordinates to go over everything again, paying special attention. As for himself – he extracted the mysterious screwdriver and started going around the flat with it, like a water diviner with a dowsing rod. The kitten dodged between his feet, looking up inquiringly.

Piss off, animal! The kitten, receiving a shrewd kick, skittered away under the cupboard and peered out with the malevolent stare of a recent poacher turned gamekeeper. Lucky for you, thought Viktor Stepanych grimly, that you can't talk, or I'd soon make short work of you! Actually, it's amazing to think how much our subjects' pets know about what we do. Just as well they're speechless.

Hallway? No. Toilet? No . . .

*

Filipp Savich always arrived at work on time, although he could have come in later, nearer ten, if he wanted. The senior staff often do so, and then express surprise at the lack of discipline among their subordinates. It wouldn't have happened in the Leader's time. People worked nights back then. Many had become lax in recent years, but not Filipp Savich.

He approached the door of his office exactly three minutes before the start of the working day, and found Viktor Stepanych pacing around, his eyes ablaze. All right, come on in.

Viktor Stepanych set out four rolls of film on the polished surface of the desk with a decisive click.

'That's our Storyteller for you!'

'Got it, eh? Where?'

'He's got this little step at the entrance to his balcony – you know the kind. Just a bit above floor level. Well, he's made the front board removable. Set it on screws at each end, and there's a space underneath . . . Simple as that – undo two screws . . .'

Viktor Stepanych was clearly keen to draw a diagram for Filipp Savich's edification, so it was time to deflate him a little.

'Then how come it took you three attempts to find it?'

'My fault.'

Right answer, succinctly put. The young fellow was learning fast.

'Fine, fine, one can overlook an initial mistake. Who would have expected a children's writer to pull a stunt like that! Did you confiscate the manuscript?'

'I left everything just as it was, Filipp Savich. Pending orders. I simply photographed it and got the film processed. The quality's good.'

'Well done, you're improving! I suppose you haven't had a wink of sleep? Go home and have a rest with my blessing. Come back around four o'clock. Leave this with me, I'll take a look at it, and we'll decide later what to do about it.'

Viktor Stepanych was sure that he wouldn't be able to sleep after such a coup. However, he went out like a light almost as soon as his head touched the pillow, dribbling a child-like drop of saliva. But even in sleep, he remained appreciative and proud: how thoughtful of Filipp Savich to send him off for a rest. Personally.

In the meantime, the Storyteller's novel reached its first outside reader. Filipp Savich ran through the work cursorily: using the viewer for a long time was tiring, for all that he was used to it. However, he could already tell that the work had considerable merit. This was no junk literature.

Pavel Pulin's opus had been a much easier proposition to deal with: his 'Apple In the Well' was pure anti-Soviet propaganda. Slander about the conditions in state-run old people's homes. Every page reeked of stale urine and unwashed bedclothes. Lice crawling all over paralysed old women. A cry of infuriated passion: look, people, at what's happening! Sabotage, no more, no less.

If that had made it to the West, the uproar would have been horrific. Even worse than the one about our psychiatric practices. And it would have been harder to hide: old people's homes aren't labour camps or specialized psychiatric institutions. Access to them cannot be refused, so anybody can go in to visit their grandmother twice removed or their ageing granddad. To check out the truth. What enormous resources would have had to be expended to quash the whole business if the subject had ignited public interest. Pulin was lucky to die when he did, or we would have shown him a thing or two!

But this work was much more subtle. It wasn't documentary, but a fantasy of sorts. Involving both a flight from reality and an unhealthy interest in it. Containing elements of surrealism, and at the same time bristling with tactless references to things as they are, but mention of which is taboo in our society. By tacit consent of the survivors. Then there is some mystical nonsense concerning doubles. You have this former Soviet intellectual –

popularly known as an 'fsi' – freely roaming round the country – and that at the present day! It's not clear what he's looking for, but he's certainly in breach of the passport laws. Nor does he work anywhere, but feeds himself by doing occasional odd jobs – thereby also breaking the law. Hangs out with tramps and similar misfits, gets into all sorts of scrapes. Matures into a tough guy with no sloppy sentiments. At the same time, he somehow enters the former lives of his doubles: each one more dubious than the last, but all in Russia, and all interwoven. Parallels emerge which act powerfully on the imagination. About love, and power, and things like that. The main character is a complex sinner of enormous charm, amazingly credible, and so typically Russian that Filipp Savich could not help sympathizing with him: he's one of us. Ours.

And the author's conclusion is that if you can't be master of your own country, you can at least be master of yourself.

A pernicious piece of writing, no doubt about it. The fact that it was so well done only aggravated the situation. Head and shoulders above Pulin's 'Apple'. Filipp Savich understood literature; were it otherwise, he would not have been appointed head of the Fifth Directorate. This work, he knew, would appeal to the avant-garde of all kinds, and even to the progressive Western intelligentsia, although it was hardly likely to provoke an anti-Soviet craze. But it would certainly make waves as samizdat. Russians would wear holes in the paper reading it, sit up nights hammering out copies. There's a growth of interest in Russian themes here.

Well, Storyteller, we certainly underestimated your calibre! We're going to have to work very hard on you. Easy enough to confiscate your manuscript, but then you'll just go and write something else. So write away – but in the right direction. It will be better for you. And a help to the state.

In fact – and this is an important point – literary merit is a secondary consideration. As is political awareness or the lack of it. If a clandestine manuscript comes to light – even an essay on the climate during the Jurassic period – it must be taken in hand. The political harm of such manuscripts, as Filipp Savich was always dinning into the heads of his juniors, has two aspects.

The first and most important is the fact of uncontrolled dissemination. Or even the possibility of it. Anyone who doesn't understand that information means power in the twentieth century shouldn't be working in the Committee. If someone has failed to understand that violation of the state's monopoly on information is anti-state activity, then clearly we like them to remain at large for as short a time as possible.

The second aspect may be present as well: that is, the work may contain material which is unacceptable to the state. At this point in time. If either aspect is present, then work must be carried out with the author. So that he can be made to see sense before he can cause any real trouble.

At four o'clock Filipp Savich instructed the happy Viktor Stepanych to continue the Storyteller operation. He even gave him increased powers. Within reason, naturally. Let him enjoy himself, he's earned it. The decision was to leave the manuscript where it was, though under surveillance. The author must be recruited.

And why not, after all? We need Storytellers, too.

Chapter Thirteen

NIKOLIN RETURNED TO Moscow feeling tired but light at heart. The manuscript was buried safe and sound in Klim's cellar, so the old man wouldn't stumble on it by chance. Klim was in good health and content, his only complaint being that his phantom foot ached because of the weather. Nikolin loved giving presents and was good at choosing, but he always worried that they might not please. However, the Finnish thermal underwear fitted Klim to perfection, and the map of Brussels filled him with delight. The old man had a weakness for maps, new or old. His favourite – of nineteenth-century Paris – was affixed to the wall above the table with rusty drawing pins.

Nikolin had breathed his fill of sky and snow, stretched his muscles doing various chores, and learned a whole lot of marvellous new details about Klim's eventful life. It would appear that if every blonde or brunette who had enjoyed Klim's favours were to apply for child maintenance, there wouldn't be enough bees in all his hives for each child to get one.

The only difficulty was that Nikolin couldn't smoke. A bee is a delicate creature, and can't stand the smell. Even though the hives were hibernating at present, once the odour of cigarette smoke permeates the house, there's no way you can get rid of it completely. So Nikolin had to go out to the little copse near the house to smoke, which meant he smoked that much less. The old man grinned knowingly: being around honey makes people shed all sorts of bad habits.

Still, it was nice to be going back. He had been a bit too much alone of late, and wouldn't mind a little socializing. He wondered how Brysik was faring – there, the little wretch had already tamed his master, had him concerned about his welfare.

Getting off the bus was a crush, and the woman in front of Nikolin landed awkwardly and fell. It looked as though she'd sprained her ankle quite badly, because she sat on the footpath, holding her foot, eyes closed and rocking in pain. Nikolin picked up her handbag and returned it to her. She thanked him with a feeble nod. Nikolin knew how to deal with sprains, but she was wearing a high boot, and probably wouldn't want to take it off in the street. He stood uncertainly beside her.

'May I help you?'

'Get a car for me, would you! To Kachalov street,' she replied in a voice tight with pain.

Nikolin had barely time to raise his hand when a car pulled up smartly: 'Where to, pal?'

Nikolin carefully helped the woman rise and get into the car. A whiff of some exotic perfume filled his nose. He put her bag on her lap. Maybe he should offer to see her home? But what if she thought he was trying to latch on to her? A woman like that must be used to men making a play for her, and very often.

'Will you be able to manage by yourself? Or is there anything else I can do?'

'Thank you, but I wouldn't dream of bothering you any further. You've already done more than enough. There's a lift in my house. Thanks again.'

When the Zhiguli had shot off into the traffic, Nikolin saw a plump, leather-bound notebook practically under his feet. Stupid of him not to have seen it earlier. She must have dropped it when she fell. He picked it up and leafed through it: addresses, telephone numbers, calendar . . . The same perfume wafted from the pages of the little book. Luckily, the first light blue page bore the name, address and telephone number of the owner: Tatyana Kuzina.

*

The investigator was a middle-aged man, neatly dressed. He looked at Dima with clear, light eyes and addressed him politely. Dima, still shell-shocked by his first body search – they'd even made him take off his underpants – sat where he had been instructed: on a stool bolted to the floor. He tried not to move his hands and betray his agitation. He confirmed his name and date of birth. He had braced himself not to answer any further questions, but this resolve proved unnecessary. He was informed that he was suspected of possessing and disseminating anti-Soviet literature. The result – detention. Arrest, in other words. Please sign here to indicate that you have been so informed. Dima signed. After this, he was transferred to his first cell.

As it turned out, everything was fairly run-of-the-mill. The prison was just as Dima had imagined. A large, echoing building, smelling of carbolic. Wire netting strung between landings on the stairways. His cell-mate was an elderly man with a pale, puffy face. He greeted Dima indifferently, and issued an immediate warning: no pacing up and down the cell, he couldn't stand that. Made him dizzy. If Dima wanted to pace around, he'd have to wait until they were taken out for exercise in the yard. Naturally, Dima agreed. Two hours later, he realized the difficulty of the undertaking: it was murder sitting still on the metal bunk, his whole body complained and demanded motion. But he'd given his word, so there was nothing he could do but fidget around where he was.

The notorious slop bucket was also not in evidence: there was a toilet bowl in the cell. One could ask for the catalogue and order books from the prison library. Dima's cell-mate lent him his book – all about the struggle against the kulaks in the Ukraine – until Dima was able to make a selection of his own. In the evening they were given some kind of soup in enamel bowls, and bread. Not the kind of bread you buy in shops, but it looked edible enough. Dima couldn't eat, anyway. His cell-mate was concerned.

'Hey, lad, don't ever think of going on hunger strike. They'll either force-feed you or cart you off to the loony-bin. Go on, eat!'

He poked a meaningful finger in the direction of the judas-hole in the door. The small aperture darkened abruptly. Clearly, they were watching Dima. He forced himself to swallow a few spoonfuls of the soup. He'd come through, just like others had before him. Yet they were heroes, and what was he? All right, he'd be a hero, too. The main thing was not to think of Mother, not even for a moment!

But the thoughts crowded in regardless, and Dima shifted from side to side on his bunk well after lights out. He tried to lie the other way around, but the hatch in the door snapped open at once, and he was told to get his head back to the other end of the bunk and lie in accordance with prison regulations. Dima clenched his teeth, but obeyed. His greatest fear was that he might burst into tears.

For two weeks Dima was left where he was. It drove him mad, wondering why this should be. He spent every moment expecting to be dragged off for questioning, and played all the possible scenarios through in his head. Should he maintain total silence? Resist? Or admit everything concerning himself but refuse to say a word about anyone else? His cell-mate kept up a flow of advice.

'You're here now, so there's no point in making a song and dance about it. These people aren't going to pander to you. The main thing is to remain on good terms with the investigator, or it will only be worse for you. Of course, there's no need to say any more than is strictly necessary, but don't try and pull a fast one, if they've got anything on you. If you try that, they'll slam you into the punishment cell, or even worse. You can't imagine yet how bad things can get. And take care of your health.'

But it seemed that Dima had been entirely forgotten. That alone was enough to drive anyone nuts. That, and the cell-mate's dark hints. So it dragged on until, finally, the hatch opened and the turnkey beckoned for Dima to follow.

The first thing which took his breath away was the sight of Pulin's manuscript on the investigator's desk. Dima froze. He had not allowed himself even to contemplate the possibility that they might find it. But they had. What should he do now? Dima had envisaged every contingency but this.

'Is this yours?'

Say yes! Protect Stella!

'Yes, it's mine.'

'And when did you write it?'

'I didn't.'

'But you said it was yours. So who did write it?'

Should he name the author? The man was dead, after all. Yes, that's it! Shift the blame on to the dead. But maybe he should pretend reluctance for a while, just to keep things credible?

'I don't know.'

The investigator shook his head in a paternal sort of way.

'It's a pity you're taking that attitude, Koretsky. You realize, young fellow, that you're ruining your own life – and for what? For some filthy anti-Soviet scribbling? Have you read it yourself?'

'No,' replied Dima honestly.

'You see, you don't even know what it was you were hiding. That's really not on. You're being manipulated like a baby by some experienced anti-Soviet elements. Who gave you this manuscript? How did it happen?'

'The author. Pavel Pulin. He asked me to keep it for him for a while. He said he'd have it back soon.'

'But you must have realized there was something illicit about it since you went to so much trouble to hide it?'

'He asked me to hide it.'

'How did you meet him?'

Dima had never actually met Pavel Pulin, but he managed to invent a sufficiently believable yarn. The investigator took notes, and Dima cheered up. Let him think that he was some innocent youth who'd been a stooge for the author. That kept Stella out of the entire business. He could even pretend regret that he had allowed himself to be drawn into the affair. He hadn't thought, he hadn't understood, he'd been played for a sucker through his own carelessness. Maybe they wouldn't put him away.

He felt quite pleased with himself, signed the official statement and was escorted back to his cell.

An unpleasant surprise was waiting for Nikolin when he got home. Auntie Xenia, lips compressed, walked in, threw his keys on the table and informed the astounded Nikolin:

'I don't know you any more.'

'Auntie Xenia! Whatever's happened? Why?'

'It's too late for questions now. If you don't know yourself – well, there it is.'

'But Auntie Xenia, what am I supposed to have done?'

'I don't have to tell you. Me – I'm a free woman. Goodbye.'

She stalked out, slamming the door. Nikolin, totally at a loss, began to ring her doorbell, hoping to get an explanation and clear things up. There was obviously some ghastly misunderstanding.

'If you don't go away,' yelled Auntie Xenia furiously from the other side of the door, 'I'll call the militia!'

Good God, thought Nikolin, whatever's got into her? He couldn't think of anything he'd done wrong, and couldn't help feeling hurt: she might have explained.

Brysik was purring his head off in the crook of Nikolin's arm. Well, at least someone was pleased to see him. Thank heaven for small mercies. He filled Brysik's dish with crab meat to make up for his absence. He took himself to task for being thrown off balance so easily: obviously the whole business wasn't worth bothering about, it would sort itself out in time. There was no need for him to ransack his conscience as though he were guilty of some crime.

The thing to do now was to forget about it and call Tatyana without wasting any more time. It had to be her, seeing the address was Kachalov street. There was a limit to coincidence. He'd intended to call her after that letter of hers, but hadn't got round to it. Now there was no reason to delay: maybe there were things in that notebook that she needed urgently.

He dialled the number and launched into a stilted explanation: he was calling about her notebook. The voice at the other end responded joyously.

'Oh, you're so kind! I don't know how I'd manage without it! When may I pick it up?'

'You should probably rest your leg. If you like, I'll bring it round to you.'

A slight snort floated down the telephone line.

'You're so helpful, it's positively suspicious!'

'Oh, I'm a very helpful fellow,' agreed Nikolin, laughing. 'I can bring it over to you straight away, if you wish.'

She wished. He bought a bottle of champagne on the way.

Tatyana was still limping slightly, twisting her pretty mouth a little. However, she looked absolutely stunning. He would never have recognized her. The Tatyana of his schooldays had hair a bit darker, but then, all women dyed their hair these days. She cocked a severe eye at the champagne.

'Oho! You drink champagne before lunch?'

'Only on special occasions.'

Nikolin felt daring and dashing: so, my old classmate! You never did manage to teach me to dance!

'Are you always so quick to seize an opportunity?'

'I never miss a single one. Young lady, you and I have met somewhere before.'

Tatyana was looking a little puzzled. Nikolin decided that

he'd teased her enough, or she'd start thinking he was some kind of crank. He pulled her notebook and the bottle out of his bag, and announced that he had brought one more present. And laid the presentation copy of his latest book on the table. He'd get his regulation number of author's copies tomorrow, so he didn't mind parting with this one. Tatyana glanced at the bright cover.

'This is for me? A children's book?'

'I write children's books mainly. Take me or leave me!'

Then she saw the author's name, and gasped.

'Anton! Antoshka! Is it really you?'

Nikolin enjoyed the effect of his surprise – it was everything he could have wished for. She was laughing and incredulous, making him turn his head this way and that beside the window, finding no trace of the Anton she knew.

'My, what a fine specimen you turned out to be! You ought to be a film star. That bit of grey hair at the temples, and so distinguished looking! And to think you were nothing special when we were at school!'

'Well, you were no oil painting yourself in those days!'

'No . . . ooh! I'll show you! You just didn't know anything about girls.'

'I humbly agree and repent. Tell me, d'you know anything about any of the others? Where's Grishka now? You were leading him around by the nose for a while, weren't you?'

'Nothing of the kind! As for Grishka – he's in Norilsk. Married, with three kids. He's an engineer.'

She hopped nimbly on one foot over to the wall unit to fetch some glasses. Nikolin helped. On the shelf beside the glasses there were some books and a photograph of a young girl with curly hair.

'Yours?'

'My Alisa. Goodness me, wouldn't she be excited if she could see you!'

'Where is she? At school?'

'In a manner of speaking. She's at school all right, but the school's down south in Evpatoria. It's for children who have had tuberculosis. My mother's working in a boarding school there, and she managed to have Alisa admitted. That makes it a little bit easier for me – at least I know she's being well looked after. If only you knew what I had to go through! And alone, all alone, nobody to lean on! Thank God they managed to cure her. Another six months, and I'll be able to bring her home. I've just returned from there, actually, from visiting her. Poor little kitten, she just clung to me and kept on saying over and over: Mummy, I want to come home, take me with you now.'

Tatyana drooped, and Nikolin hastened to uncork the champagne.

'Come on, let's drink to our meeting!'

She tossed her fringe and smiled.

There would be no need to resort to the tablets, she realized. She could keep all three. This assignment could be managed without them. He was ripe to be worked. Lovely man.

When Viktor Stepanych received her first report, he shook his head in admiration: Forget-me-not certainly delivered. Nobody could do the job as well as that woman! He resolved never to question her requisitions for special clothes again.

Chapter Fourteen

PETYA WAS SHAKEN: it emerged that Filipp Savich was better versed in samizdat than Petya himself. And treated his knowledge as nothing special. And why shouldn't he? He'd read Orwell, after all . . . maybe he'd let Petya borrow it? By all means! Admittedly, his copy wasn't an original. Could Petya read English? We-e-ll, at student level . . . in other words – no.

Filipp Savich gazed at Petya understandingly, a benign look on his face, his large head with its square balding patches leaning to one side. Petya was no longer on his guard, and listened attentively. This was a true man-to-man talk, with a bottle of Georgian wine to help things along.

'I respect your convictions, and I'm not trying to force things out of you,' said Filipp Savich. 'I won't deny that there are a lot of things happening which decent people would wish otherwise. But the question is: what should be done about it? You're a thinking person, so you should understand that every action is judged on the basis of its results. And I'll tell you honestly that I don't have much respect for the majority of those dissidents. They cause a lot of trouble, make a name for themselves, and then clear off abroad. Where there's plenty to eat and it's safe.'

'Or they land in the camps,' countered Petya hotly. He was not going to let that pass: what humbug! There had been some fifty political trials in the past five years, and those only the ones we knew of! How many more had there been of which nothing was known?

'Or the camps,' agreed Filipp Savich equably. 'And they'll

drag a few more in with them. No problem. So let them be heroes. But where does it all lead? Is society any better off? It only makes the people at the top tighten the screws. So we get psychiatric prisons instead of the camps. I once saw someone who'd come out of psychiatric treatment. He didn't even recognize his own wife. He was a completely broken man. Not even a man any more, I daresay. A totally obliterated personality. All that was left was his body, which was strong enough to live for another thirty or forty years. A real consolation to his wife and children that was!'

'But, Filipp Savich, what do you suggest? Stay silent, avoid protest, take part in those moronic elections where there's only one candidate? Go along with all this?'

Filipp Savich took a sip of his drink and refilled both their glasses.

'Life, my friend, consists of more than just politics. And even politics aren't the main thing. Look: we were building communism fifty years ago, and still are. From the political point of view, things haven't changed. But life has changed, and so have people. You'd have to be blind not to see it. Throughout this time people have fallen in love, had children, engaged in their chosen occupations, even while cursing every obstacle. They've read books, and listened to music, and complained about their bosses, whom they've usually managed to outwit. Life flows on and a great deal gets smoothed away. There may be some huge obstacle in its path, but time passes and what happens? – that obstacle disappears, and the river follows a new course.

'As for you – you don't know life yet. So you're ready to go off at a tangent. How will it help this Dima of yours if you go out into the middle of a square with a placard? All by yourself, at that. I know these dissidents – they only care about people whose names count for something.'

'So you're saying that I should betray him?'

'What kind of a swine do you take me for, eh? Am I advising you to take part in his investigation? On the contrary, I'm saying you should steer clear! And there's one more person you have no right to betray: your mother. Just think how hard it was for her, a woman alone, to set you on your feet, and now you're hell bent on winding up in a lunatic asylum! And just when you should be starting to be a support to her. She's got nobody else to look to, and you know it.'

That was something Petya did understand, and it rang painfully true. Indeed, how would she manage? Meanwhile, Filipp Savich continued bitterly:

'Why did she never remarry, young and beautiful as she was? I remember what she was like. She's beautiful even now. Do you think she's deserved no happiness in her life? She's an angel, I tell you. Let's drink to her!'

They raised their glasses and drank.

'Filipp Savich, would you go off – just like that? If a friend of yours had just been put away?'

'I was young and hot-headed once, too. So I'll tell you to your face, it's not for you, but for people like me to try to do something for your Dima – who know what life's all about.'

'Is there really some way you can help?'

'I'm not promising anything. And don't you ever make promises. One judges by results, understand? You know, it occurred to me that maybe it's your samizdat that landed Dima in this mess. I don't need an answer from you, but ask yourself, what could they have found? Maybe some journal published on the other side, or, at worst, the *Chronicle*. Possibly some retyped poetry or other. If that were a cause to put people away these days, half the country would be behind bars. Half of Moscow, at any rate. But maybe there was something else, something he didn't trust you with?'

'But what else could there be?'

'For one thing, could he have been involved in black market dealings? Didn't you say he was a dab hand at getting hold of things?'

'Well, his father's a gynaecologist – he's got lots of contacts.'

'I'm a father with contacts, too, but do you think I try to get my daughters everything they want? Fathers can get fed up, too. My Inna, for instance, was only five years old when she got it into her head that she wanted a pair of patent leather shoes. Even though she couldn't say the words properly, she went around screaming: papem toos, papem toos . . .!

'Now, you're not into wanting all sorts of flash gear, so you've no idea how easily people get strung along. You wouldn't believe the number of youngsters who have landed in jail for dealing on the black.' Filipp Savich artfully laced his speech with as much current slang as he knew. 'Many more than were ever taken in for samizdat over the years. Still, charges of black market dealings are easier to quash. Now just suppose somebody sets inquiries afoot to find out at least what your friend was taken in for. And at the same time you, with your idiotic public protest, push him out of the black market category into the political sphere. I doubt very much if he'd thank you for that.'

This was an angle that had not occurred to Petya. True, Dima was very interested in all sorts of imported goods, knew the differences between various Western firms, showed off labels of all kinds. It was very likely that Petya might not know his contacts in that area, just as Dima wouldn't know where Petya got his beloved irons.

Filipp Savich managed to convince him, just as he'd known he would. Petya was a good lad, but his head was still full of youthful nonsense. He was looking for romance in the wrong quarters. Still, he was amenable to instruction. For instance, just think how he'd come back at Filipp Savich at the very end: 'I haven't promised you anything!' Sounding exactly like Filipp Savich himself, the scoundrel!

When he got back, Filipp Savich would have to think seriously about steering the boy in the right direction, but this would require a very light touch. As for Koretsky – they could always sentence him to a further term in the camps if need be.

So he wouldn't lead Petya astray. For the time being. And no matter how much longer Koretsky had to serve, he could at least be grateful for the hope that he would one day be released. Now that everything was settled to his satisfaction, Filipp Savich's fury almost subsided. Only now and again, he would feel a sudden rush of anger at any mention of Koretsky: the son-of-a-bitch! Ruin my Petya's life, would he? And the underhand way of doing it, too: Petya hadn't found his way in life yet, and here he was already being drawn into some kind of scrape. Come on, this is what you have to do – and if you don't, you're a chicken! Petya was a talented youngster, bright, full of character, but he would have found all roads barred to him but one. No you don't, you bastards! You don't know Filipp Savich. He'll cut the throat of anyone for his son's sake, anyone at all. Just let them try!

Filipp Savich was especially anxious to safeguard Petya's opportunity to choose, because he himself had been forced to make his choices too early, back during the war. What had he feared then? That he would be killed. He had seen how it happened in battle, heard how it was done in the prisons, and then learned yet more from the archives. It was hair-raising.

What had Filipp Savich wanted then, when he was a boy like Petya? He didn't know exactly, his desires were still in a state of youthful chaos, and difficult to determine precisely. Probably, what he wanted most was power. And something else, but there was no time to pin it down. Life did not afford him the chance to settle matters in his own mind. So he pitched in: in those days, there was only one form of power that he could see; any alternative was unthinkable. So he knuckled down and followed its lead determinedly, but with close attention too. Analysing situations, considering variations. In order to stay alive.

Yes, Filipp Savich possessed considerable power. He knew how to use it, and how to enjoy it. And would not be averse to increasing it. Only now power was no longer monolithic. There were alternatives these days. That damned Solzhenitsyn, for example: how much power he manages to exercise over his readers: thousands of them, and if we don't take care, there'll be millions. He knows it, too, and writes like some latter-day prophet. His insolent attitude towards us just goes to show . . .

And what about that fellow Amosov? So he's a surgeon, but that fiddling pill-pusher bosses the leaders of the country around any way he wants, can't even keep a civil tongue in his head. Because he knows that he's the only one of his kind in the country. A miracle worker. When all is said and done, everybody has only one heart, including those at the pinnacle of power. So Amosov doesn't have to kow-tow to anyone, he's got his own power over life and death.

Then again, what about our scientists? How many times has the president of the Academy of Sciences, Keldysh, told Party bosses and regional secretaries exactly where they can get off, with their various ideas and demands? And all we can do is put a good face on it, and smile avuncularly, as if all this was no more than some endearing childish prank. We can't complain about writers, true, but will our academics – always excluding Sakharov, of course – vote the right way with a president like that? There's nothing we can do to them, and they know it: what progress can we expect to make otherwise in scientific research, let alone defence matters, without them?

As if that weren't enough, there are the churchmen to worry about, too. Twenty thousand priests and monks were shot, uncounted numbers were packed off to prisons and camps, yet you just take a close look at today's young people, and you'll see practically one in ten sporting a cross round his neck. Openly, at that. It's just a craze? Sure, we can claim in the papers that this is all it is, but we know that crazes are short-lived, and this one's dragged on a bit too long. The clergy's power is growing, and it's not surprising that our colleagues in the Council for Religious Affairs are complaining: you'd think that with every priest accounted for, they'd be under control. But they are, and they aren't.

Filipp Savich would occasionally wonder if there hadn't been something lacking in him when he made his choice as a young man, whether in fact he had grasped all the happiness he might have been destined to have. But what was done, was done, and there was no going back. But he would shield Petya from any efforts to push him. Let the lad sort himself out, get his priorities straight, and then Filipp Savich would do everything in his power to support his son's choice. Whatever that choice might be.

Petya wandered the streets at random, saying goodbye to the city. His academic leave had been approved, and all the details of the expedition arranged. They were sailing tomorrow. The South Seas! The places he would visit! He had seen a photo of the *Meridian*, two huge white spheres mounted on its decks the purpose of which was still a mystery to him. Still, you could tell at a glance that this was a scientific research vessel. The imminent journey beckoned mysteriously, murmured like a sea-shell, filled one with heart-stopping excitement.

But something worried Petya, too, something he could not quite put his finger on. Filipp Savich's reasoning had been impeccable. Yet hadn't Petya, who had never had an inordinate amount of respect for his elders, succumbed to his influence far too easily? In fact, he had permitted outright interference in his affairs! Maybe it was just that he missed having an older and wiser man to defer to? He had never had anyone like that. Or had he been seduced by Filipp Savich's contacts? It's so nice when everything falls into place with no effort.

Petya examined his conscience closely. No, it wasn't that. He wasn't that much of an opportunist. He liked Filipp Savich not just for his mysterious air or his contacts. How warmly he'd spoken of Petya's mother. And Petya, too – to whom, when all was said and done, he owed nothing – he had dealt with very fairly, if in a strict, somewhat paternalistic fashion. Would Petya have allowed anyone else to describe the people he most admired as 'that dissident mob'? But in this instance, he had. It was clear that Filipp Savich had the right to his own opinion, and that there was a reason for it.

Nevertheless, something nagged away at Petya inside, seeking a way out. Something in his life was changing – no, everything was changing! The chain of school–institute–work, which had seemed indissoluble before, had suddenly been broken. Would it be worth his while to return to the Institute? Was he really all that interested in physics and electronics? Hadn't he chosen them merely because they meant an assured income in the future? Yet why should he, with his convictions, need an assured income? And what were his convictions, when any alternative seemed right? For some reason, he remembered the jam sandwich he had made for himself when he heard of Dima's arrest.

He passed the church of the Representation of the Antioch Diocese, where a service was in progress. Suddenly, he wanted to go in and light a candle. He entered quietly. The liturgy was ending, so nobody paid him any attention. He was a little afraid of the fierce old women who seemed to be part of every congregation, and were always ready to snap at you for not crossing yourself at the right moment or standing in the wrong place. The priest came out with a chalice, everyone bowed their heads and some people knelt. Petya bowed his head, too. There was already a line of women with children of various ages, hands crossed on their breasts. Among them was a grown man, also waiting to take communion.

Petya stood well to the side, out of everyone's way, waiting for the moment to place his candle. In the meantime, he watched the faces around him. A slim young woman with a dark shawl thrown casually over her head stood in deep concentration, holding a fair-haired little boy in her arms. The boy's eyes were very round and a little apprehensive. After communion, this young woman and her child moved over to where Petya was standing. She was bending down to put the child on the floor, when he suddenly tightened his arms around her neck, pulling at her shawl and exclaiming loudly and happily:

'Mamma, I love you!'

You could hear him all over the church, but none of the old women said a word.

She smiled, and whispered back, and he buried his embarrassed face in the folds of her skirt. Petya could see that something very important had happened to the child, and at the sight of them together he felt an unexpected surge of emotion. Could holy communion cause that?

He lit his candle, not praying and not thinking about anything. There were already a lot of candles on the stand, there might as well be one more. But he stayed on. He waited until everyone had venerated the cross and the priest had retreated into the sanctuary. Clearly, he was expected to come out again, however, because a number of people lingered, waiting. Finally, he emerged and Petya, suddenly brave, marched up to him.

'Father, may I have a word with you?'

The priest, dressed now in a simple black cassock, looked at Petya inquiringly, then nodded.

'If you wouldn't mind waiting a few minutes?'

He spoke briefly and quietly to each of the other people waiting for him, and finally turned to Petya.

'Father . . . I'd like you to baptize me, please.'

Petya emerged from the church, though not after the eternity it had seemed. Now he didn't care whether he went right or left. He was in no hurry, he walked as he had before, just the same. In fact, nothing had actually happened. The priest had refused to baptize him then and there, explaining that this was something that required preparation. He instructed Petya how to pray while he was at sea. He also asked a number of unexpected questions. He promised to pray for Petya and blessed him in parting.

'Go with God,' he added with a smile.

So Petya went. Fearing to lose this feeling, the feeling that he was really going with God.

Olga Belokon returned home with Denis, thinking that it would be good to lie down for a bit. It's hard to pray when you're with a small child, because you have to be constantly on the lookout that he doesn't make a noise, start whining or annoy anyone. But Denis, as always after communion, was quiet and amenable. So she had hopes that he would play happily with his building blocks and let her do nothing for half an hour or so. She was just unhooking the clasps on his jacket when the phone rang.

At first, she simply couldn't believe what she was hearing. Then she realized that Mila wouldn't invent something like that, she always knew everything before anyone else. Yes, such things happened very rarely, but in principle, they could: if the literary powers-that-be suddenly decided that there was an 'error' in a book, it would be withdrawn, even if it had passed through all the stages of censorship. Even if it had already gone on sale. In this case, the book would have gone on sale the day after tomorrow. So the entire print run would be confiscated.

She recalled several such cases, but never involving children's books. What are They doing, what are those no-good bastards doing now? Hadn't there been enough wear and tear on the nerves already? And then, the seemingly happy outcome, that moment of satisfaction she and Nikolin had had . . .

While she was on the phone, Denis occupied himself with emptying the sugar from the basin on the table and making little pyramids out of it.

'What are you doing, you little horror?' yelled Olga, and Denis raised surprised eyes.

Olga flopped down on the couch and began to cry, like a child who'd been hurt for no reason. Denis tried to comfort her, smearing her tears all over her face with his pudgy little hands, wiping her nose with his blue scarf. Finally, she checked herself, washed her face with cold water. For the next hour she and Denis, in perfect accord and to spite their enemies, read that very book: the one about Old Man Andron and the royal blue mouse. That book was probably a bibliographical rarity by now, to be found in a total of two presentation copies.

Olga didn't have the heart to phone Nikolin. He'd find out soon enough, anyway, so why should she break the bad news?

As it happened, Nikolin already knew. And didn't phone Olga for the same reason.

Chapter Fifteen

THE GOOD THING about Soviet life is that it doesn't give you much time to indulge in disappointment. You get kicked – then keep on moving. No hanging around and getting depressed. Life has to go on, come what may. And life means laying your hands, if not on one thing, then another. Whatever one needs to go on living.

While Nikolin fumed about the book, Brysik wasted no time. From his first day with Nikolin, he had been fascinated by the movement of the typewriter ribbon, and had done his best to capture it. However, Nikolin remained vigilant and would chase him away. Now the master's attention was distracted, and he was not near the machine, just stood there smoking and muttering, his back to the object of Brysik's burning interest. Staring at nothing. Perfect!

When Nikolin finally turned round – well . . . The ribbon was half out of the typewriter, hanging in shreds, with Brysik firmly snared in its toils. However, even half-strangled, the kitten fought on valiantly. Nikolin hurried to part the warring sides and got his hands filthy. The kitten was a sight to see, too: scarcely a trace remained of the three colours of its fur. The worst of it was that this was Nikolin's last decent ribbon. That is, he did have two spare spools, but they were of domestic manufacture, sitting in his desk drawer in case of emergencies which Nikolin devoutly hoped would never occur. The only decent typewriter ribbons were of East German manufacture. There were even better ones, of course, but they were special import goods of a quality quite out of Nikolin's reach.

So where does a Soviet writer acquire an East German type-writer ribbon? One that would not run and smear or go into holes the first time you typed a sentence, but would last, say through about four full-stops? There had been a time when Nikolin was unaware of these mysteries, but when he had to apply himself to the problem it reminded him (as he was a story-teller) of the tale about Kaschey-the-immortal's egg, only in reverse. In the tale there is a hollow oak tree, in the oak tree there's a rabbit, inside the rabbit there's a duck, inside the duck there's an egg, and only inside the egg is the magic needle which can kill Kaschey.

In this instance, there is a typewriter ribbon which is held by Glafira Markovna, who in turn inhabits the writers' supply depot, which belongs to the Literary Fund, which is a branch of the Union of Soviet Writers. The Union is a social organization, and social organizations are under the caring wing of the state. This means that you can order a typewriter, a stack of carbon paper, or whatever your heart desires. Glafira Markovna will take down your order and get it processed.

There are so many Soviet writers that it is impossible to know them all individually. You sit at one of the Union meetings and find yourself wondering, who the hell is that on the podium? So you have to ask the person sitting next to you. Yet everyone knows Glafira Markovna. Especially as her appearance is so memorable. A lesser woman would have started shaving, but not Glafira Markovna. And why should she bother? She gets her hands kissed and is showered with gifts of perfume and choco-lates all year round, not just on International Women's Day on March the 8th.

To cut a long story short, the cat had done its worst, and lapsed into a deep and untroubled sleep while his master went off in pursuit of a typewriter ribbon. Nikolin reacted to the weather like a small child, squinting in the bright sunlight and pulling off his scarf. The breeze was moist and friendly, like a dog's tongue.

Funny, thought Nikolin, how city-dwellers react to the slightest hint, the slightest sign of a still far-off spring. In Lipetsk, and especially during his sojourns in the country, Nikolin had been accustomed to wide open spaces: when the snows started melting, the thaw would stretch to the horizon; when birds were migrating, they'd fill half the sky; when the apple trees started blooming, there would be a sea full of blossoms. But here in the city, the sight of an icicle falling and shattering on the ground or the sound of a small bundle of feathers venturing a chirp from rooftop or tree was enough to throw one into ecstasy.

City minimalism, that's what it was. It affects writing, too: you live in a big city, you'll write in telegraphese. A little detail, a slight hint – and the reader understands, and races ahead. But he'd certainly have got himself a little place in the country had he lived in the last century. Or the one before. He'd stroll around with a cheeky tuft of hair sticking up on his head, and instead of chasing around after typewriter ribbons, he'd write with a goose-quill. He'd pluck the quills from his own geese, and mend them himself. He'd write at his leisure, too, novels of no less than five volumes. Four pages to a description, say, of the wind changing quarter; a page at least to describe a girl's appearance, and as to her smell – another six!

In the forecourt, Nikolin encountered Auntie Xenia. She pursed her lips and turned her head away in response to his greeting. Fine, be like that, you old battle-axe, I'm going to go on being civil as though nothing had happened. You be the one to feel awkward.

Returning from the depot, Nikolin felt that the last thing he wanted was to go home to his own four walls. What he really wanted was to go and see Tatyana: bad luck was bad luck, but it was just at such times that one needed feminine appreciation. And Tatyana's appreciation – as expressed when she knelt down before him – was not something it was wise to recall in public, in the middle of a bustling, salt-strewn street.

He phoned her and they agreed that he would come over around five o'clock. That gave him time to buy a box of chocolates and what-have-you for a romantic evening for two.

She opened the door stark naked, drops of water beading her nipples. She hadn't even stopped to towel herself dry.

'Are you out of your mind? What if it had been someone else?'

Tatyana laughed uproariously.

'So what? Two pensioners came around here once when I was in the shower. You should have seen their faces! And you know what those two old biddies came for? They were taking part in a district socialist competition to find the best maintained plumbing, if you please! Poking their noses into other people's kitchens, checking out how clean they were. Bloody activists! And I said to them – politely as you please, just as though I wasn't starkers: please come in, would you like to examine the bathroom first? And yelled: hey, Janek, whip the foam up a bit higher, there're two ladies here from the housing administration. You couldn't see their heels for dust!'

Nikolin imagined the picture and snorted with laughter. But immediately after, asked severely who this 'Janek' was.

'You're jealous? My poor angel! No Moors in your ancestry, I hope? Calm down, there wasn't any Janek, but they would have heard the water running. I couldn't resist shocking them. Why are you so glum all of a sudden?'

She dragged off his scarf, and then the rest of his clothes.

Stella phoned everyone she could think of. He's been arrested! Something's got to be done! But not everyone could do something. That required a certain position. And Kir, who did have a name of sorts, was in Mexico, drinking pulque and feeding the local progressive writers a load of rubbish. She got through to him only a week later, and went straight for the jugular.

'He's your protégé, so get him out of this mess!'

That was all Kir needed. He floundered awkwardly.

'Why me? And he's not mine! If you want to know, he doesn't even speak to me.'

'This is no time for settling scores! Haven't you a scrap of decency?'

So it turned out that he – how do you like that! – was guilty of settling scores with the poor kid. The voice on the phone continued relentlessly: 'your protégé . . . I don't give a damn about your differences . . . you'll be able to live with that?' and finally: 'no wonder he won't speak to you . . . you toadying bastard!'

Kir fell back in his chair after hanging up the phone. Katerina, his third and probably last wife, exhibited tact and understanding: filled him a glass and put an ashtray by his elbow.

'Trouble?'

She cocked her head above a shoulder clad in a Mexican poncho. She was dying to get back to the as yet unpacked suitcases and try on everything else that Kir had brought back, but she checked herself and stayed put, sympathizing and stroking Kir's head. She kept darting glances at herself in the mirror out of the corner of her eye, not having had a proper chance to pirouette around in front of Kir in the poncho yet. Katerina was a fine woman, easy to live with. She appreciated every attention, not like that high-principled bitch Olga. He should have married a colonel's daughter straight away. They know how to keep women in their place in military families, and raise their daughters in the same style. But Kir had wanted to get into the Union of Writers very badly, and Belokon was a powerful figure.

Kir decided to forget the whole thing: people spitting in his face, and then expecting him to use his precious connections! Dima had got himself into this mess, and reaped the results of his stupidity. Hadn't Kir taught him, hadn't he put his soul into that kid, telling him not to cross the line? Feel the times. What kind of a master doesn't know his time? But all his teachings had gone for nothing. Some protégé, who pours scorn on his mentor! Talk about vipers in bosoms . . .

Yet at the same time he was wondering whom he could turn to. He thought of Belokon, but that was purely instinctive. No help was to be expected from that quarter. Not these days. For Kir, at any rate. Just be grateful for what he'd done earlier.

He ran through a mental list of several names, but they were not right for this. They would be all right for staging a citizens' protest, but Kir had already had his fingers burnt once, and wasn't going to repeat the mistake. The Secretariat was no use, either: that was the same as applying to the Committee. And yet – why not approach the Committee? Phone Filipp Savich himself, ask to see him . . .

He must be mad to contemplate approaching Filipp Savich over some ungrateful kid. He might get something more than a mere 'no' for his pains.

Katerina fussed around her husband, raining kisses on his forehead and generally soothing his ruffled composure. She refrained from asking any questions. Kir remained restless until the evening, vacillating between civic duty, fear, pity and his own hurt feelings.

If only none of this had happened. Some welcome home he'd had from his foreign travels! Just when he should have been able to have a good time, go somewhere special, reminisce about cacti and Aztec culture. Put on his suede jacket. But no, everything was ruined straight away. They'd landed him in it on his first day back.

Dima had people to look out for him, but who had ever looked out for Kir? Had anyone shown the slightest interest in a kid from a children's home? When he and his friends had to steal food from market stalls, wouldn't they have been beaten to death if caught? He had once seen a small, dark, twisted bundle of flesh, hardly recognizable as a body, dumped on the ground after being beaten to death, and the memory of it still haunted him. When Kir was small, he often imagined himself as a mighty magician. He would only do good, make sure everyone had enough to eat, he would protect and comfort people and never, never punish anyone: not even those who tortured cats or people. Because life is a frightening thing, and death is dark and twisted, and there is no corner where one can find protection and comfort.

Yes, he had been a good-hearted boy, but what would he be today with dreams and thoughts like that? Nobody. Nothing. At best, an item to be counted among others being off-loaded from a wagon or a ration-issue list. Remember when they'd left his name off the list, and the authorities took two ghastly days to establish under which category he came? And the rations, which were never enough! Of course it was his own fault that he was growing. He should have stayed as he was, and nobody would have noticed. Then there were the Germans, who were coming from the west to get him and his mother. They had been told in the children's home that the Germans did not think of Russians as human beings. Just Russian pigs. People from the occupied territories, they were told, even boys, were sent off to German farms. He did not realize at the time that this meant slave labour, he decided that it was for meat. Pork to be eaten. Later he understood the truth, but the childish fear remained.

There was war with the Germans, and the denizens of the children's home were told that they were being protected. But Kir had trouble believing that anyone was defending him. Who cared about him? Sometime later, he and his mother received notification of his father's death, and a letter from the regiment, informing them that he had been leading his platoon into action with the cry of 'For Stalin!', and died in the attack. Much later, as an adult, he understood that nothing else could have been written, that was the standard formula. But at the time he had felt a burning resentment that his father had been defending Stalin, and not him. Yet what doubts could there be about Stalin? He was our Great Leader, and it was only to be expected that a soldier would die with his name on his lips. Not the name of some young kid. His, Kir's name, was not the most important thing even to his own father.

Mother found him, took him back and loved him. But what could she do, exhausted and rapidly losing her health as a seamstress over such troublesome fabrics as felt and padding? There was no eight-hour working day then. Everything was 'for the war effort', and at times his mother would have to stay at work all night. The end of the war was followed by years of hunger, and here, too, there was little she could do.

At home she would make him chest compresses out of mashed potatoes if he had a cold, and kissed him, and stole enough cotton wool from work to make him a patchwork quilt. But could she help him to become someone? To transform an expendable item on a list into a man with a name that would not be easily forgotten, who would enjoy some position in life? Everything he had, he had achieved through his own efforts; nobody had helped him, but he had forged his way ahead and made a name for himself.

Why should he risk all this for some arrogant youth? Because if he didn't, that lad would become a nobody. An item on a list of camp inmates. A defenceless, scared kid. It would be a few years yet before he outgrew the first prisoner's uniform he was issued with.

And anyway, hadn't Kir once dreamed of being a kindly magician? Maybe he was imagining insuperable problems. Maybe he would talk to Filipp Savich, and the young man would be freed after a single magic phone call. What possible use was Dima to the Committee? So he'd read samizdat. The same could be said of thousands of people in Moscow alone. Let him go free, and let him continue to ignore Kir if he wanted, the silly young fool!

Katerina, having exhausted her attentions, sat beside him, quiet as a mouse. Kir felt ashamed of himself for this rush of self-pity. He wasn't the only one to have suffered deprivations. The war had been hard on everyone. It wasn't easy now, either, just different. Here was someone who cared for him, looking at him expectantly, all love, all sympathy.

He urged Katerina to put on her new dress. There was still time to go out. Would you like to go to the Bolshoi, darling? Don't worry, they'll always find a couple of tickets for your Kir. Or would you prefer to go to a restaurant? Which one? Heck, we only live once, let's celebrate being together again!

Katerina, delighted at the outcome of her manoeuvrings, dressed with the lightning speed of a well-trained soldier. A few seconds likewise sufficed to put on her make-up, which is not an accomplishment demanded of even the best-trained cadet.

Dima stuck to his chosen line: a poor stray lamb, he had been duped by the late writer, Pavel Pulin. The investigator was understanding and sympathetic. He expressed regret that a good Soviet lad like Dima had become involved in such a business.

They brought Dima his first parcel from home: the toothbrush he'd longed for, clean underwear, woollen socks, his favourite sweater with the letter 'Y' on the front. There were also some home-baked biscuits, a stick of smoked sausage, some oranges. A sum of money was deposited for him in a prison account, so he could buy whatever was permitted from the prison kiosk.

Dima swallowed his tears but sniffed audibly. The parcel meant that his parents still loved and cared for him. Mother had made only one mistake, and that was to send his best pair of trainers. Who needs trainers in prison? They lace up, and prisoners are not permitted to have shoelaces. Just in case they use them to hang themselves and mess up the investigation. It would have been better if she'd sent his slippers, even though he hated them at home. But Dima was not eligible for correspondence or meetings with relatives, so how could he let them know?

The trainers flopped about without laces, and quickly wore a hole in the heels of his woollen socks. Darning was permitted:

prisoners would be issued half a metre of thin thread and a needle. The guard kept watch through the door hatch while Dima tried to mend the socks: a needle, after all, is a sharp metal object in the prisoner's hands. Dima tacked the edges of the holes together anyhow, then gave up: to hell with it, we'll make do somehow, live through the winter.

Meanwhile, the investigator was wavering between charging Dima under articles 70 and 190. Both related to anti-Soviet agitation and propaganda; article 70, however, assumed an intention to undermine the Soviet system, whilst article 190 excluded such an intention. Article 70 carried a maximum penalty of seven years in the camps to be followed by five years of internal exile. The punishment decreed by article 190 was a maximum of three years' deprivation of liberty, and in general rather than strict regime camps, which made quite a difference.

He shared his hesitation with Dima: well, what are we going to do, young fellow? He, personally, did not doubt that Dima had harboured no such intention. But the investigation had to have proof of things. How could Dima prove that his apparently negative attitude towards the Soviet regime was, on the contrary, quite positive?

The investigator was no monster. He was only too glad to help, to advise. It's wrong to think that the investigator's only aim is to put people behind bars. That was for enemies of the state, not someone who'd merely slipped up the way Dima had. A boy from such a nice family, too. How his mother had wept when she brought the parcel for her son and pleaded on his behalf. It had really wrung the investigator's heart. He had a mother himself, a very old lady now.

In short, there was one way out. Before formal charges were laid, Dima should draw up a declaration of repentance affirming that there had been no malice aforethought on his part. Then, as proof of his good intentions, sign an undertaking to cooperate with the state organs, should such cooperation ever be solicited.

Now, there's no need to get upset! We don't ask such young and – if I may say so – unreliable people to work for us. The state organs had no need of Dima's assistance as such. It was Dima who needed this undertaking, not the state. It would save Dima from the camps. Three years was the maximum under 190, not the minimum. The minimum was a suspended sentence, so Dima stood a good chance of walking free from the courtroom straight into his mother's arms. Court officials are human beings too, not without understanding. Why should anyone want to ruin a young life like that?

Even if the judge proved to be a strict one – well, he'd be sentenced to six months. Provided there was the declaration of repentance and an undertaking to cooperate. Dima would have spent some time in custody before the hearing, and this time would count as part of the sentence. And given the difference of a month or so, nobody was going to trouble to send him to the camps for just a few weeks. He'd be left here to perform various duties around the prison until the date of his release, and that would be that.

And he, the investigator, had no particular wish to charge Dima. After all, he's not obliged to charge every suspect. Let Dima show a little good will, and he'd be home before he knew it. He'd be back at his studies and life could go on as before. Only it was to be hoped that he'd be a bit wiser in future, and not get involved with just anybody who came along. There's paper and a pen in the cell? Fine, see you tomorrow.

Dima paced the cell in his agitation, paying no attention to his cell-mate's grumbling. Evening tea was brought around, a pale yellowish fluid. Coffee was not served in the prison, it was forbidden for some reason. So the prisoners – *zeks* – were like English aristocrats. Dima had read somewhere that the English aristocracy never drank coffee.

Could it be possible that he'd be home tomorrow? He'd done

right to feign hesitation back there in the office. That made the investigator show his trump card: a trial could be avoided! Clearly, he did not want to put Dima away.

All right, let's leave personal liking and sympathy out of the question. Maybe the authorities simply didn't want to put people away at the moment, they had this thing about dates and anniversaries. Maybe they didn't want any trials coinciding with the approaching centenary. Or maybe his father had found some influential friend who had applied pressure in the right places. Yes, it certainly looked as though Dima had managed to wind them round his finger. And without incriminating anyone else, pointing the guilt firmly in the direction of Vagankovskoye cemetery. To cap it all, he'd even managed to avoid being tried.

The paper had to be written. But a paper is nothing. It would be like that essay they'd had to write at school: 'Hail the Beloved Army!' Dima needed full marks to gain entrance into the institute, so he'd penned the required essay with great feeling, expressing a burning desire to join the ranks right away. It was a paradox that the burning desire meant full marks, which, in turn, meant entrance into the institute, which excluded the need to join the ranks. Dima dashed off the paper as easily as he had written that essay. School had its uses.

He clambered up on his bunk, drew his feet under him and studied his reflection in the murky window. His cheeks had sunk, which made his eyes look bigger. And his hair had grown. People under investigation don't get their heads shaved, that only happens to convicted prisoners. He liked what he saw in the glass. A tough nut. A man who had suffered much, with tired and wise eyes. He folded his lips into lines of long-suffering and peered closer to see if he'd acquired any grey hairs. However, the light was too poor to spot such fine details, and, in any case, just at that moment the guard flung open the hatch and ordered Dima to climb down. Dima looked at him with lofty disdain: you'll still be here tomorrow, my fine friend, and the day after, stomping up and down these corridors. Go on, earn your Moscow residence permit!

For the first time since it all began, he allowed himself to contemplate his return home. Would he take a bath with 'Bad-u-san' first and have a cup of coffee later, or vice versa?

Chapter Sixteen

THE NEXT MORNING Kir couldn't bring himself to pick up the phone. He drank three cups of tea, sat there for a while changing television channels in an aimless sort of way, smoked a couple of cigarettes. He tried to put everything out of his mind and sat down at his desk to do some work, but couldn't. It was always the same after a break: the horror of sitting down before a blank sheet of paper, the difficulty of getting back into routine. Absently, he doodled some figures of imps on the virgin sheet, just to get his hand moving. The imps came out very lively, with sneering little faces. Was this his subconscious acting up? He felt a flash of anger at himself, and plunged towards the phone, like a swimmer taking a dive into icy water. He hoped inwardly that nobody would answer at the other end, but the receiver was picked up instantly, and, by some miracle, he was connected to Filipp Savich straight away.

This took him by surprise, and at once Kir began to hem and haw. What was the problem, Filipp Savich had to ask impatiently. Meet? Something particularly urgent? Actually, Filipp Savich was extremely busy right now, but for an author of Kir's international reputation – very well, he'd make the time somehow. Come to such and such an address at around four. Yes, today.

Kir wrote down the address, which meant nothing to him.

Filipp Savich had no idea why Kir should request a meeting with him. All the recordings of Kir's conversations in Mexico were already in the Department: our people don't know

Spanish, so the Soviet embassy there had supplied Kir with interpreters. He took a quick glance at the transcripts: nothing unusual there.

As a matter of fact, that discussion of his with one of their progressive priests was highly satisfactory. Heartfelt and full of a sincere mutual hatred of Americans. Kir had made a timely mention of '47, and had expressed just the right degree of interest in composing some verse to celebrate those heroic youngsters, and to remind the world of that forgotten tragedy. Filipp Savich particularly liked the phrase about the supremacy of the System: 'Communists are not obliged to pray for their enemies.' That was exactly to the point.

With the priest now being worked by the embassy interpreter, there seemed to be some very promising contacts in that direction.

Kir made his way to the address he'd been given, having prepared what he was going to say, and trying to maintain his composure. In order to calm his nerves, he studied his surroundings: people were going about their business more briskly than usual, cheered by the almost spring-like weather. Slush of all shades from beige to dark brown saturated shoes and boots. The snow had been sprinkled with large grains of salt to help it melt, shortening the life of footwear at the same time. No doubt, this gives the economy a boost and the populace new strength to maintain a purposeful trot.

Queues jostled along the pavements, a stand of oranges on the corner beckoned invitingly. A man in a leather cap with the earflaps down hurried past with a string bag full of large white loaves. You'd think the fool would at least buy the longer ones, though what did it matter? They'd be frozen by the time he delivered them back to whatever God-forsaken village he came from. It was disgraceful, the way they were letting just anyone crowd into Moscow these days: these outsiders bought up everything in sight, and how were native Muscovites supposed to live? Start growing potatoes on their balconies?

Kir was not at all surprised that he did not know the address to which he had been directed. He had had experience enough, but someone with less might have been puzzled to know where and how members of the KGB met with their agents. There were the wildest rumours about it: so-and-so, for example, has been noticed near a building adjacent to the Department virtually every day, so he's probably an informer.

In fairness, it must be noted that in such a case it was far more likely that the suspect genuinely worked close by, or had some other perfectly innocent reason to be there, and was in no way an informer. The truth was that real agents never came to the KGB directly, and could not. They went where they were told. To some other place, such as the army enlistment headquarters, for instance. Or they're summoned to the personnel department at their own place of work, or to an empty room in the local clinic, or the house administration office.

There are also apartments in every town which belong to the KGB. Naturally, the neighbours suspect nothing. They assume the tenant is a private tutor, or a masseur, and that's why all sorts of people are seen entering the place. Apartments like these are carefully selected, preferably with a separate entrance rather than a shared entrance hall, so that no neighbour should take it into his or her head to try to make an appointment for a back rub. Such places are known as briefing points, in the best traditions of revolutionary romanticism.

Briefing points are especially useful for receiving trusting foreigners. They are usually well-furnished, even though some of them may be a bit heavy on the samovars and the wooden *matrioshka* dolls.

It is worth noting, though, that visitors to briefing points are not necessarily agents, either: they may not have the slightest suspicion of where they are. That was the case with Nikolin, also known as the Storyteller, who came clutching boxes of chocolates for Tatyana, also known as Forget-me-not. Because Forget-me-not, whose passport bore the name of neither Tatyana nor Kuzina, was registered for residence with her husband at a totally different Moscow address.

Filipp Savich greeted Kir expansively.

'So, our traveller's back! How are things? Good trip? I hope you didn't short-change your lovely Katerina and bought everything you should?'

'Actually, Filipp Savich, I don't regard overseas trips as an endless shopping spree. A fascinating country like Mexico, the cultural contacts, the –'

'Yes, yes, that goes without saying: Popocatepetl, Istaxiutal and all that . . . I daresay you've brought back a mountain of slides, a host of creative impressions . . . But, between ourselves, I must say that shopping is an integral part of foreign travel, and there's nothing wrong with that. The First Commandment is to love our neighbour, and this is where they are, not in Mexico. You just try and forget to bring back something for someone who expects it – they'll take it as a sign that you don't care about them. Why, there have been divorces because somebody forgot a present for their mother-in-law – ha, ha!'

Kir laughed dutifully. He knew about the Ten Commandments, having read them once, but he wasn't disposed to argue with Filipp Savich, who continued his train of thought.

'No interest in shopping is a bad sign. It means that either the person's a bad family man, or he's thinking of doing a runner. I hope there weren't any like that in your delegation?'

'No, no, Filipp Savich. We didn't even get as far as the Teitucuana pyramids, everyone stayed on at the local market-place.'

'That's more like it! Let the envious sneer. So, Katerina's pleased? Now, did you want to tell me something about the trip? Outside the framework of the report?'

'Well, not quite . . . The thing I wanted to talk to you about is this . . . you see . . .'

If there was one thing Filipp Savich couldn't stand, it was unnecessary beating about the bush. What impertinence it was, in our busy day and age, to waste people's time! Let alone that of one's superiors, whose every moment is valuable. All his staff knew this, and those who didn't were in for a nasty shock. But in this instance, he merely steepled his fingers and listened. Let the comrade agent go his length. Maybe he had done something stupid over there and was having a hard time finding the words to admit it.

But the moment he heard the name Dima Koretsky, Filipp Savich exploded. So this Kir, this nonentity, assumed he was some kind of international celebrity and had decided to embark on charity work! And had the temerity to drag Filipp Savich away from his desk, where he had to contend with people who posed a real danger to the state! Filipp Savich had already wasted enough time over this Koretsky. There were other matters of real importance that had to be dealt with.

A conspiracy had been uncovered in the Baltic fleet, and what guarantee was there that conspirators weren't hard at work in the army? That nuisance Gorbanevskaya had been put away, yet not a week had passed before the next issue of the *Chronicle of Current Events* lay on Filipp Savich's desk. Issue number eleven, if you please. Bukovsky had been released after serving three years, and was up to his old tricks again. Started poking his nose into matters concerning psychiatry. A subject close to his heart. And you're bothering me with trifles!

You pot-bellied little twerp! You can go around in your intellectual circles boasting about your past, playing the genius and handing out autographs to silly schoolgirls! As far as we're concerned, you're nothing more than an agent with a number and a code-name, you mongrel son-of-a-bitch.

Filipp Savich pinned Kir with a relentless stare.

'It seems to me, Arseni, that you are poking your nose into

matters which don't concern you. And – if I may say – which are out of your domain,' he said calmly and precisely. He paused slightly, to allow this to sink in, then added:

'In future, I'd be grateful if you didn't trouble me with your initiatives. You will continue to meet your controller, in the standard manner. Have you anything else to say?'

'No, Filipp Savich,' muttered the shattered Kir.

'In that case – goodbye.'

Filipp Savich deliberately refrained from rising and escorting Kir to the door. Just to stress his point. He'd have to have a word with those who were handling the agents – discipline was slipping badly. This one needs to be reined in, for one. Harping on his youth, damn it. We didn't work hard enough on them, at the beginning of the sixties, and this is the result. And to think where he was presuming to meddle! There'd been no anticipating that: it had been the last thing in Filipp Savich's mind. Who knows where else he might start shoving his oar in? It looked as though some of his old habits had endured, after all.

He looked hard at Kir, using his code-name on purpose. And suddenly he caught a very unpleasant flash in those blue eyes.

Tatyana was very morose today, not looking at all her usual self. Nikolin tried to persuade her to take a trip with him to Lipetsk, visit the old haunts. The book might have been confiscated, but Nikolin had received an advance, so money was no problem and it would be nice to get away for a while.

'Take some unpaid leave,' he urged her. 'A week or so – surely they'll let you go? Can't that lab of yours manage without one of its assistants? We'll have a good time, get a bit of rest. Maybe we can even find someone from the old crowd, call in at the school, reminisce about old times . . .'

He had been surprised how reluctant Tatyana always was to recall their schooldays. It was as if she had wanted to wipe the slate clean. She was slow to recall the names of the teachers.

Even the young German teacher whose life Tatyana had made such a misery that it got as far as the headmaster: sabotage in the eighth grade, they refused to learn German! They had all been little more than irresponsible youngsters then, but it was fun to remember it now. Tatyana, however, seemed to derive no pleasure from such recollections.

To cheer her up, he told her about the gypsy and her warning about a chestnut-haired woman.

'See what a femme fatale you are! You capture my heart, and then refuse to come when I try to steal you away. Come on, take a bit of leave!'

'Leave, leave!' muttered Tatyana, jerking an emery board across her nails. She was sitting with her feet tucked up on the sofa, her knees in their fishnet stockings protruding from under her. A true woman, she despised tights.

'It may be that I'll soon have to take more than a few weeks' leave!'

'What do you mean?' asked Nikolin, puzzled.

'I mean that I'm two weeks overdue, that's what I mean!'

'But you checked out your safe days on the calendar . . .'

'Well, it looks as though I was out in my calculations. Remember that time when you didn't have a condom with you? That must have been when you hit the bullseye.'

Nikolin began to feel worried.

'Maybe you're mistaken? Perhaps you should have a check-up?'

'I have. There's no mistake. I wouldn't have said anything otherwise.'

'Listen, I've got money –'

'Money?' screeched Tatyana with unexpected fury. 'You get me pregnant, and now you want to pack me off for an abortion? Have you any idea how many women in this country end up unable to have a child ever again after that? This could be my last chance! Maybe I've always dreamed of having a son, and you want me to kill him off?'

She began to cry wildly, banging her head against the arm of the sofa. Nikolin was about to run out into the kitchen for a glass of water when suddenly she gave a final sob and stood up.

'I'm sorry. I didn't mean to make a scene, it's just that my nerves are shot to pieces at the moment. I'm in bad shape, so it's better if you leave. I'll call you later, when I've pulled myself together. Go on, go on! No, don't worry, I just feel a bit nauseous, that's all.'

Tatyana practically pushed him out of the door, giving him a quick peck on the forehead.

They didn't force Dima to wait long the following morning, but summoned him straight to the investigator's office from the wire-enclosed exercise yard. He asked to be taken to his cell first, to collect the paper, and the guard escorted him there without demur.

The investigator was not alone. There was another man with him, also in civilian dress. An elderly man with dark hair and a bulldog-like face.

'You've got your statement there?' asked the investigator with a friendly smile. He ran a quick eye over the sheet of paper, put it away in a file and smiled again.

'That's fine. I shan't detain you any longer. I daresay you've had enough of this place, anyway.'

Then his voice became a shade more businesslike.

'I am able to inform you officially, Koretsky, that I see no reason to press charges against you for the literature found in your possession. I'm sure you've learned a valuable lesson for the future, and sincerely hope that you and I will never meet again inside these walls. I wish you all the best. My regards to your family.'

He rose, extending his hand.

'Thank you . . .' was all Dima managed to say. Although this was what he had been waiting and hoping for, he was a bit bowled over by the speed of events. 'Does that mean . . . I can go home?'

'I'll not take up any more of your time. However, as you're here, my colleague has just one question for you. I expect you'll be through in no time. As for the case of anti-Soviet propaganda against you – yes, it's closed. Just sign here to say you have been officially informed. Thank you. Good luck.'

The investigator gave Dima a final smile, picked up his papers and went out, leaving him alone with the man with dark hair, who looked him over unhurriedly and said:

'Sit down for a moment, Koretsky. I want to ask you about the twenty-four American dollars which were found during the search. Before we finally say goodbye, I'd like you to explain how you came by them.'

Good Lord! Dima, completely rattled by the house search, had clean forgotten about those dollars in his anxiety about the samizdat. The money had been in the hollow with Pulin's manuscript. Of course they had found it when they found the manuscript! What on earth was he to do now? Tell them about Kemal? After all, they were hardly likely to do anything over a trifle like that. It's not as though the sum amounted to thousands. What should he say?

But this investigator was clearly not inclined to give Dima time to think.

'When did you get this money? Who from?'

Dima hung his head in silence, thinking furiously.

'Are you refusing to talk to me, Koretsky? And Pyotr Afanasyevich told me that you were such a sensible young fellow. All right, let's try another way. Do you know this object?'

He lay an Order of Lenin medal on the table with a loud clink. The familiar profile squinted at Dima with one bird-like eye.

Dima's nerves, already stretched to their limit, could hardly bear this additional stress, but seemed to start snapping apart almost audibly one after another, like over-taut guitar strings.

Something inside his head buzzed like an angry alarm-clock. He buried his face in his hands and began to wail thinly.

This was yet another version of the Swings, based on the general principle that the untrained human psyche can take only so many consecutive stretches and compressions. And what possible training could Dima have had? He didn't even know what the routine was called. To know the name of something is to be at least half-prepared for it.

The bulldog-like investigator was not one to tolerate hysterics.

'Stop playing the fool, Koretsky!' he barked, so loud that Dima could not fail to obey.

No longer making any attempt at resistance, and driven relentlessly by the investigator every time he slowed down, he poured out the whole story. How Vova had taken a pair of jeans that were not Dima's size, promised to pay later and left that medal as collateral. No, Dima didn't know whose it was. Vova said it had belonged to his grandfather's cousin. Vova still hadn't paid for the jeans, although the time limit had long since passed.

Then Kemal had turned up, an African student from their faculty who was going home on leave to get married. He'd asked Dima if he had any contacts with people who might have medals for sale, because Kemal's future father-in-law was an avid collector. So Dima offered him that medal. How much did he get for it? Those twenty-four dollars. They'd agreed on twenty-five, but Kemal had only twenty-four on him. Said he'd give Dima the outstanding dollar later . . .

The investigator of illegal currency dealings was looking at Dima with undisguised contempt.

'You couldn't even jack the price up to thirty pieces of silver, Koretsky? You're a real cheapskate, you know that? If you were a bit smarter, you could have got a full hundred. But what did you do? Sold off a major award, earned with the blood of an old Communist, for a few pence! Just as well our customs people found this medal on Kemal, or it would have disappeared abroad for ever. To think that we have to sort out grubby dealings like this just at a time when the country's preparing to celebrate the Lenin centenary! Selling off an Order of Lenin, a sacred relic like that, abroad? I tell you, the country won't stand for it!'

The investigator crashed a fist on the table, overcome with indignation.

'So what other currency fiddles have you been engaged in? You'd better tell me everything, because we'll find out anyway.'

'None! I give you my word – none!'

'Your word's nothing to boast about. All right, sit there and keep quiet while I make a note of everything.'

Dima, completely crushed, signed the interrogation record. One concerning an entirely new case, in which citizen Dmitri Borisovich Koretsky was held on suspicion of illegal currency dealings.

He was taken back to his cell for his things, and transferred to another, on the next floor, designated to hold three people.

A couple of days later the rumour went round Moscow that the student Dima Koretsky had been an informer and a provocateur, and had hung around in samizdat circles for this reason. He was in prison, however, for nothing to do with samizdat, but because he'd been caught in black market dealings – selling an Order of Lenin to some foreigner. Currency dealings fall into a completely different category, and even an informer can be arrested for them. It did not take long for the rumour to reach Stella's salon.

Two weeks later, the Moscow Komsomol newspaper published an article denouncing him under the title 'Twenty-four Pieces of Silver'.

Stella had no trouble guessing what had been the real cause of Dima's arrest. After all, there had been a house search. For obvious reasons, though, she couldn't say a word to anyone. All she could do was fret and fume, and loudly declare that she didn't believe a word of it. It was all lies and slander! A plant! A frame-up!

She even quarrelled with several of her friends about it. As for Petrovich, who had previously been regarded as infallible – she barred him from her house. Ordered him out point-blank for some of his remarks about Dima.

She was a nervous wreck, her face was bloated from tears and she seemed to have aged ten years over the couple of months of the investigation.

Dima was sentenced to three years in general regime camps. He'd got off lightly, considering that the prosecution had called for five. Stella would wait for him. She wouldn't abandon him, betray him. She loves him, after all – surely by now she must have realized how much! And would go on loving him – alone, against the whole world. As for how much younger he was than she – that was nobody else's damned business!

Chapter Seventeen

BELOKON NEVER NEEDED to be told anything twice. He had nothing personal against Kir Usmanov, and thought Olga had been a fool to divorce him. What more did she want? She'd had a husband who was a member of the Union of Writers, earned good money, travelled abroad . . . she could have had it easy, and sat back and raised Denis in comfort. In a self-contained apartment with a room for everyone. Kir had been brought to see sense, but she hadn't, silly cat.

Still, if those were his instructions, that's what he would do. Filipp Savich knew best. So what did Kir have in the works at the moment? A selection of poems with mystical overtones in *Baikal* – that would pose no problem. Kir would spend a long time waiting for that publication. Belokon's influence extended to *Baikal*.

New World had enough problems of its own: it was about to go under. In any case, they had disdained anything by comrade Usmanov in recent times . . . Give them something with a bit more sting . . . your time has passed, O white swans!

As for the journal *Youth* – it should be simple enough to wean them away. They always had droves of talented young individuals on their doorstep; all that would be needed would be to point out that Kir was not exactly a fresh-faced youngster any more. It should be easy enough to promote some kid fresh from the farm, who would be overjoyed to fill his place.

Kir's collection in the Soviet Writer publishing house could be easily replaced, too. Let them publish someone else, whom Belokon would support. There was that very promising young fellow who seemed at first glance to belong to the newly popular 'village writers' school – but only at first glance. Belokon knew him personally: he was an outstanding exception in the current no-good generation! Affronted, angry – but in the right direction: he'd gladly have taken it on himself personally to wipe out all those the Leader had missed.

Cinema contacts would be checked, and if Kir had a screenplay under consideration, it could be shelved. Dealing with cinema people was easy, they always worked as a unit. Your orders will be carried out, Filipp Savich, yes sir! To the letter.

Belokon, smiling benignly, pulled a thorny branch away from his sleeve. It's a mistake to think that climbing roses don't need pruning. All roses have to be pruned, that only makes them bloom better. This could be said of literature, too. It's the same process. You loosen the soil around the roots, and keep the weeds down, add a bit of fertilizer at times without minding if it got your hands dirty. Some branches have to be spotted in time and ruthlessly lopped off, or they'll ruin the whole bush. The Leader understood this, and in his immortal works had likened the burden of power to the patient toil of a careful gardener.

Belokon breathed deeply and evenly, his whole body enjoying the fine day. The weather forecasters had said there would be no more frosts, it was just the moment to start tending the garden. He loved and understood roses, and acquired new ones with all the dedication of a keen stamp-collector. His favourite occupation down at the dacha was pottering around among his rose bushes.

What could be better: you'd don a padded jacket – one of ours, a collective farm one: a present from the girls in the dairy – and feel an immediate bond with the people. Half the country goes around in jackets like this. It's warm, but not too warm, and even the nastiest thorn can't penetrate it, just leaves a little curl of fluff, at worst. No thorn was a threat! Belokon was scrupulous about attending meetings with collective farm workers, not like some people he would name at the right moment when the

Prose Section held its general meeting. A Soviet writer's duty is to bring enlightenment to the masses, and he has no right to decline this sacred obligation.

Unlike the jacket, Belokon's gardening gloves were not collective farm issue. Kir had brought them back from his first trip abroad. He'd certainly known what would please the old man. Those English capitalists knew how to make gardening gloves; these had lasted for years.

Having filled a barrow full, Belokon headed for the far corner, breaking through the soft, crusty ice, where he had a large drum for burning garden refuse. The drum sat on a square of concrete, just as it should. Four more bushes to go, and he'd be through. Fertilizing would have to wait until all the snow was gone. The pruned off branches could be burned later, too, when they were dry.

Belokon stretched, and his joints popped pleasantly. Paradise! He'd bet that if his blood pressure were measured now, it would be like that of a young man attending his first call-up. He was good for a while yet, that was certain. He'd still be digging around in this garden twenty years hence. Why worry about age? His late grandfather had become the father of twins at the age of fifty, and Belokon was still a little way off that. He'd be marking his half century only in May.

It was a pity he had to leave the dacha, he'd planned to stay here another day, taking in the fresh country air. But if he must, he must. He sighed, phoned for the company Volga. There was still time to drink a cup of tea dacha-style, with rowan berries, and lounge around in an undershirt and training pants. Later he'd have to change into his working clothes, and put on the striped tie. Belokon hated ties, striped or spotted. He'd never really accepted them, but wearing them came with the job.

Kir was in a restaurant with a young lady, and in his most audacious mood. The young lady, a soloist with a visiting song and dance troupe, was charmingly shy, and clearly unspoiled by the mysteries of restaurant life in the capital. The troupe was from Ternopol, her name was Oxana, and she was a brown-eyed, black-browed charmer with unbelievably long eyelashes. She was tactfully searching the menu for the cheaper items.

With a cheerful grunt, Kir took matters into his own capable hands.

However, no sooner was their order on the table than another waiter shot over with a bottle of champagne.

'A present for you,' the waiter said, jerking his chin in the direction of another table.

'From our table to yours!' came a friendly bellow with a marked Georgian accent.

Kir was not particularly pleased. There were times when he enjoyed Georgian hospitality, with its elegance and flair, but this was not one of them. Right now he wanted to be left alone with Oxana. So he limited himself to a slight nod, and sent no reciprocal bottle back. Moscow wasn't Georgia, after all, and there was no reason for him to observe their customs.

One would have thought this would be enough to discourage any further advances, but no. Oh, the Georgians were offended, but not at all put off. Just then the band began to play a dance tune, and one of them, thickly moustached and clearly somewhat the worse for wear, appeared by their table.

'May I have the pleasure, lovely lady?' he slurred.

He paid not the slightest attention to Kir: you ignore us, we'll ignore you.

Kir had no choice but to insert himself between the Georgian and Oxana.

'The lady isn't dancing tonight.'

The Georgian pretended injured dismay.

'Listen, friend, nobody's talking to you, right?'

'Go on, go on, get out of here,' replied Kir, taking the man by the elbows and turning him back towards his own table.

'Hands off!' roared the Georgian, loud enough to be heard

right round the restaurant and, seizing the tablecloth, he jerked it off the table in one swift move. Dishes and cutlery scattered over the floor. Oxana jumped up, swabbing at a spreading red wine stain on her Crimplene dress.

The head waiter made a belated arrival, but, for some reason, his ire was directed solely at Kir.

'Causing a disturbance, are you? Do you want me to call the militia?'

Oxana stared at her erstwhile cavalier in helpless despair, ready to burst into tears. The head waiter fastened his hand firmly on Kir's sleeve.

'Come with me, please.'

This was the last straw. Kir grabbed the man by the front of his jacket so hard that the buttons popped off.

Nikolin was going through a very bad time: Tatyana was behaving as though she were going off her head, and seemed determined to drive him mad, too. The worst thing was that he couldn't tell what she was after. She did not want to marry him, and never said a word to indicate otherwise, either directly or indirectly. Thank God for that, at least! But one moment she wanted to have the baby, the next she didn't; she flatly refused to have an abortion, and threw terrible scenes, railing at Nikolin, and yelling hysterically:

'I'll go to your Secretariat, let everybody know! Get them to order you to pay maintenance!'

Then she would cry and apologize, blaming everything on feeling unwell. She was capricious, demanding first pickled gherkins, then black caviare, then tinned pineapple if Nikolin was such a helpless idiot that he couldn't get her a fresh one. But who has the right to such whims if not a pregnant woman? Just try refusing.

Worn and unkempt, Nikolin ran around Moscow searching for one thing after another. The janitors were out in full force, scraping the remains of the packed March snow off the streets and footpaths. The larger streets were already clear and almost dry. Just about every second passer-by seemed to be pushing a pram with an infant: either there had been a baby boom, or Nikolin was unusually aware of the circumstance.

Everything inside him seemed turned upside-down. Having a baby on the side? He didn't want that at all. Not only because of Tatyana's explosive temperament, either, but because of his recollections of what it meant. Having a baby, he knew, could mean going out of your mind.

Nikolin no longer tried to suppress the memories, and they came crowding back. The first time he had taken Dasha in his arms: that weightless, breathing little scrap in a blanket. How she would clamber out of her cot and, puffing heavily with concentration, work her way into bed with her parents. And how she'd squeal triumphantly, bouncing up and down on Daddy's stomach.

He remembered how he and Lucia had huddled in the corridors of the intensive care wing, looking with pleading spaniel-like eyes at every passing white coat. They weren't allowed in to see Dasha, not the first day, nor the next. When they were finally admitted, it was all over. She lay there, white and tiny, her fluffy hair on end. There were dark blue stripes on her little hands – so dark they were almost black. Had they tied her down, or what?

No, they hadn't tied her down, they'd just had to put bandages round her hands to stop her from trying to tear the tubes out of her nose, that was the only way to stop her . . .

And Lucia's terrible silence, as though she were dead, too, and how, when Nikolin got her into a taxi, she let out an animal howl and started to thrash around, so the driver refused to take them.

In this instance he knew that it was not for him to decide whether Tatyana would have the baby or not. He avoided her hysterics as much as he could, but even at home she gave him no peace: she would phone him several times a day, and once again he could not work out what it was that she wanted. Sometimes she would phone only to shout one sentence down the line, something like:

'Don't dare come anywhere near me again, I never want to see you, I won't let you in!'

Then, half an hour later, the phone would ring again and she would beg him to come over, because she was suddenly afraid, so afraid to be alone . . .

Faint-hearted, Nikolin sought sanctuary with Nastenka out at Borisovy Prudy whenever she wasn't filming. Nastenka asked him no questions. She was glad when he came, would cook up *pelmeni* or something. She liked to feed him, and was always good-humoured and warm. Even when describing her successes and failures at work, she always treated the matter lightly.

The single room of her apartment was full of icons, and she would describe with enthusiasm how she had got this one in some obscure village, or coaxed that one out of a foreman on a demolition site. Just look at the amazing reverse perspective on this one, and the positively cosmic rays on that!

This abundance of icons embarrassed Nikolin whenever he slept at her place: he felt uneasy with such a multitude of stern eyes looking at him. Yet Nastenka did not seem in the least affected, even though she was not possessed of anything like Tatyana's uninhibited sexual appetites.

He also appreciated the fact that she made no attempt to pretend to some great passion. She never said anything to Nikolin about other attachments she might have; it was tacitly assumed that they both might have them. And why not? It was as though they were able to rest together from more turbulent emotions and get their wind back.

Nastenka hardly ever phoned Nikolin and appeared at the flat only once. She had torn her boot fooling around on an icy path watered smooth by some kids. Nikolin hauled her inside, since the incident had occurred close by, got her to rub her foot and put on a woollen sock. Then he made her a hot drink and put her in a taxi home.

This was why he was slightly surprised when she rang his doorbell this time without phoning him first. Had something happened?

'Oh, how lucky you're home,' she cried happily. 'I stopped by on the off-chance that you'd be in. No, I won't take off my coat, I'm in a tearing hurry. The thing is, I have to be on set, and I've just bought this most fabulous icon. But I can't drag it to the studio, and there's not enough time for me to take it home. Can I leave it here? Mind you don't drop it, it's heavy as anything. You can unwrap it and take a look, it's the most beautiful thing you ever saw. Right, I must run!'

'Let me at least take you as far as the bus stop,' volunteered Nikolin. 'Or shall I order you a cab?'

'No cab! I'm going to be living on processed cheese for the next month, my dear. But you can take me to the bus if you like, so long as we hurry.'

Nikolin already knew that it would be useless to try to get her to accept three roubles for a car. She would never take money, even as a loan. This was not due to some perverted sense of pride, he knew that by now. It was simply that she was terrified of other people's money. She would laugh and say that probably one of her ancestors had wound up in a debtors' prison and left his family penniless, so she had an inborn dread of owing money. Nikolin had no choice but to accept this explanation.

He helped her into a passing trolley bus, and waved. Then he went back home to feed Brysik.

Auntie Xenia stood downstairs, waiting for the lift. He said good day. She made no response. They ascended to their floor in silence. Then suddenly Auntie Xenia looked at him woefully, and said something he did not understand, but in the same friendly tone she used to use in the past:

'Don't take offence, Anton Semyonych. It's not my fault, and it's not yours. But it can't be helped.'

Then she dropped her eyes again, staring at the wall. There was no way, Nikolin realized, that he would get another word out of her.

Try as he might, Nikolin could not guess what lay behind that cryptic remark. Nevertheless, it seemed to shift a little of the load off his heart. If no one was at fault, that was a good thing in itself. Let events take their course. The mystery would be cleared up one of these days, and they might well share a laugh over it.

From that day on, Nikolin felt no awkwardness at meeting Auntie Xenia. He carried the burden of their strange relationship with easy acceptance. Like a Catholic novice, patiently watering a dry stalk for no discernible reason. He looked at her amiably, and said his cheerful hellos. After a while she melted a little, began to say something like 'G'ning' in reply. And Nikolin allowed himself to believe that this was short for 'Good morning'.

Chapter Eighteen

FILIPP SAVICH DROPPED round to Natasha's in case there was a letter from Petya. There was. Everything was fine, Petya was delighted with everything. The people were great, the work in prospect was interesting. In order not to waste time later, he was using the voyage to study the experiments they would be conducting when they reached the South Seas. They had run into a storm and he had been a bit sea-sick, but not any more. He sent lots of affectionate messages to his mother and assured her that there was no need to worry about him, because everything was tip-top. Some of the experiments concerned sharks, so he intended to bring her back a shark's tooth as a souvenir.

What a lad! He could keep his end up in any situation! In Petya's absence, Filipp Savich realized he was much more attached to the boy than he had thought. He took pleasure in recalling their earlier discussions. Even as a youngster the boy had an independent line of thought – how he'd reasoned about the emperor Paul I, for instance! He wasn't just repeating something he had read, because there were no books available from which to draw such conclusions. No, he had marshalled his facts and set them out cogently to Filipp Savich. Who had reduced the serfs' obligatory period of work for their owners to three days a week? Why, that came to less than current taxes in some countries! And who tightened the reins on the galloping growth of aristocratic privilege? No wonder the aristocracy lined up against him, had him murdered, and slandered him posthumously: the dead can't reply.

Once Petya got back, Filipp Savich decided to arrange for him to have some access to archives. Let him do historical research until he developed other passions. There were enough people to research the twentieth century as it was.

A good thing that Filipp Savich had managed to get that friend of his put away. Just in time, too, before he'd had a chance to involve Petya in anti-Soviet activity. Petya was not the kind to engage in black marketeering, that wasn't his sort of thing at all. And anyway, who better to protect a son's interests than his father? One day, son, you will find out who is your real father. One day we'll come to understand each other better. But even then, I won't be able to tell you everything. That kind of history I'll keep to myself. To spare your feelings.

Viktor Stepanych came round with his latest progress report. Filipp Savich nodded with satisfaction.

'Always knew you had a good head on you.'

He could praise Viktor Stepanych now without reserve. The young fellow had done well and learned quickly on the job. His cheeks were still youthfully round, but he'd gained much in stature, was no longer the puppy he'd been just a short while ago. In fact, Filipp Savich thought he might well, with a clear conscience, pass over the whole Storyteller business to him: he himself had much more important fish to fry.

It had been decided to commit the historian Roy Medvedev to a psychiatric hospital in May, but Filipp Savich didn't know whether he'd manage this in time. It was a matter that had to be approved at Central Committee level. Clearly, chucking Solzhenitsyn out of the country was the best solution to that problem; even so, the comrades at the top couldn't see this simple truth, and had to be persuaded and offered various options. God knows how many analysts were at work on nothing but alternative schemes! At the same time, Filipp Savich was under pressure to get the operation set up, put the press on the job, even though there was every chance that the top brass would withhold its approval. Find another solution, they'd order Filipp Savich, we don't want any trouble abroad at the moment. On top of this, Lidia Chukovskaya had managed to slip her book past the KGB. They'd fallen down on the job there. Not shown enough vigilance. Her father had been more careful, and kept her in check. But now here she was going off at a tangent, for all that she wasn't in the first flush of youth. What's more, this was probably just the beginning.

In fact, Filipp Savich even felt a trace of envy. There he was, a young operative, working a case with a run-of-the-mill writer, taking it step by step without undue waste of time, showing initiative and always winning through. And why? Because Filipp Savich trusted him and didn't interfere.

But when it came to dealing with writers out of the common ruck, it meant having to refer every step to the Central Committee or the Politburo for approval. Of course, where you have an enormous apparatus involved, the wheels will turn that much more slowly. You finally secure approval for a brilliant operation – and it all proves in vain, because the wretched writer in question has gone on and done something worse in the meantime. He would get some new idea into his head, and you were back to planning further counter-measures and referring them up the ladder for authorization.

Moreover, Viktor had every reason to hurry things along. He wanted promotion, so he was not going to let matters slide. Members of the Politburo, however, had nowhere higher to aim, unless it was for the post of Secretary-General . . . They'd no call for dynamism, they wanted stability. So they liked to take their time, and tended to be wary of non-standard solutions. Everything, everything was done too late. Even though the whole world by now was laughing, and hostile radios were chortling: a mighty machine like that, and it couldn't cope with a lone anti-Soviet writer! Of course, that was the whole reason – the fact that it was a huge machine. Try running down a sparrow with a lorry.

Still, we'll get there eventually. At least the higher-ups had come down firmly on one issue: psychiatry. No need to wait till April! Let the enemy go hang . . . Something to be thankful for at last.

The customary chatter in the vestibule of the Writers' Club was livelier than usual: have you heard what Usmanov did over at that restaurant, the Swallow?

'. . . Just swept up the tablecloth – food, cutlery, everything – and whacked the head waiter across the face with it!'

'Who got whom? Did he get the Georgians, or did they get him?' laughed a jovial, elderly man with a bald head covered with liver spots, whose claim to fame was to have written back in '47 a collection of verse entitled *Jewish Folk Songs on the Collective Farm* almost alone and unaided. Few people remembered this now, but behind his back malicious tongues still called him 'Yankele' after the immortal line:

Yankele, my Yankele, the tractor's bust, oy vey, oy vey!

'It didn't get that far, the militia broke up the fight,' mourned an international journalist, a personable figure dressed entirely in non-domestic clothing.

'That'll be article 206, carrying one to three years,' commented a man with a friendly, open face, reminiscent of a good-natured St Bernard. Nobody disputed this statement: he wrote detective stories and knew the Criminal Code back to front.

Kir's exploit excited not a word of condemnation: if anything, his colleagues felt grateful to him for providing such a diversion. The only exception was a lady in her third youth, with a clutch of medals pinned to a jacket faintly redolent of mothballs.

'I don't see anything funny in this, comrades! Usmanov's behaviour was disgraceful, yet you're all treating it as a joke . . . The whole business is going to come up before the Secretariat, so it might be better if we all took it a little more seriously. He's taken liberties in the past, too, attacked civil order volunteer workers back in '60.'

'Heavens, Marfa Nikitichna, that was way back when,' replied the crime writer in an attempt to mollify her. 'He didn't go around throwing himself at tanks by the time '68 came around.'

'Just what do you mean by that? I should think not, indeed! No, comrades, I simply can't understand how you can take all this so lightly!'

She sailed off triumphantly, leaving the others to exchange meaningful glances behind her back. A translator of Albanian prose made clapping motions in the air, as though catching at moths.

Nikolin encountered Stella by chance, at a showing of a controversial film in the Cinema House – one of those films which are not banned, but are generally kept from a wide public screening. From time to time, however, such films are exhibited abroad and even win prizes. The original intention had been to show this film only to the privileged few, but experienced Muscovites had managed with practised ease to get round this difficulty. Thanks to Nastenka, Nikolin had acquired a taste for these shows.

That evening he had absolutely nothing to do: Nastenka had phoned to say that she was flying down to the Crimea with a film crew, and had no idea how long she'd be away. It all depended on the weather. Could be two weeks, could be four. Hugs and kisses, don't mope. Well, he wasn't moping, but it would be better not to try working in his current hag-ridden state.

Stella headed straight for Nikolin, like a jet-fighter cutting through heavy cloud. Did he know? Had he heard?

Heard what? Who had been imprisoned? Oh, that student . . . There was no understanding Stella: people of enormous reputa-

tion were being packed off to lunatic asylums, all hell was breaking loose, and she was going on about young Koretsky. Nikolin
had heard of him vaguely, but he wasn't about to repeat gossip
to Stella. Yes, the article in the paper was sickening, yes . . .

The more she tried to involve him, the more he resisted. There
was no way, of course, of knowing what had really happened,
but the story *did* seem suspicious . . . She, however, pressed her
point: something must be done! It will soon be too late. Just look
at what They are doing: whatever They want, that's what!
Putting sane people away in psychiatric asylums is one thing,
but now, by the looks of it, anyone and everyone can find themselves facing criminal charges! All it takes is to plant a few
dollars, or bring charges of rape, or homosexuality . . . They only
have to get a cleaner to inform, or set them up with a woman . . .
She went on and on.

Well, yes, They could. But still there was a time and place for
saying these things. Anybody in the surrounding crowd might
be listening . . . Then again, was it so certain that Koretsky had
been framed? And why concentrate on this issue, when there
was the business of psychiatric internment to worry about? No,
any involvement with Stella was best avoided, the woman had
taken leave of her senses. Her manner, too, of trying to coerce
people into doing what they didn't want was far too abrasive.

Luckily, the signal sounded for people to take their seats, and
Nikolin was able to make his escape. He much enjoyed the film,
and left feeling exhilarated. In order not to run into Stella again,
he was the first out of the auditorium, and fled like a naughty
schoolboy.

Back home, however, he couldn't shake off the unpleasant
aftermath of that encounter. Something about it caught at a raw
nerve. What was it she'd flung at his retreating back? 'You're all
the same – we'll see what kind of tune you sing once They get
to you!' Nikolin wouldn't have been the only one she'd said that
to, offended at his indifference.

On this issue, though, Nikolin took a firm line: he was bent on keeping a low profile. After all, he had something to lose: that novel of which she knew nothing, and which was biding its time. There was also something else he stood to lose: himself. Himself as an individual. He had been in total accord with the late Pavel over this: the camps could be faced, death could be faced. But psychiatric internment was something else altogether. The worst thing was not knowing what precisely They could do to you, and what was simply hearsay. Nikolin tried to remain unaffected by his friend's fears, which at that time had seemed out of all proportion. Yet it had started: people were being taken one after another and despatched – there . . . The threat of this struck real fear into Nikolin: he admitted as much to himself. If he were to find himself in that position, he'd commit suicide rather than submit. If he got the chance, that is.

Well, if They take us, then we'll sing, he thought, and suddenly something clicked into place in his mind: 'get a cleaner to inform . . . set them up with a woman . . .' Auntie Xenia! That was the answer to her inexplicable behaviour.

Not his fault, not her fault . . . It can't be helped!

They had ordered her to spy on him, and for all her strength of character she had been unable to refuse: this was worse than facing a tank – at least with a tank the odds were better. But she also didn't want to inform on him, so she'd contrived a quarrel between them, purely to do him a good turn. Now he understood, and was duly grateful: sabotage like that was no mean feat.

But what did it all mean? Why should he suddenly come under scrutiny? As far as he knew, he hadn't done anything to give cause . . . So what should he do now?

He sat up with a jerk: the hiding place! He had kept his promise to himself and not opened it for more than a month. What if his apartment had been searched while he was away, and the manuscript found? He rushed to get his screwdriver, pushing away Brysik who began to play with a screw he dropped in his haste.

187

The manuscript was there. Nikolin sighed with relief. Even if the KGB had been while he was away, They evidently hadn't found it. He offered a silent word of thanks to the late Pavel, who had taught him all about hiding places. There was no need to worry or resort to panic measures. In any case, he had no better place, and destroying the manuscript was unthinkable. What point would there be in living if he were to do that? There was, of course, the copy hidden at Klim's, but it would be madness to go there now: two trips so soon after each other would be bound to attract attention. No, it would be better to forget about the second copy, keep it for emergencies only.

The phone shrilled. Tatyana. Of course.

'Anton, come round, will you?'

'Do you know what time it is?'

'So what? It's only just after ten. Look, I think I've finally made up my mind. Let's talk it over, I'm perfectly calm . . .'

'So what have you decided?'

'No, not over the phone . . . Please come over. Please!'

She did sound perfectly calm, her voice humming smoothly like high-voltage wires in a slight breeze.

Nikolin's mind continued to turn over like the meter of the taxi he caught to Kachalov street, reaching a number of conclusions.

Tatyana was all dressed up, looking once again at her most seductive. She was even wearing a cut-glass necklace which flashed in the light of the candles she had already lit. She knew that he liked candlelight. However, the overhead chandelier was on, too, so he could appreciate the plunging neckline of her dress.

'So what have you finally decided?'

'Later. Let me get my thoughts together. In any case, is that all we have to talk about? Do I look so unattractive these days?'

'On the contrary, I haven't seen you look so magnificent in ages. You seem to have stepped out of a different century. That dress is incredible. As for the necklace . . .'

'At last, a lady finally gets a compliment out of you! The beads are beautiful, aren't they? Someone brought them back from Venice for my grandmother.'

As it happened, Nikolin knew that the necklace was made of Czechoslovak glass and could be bought at the Beriozka shop. Kir had once shown him an identical string he had bought for Katerina and paid for with hard currency vouchers.

However – let it be Venice. Nikolin grinned, and continued his flow of compliments.

'You know, I can't help thinking how much time we lost! Just the other day I came across a photo of our class, and one could see that you were going to be a beauty even then. As for me – I was too dumb to see it, and ran around after Natka Davydova. How blind can you be!'

'Natka Davydova!' snorted Tatyana disdainfully. 'I remember her. She was always plucking her eyebrows, not that it did her much good,' she added with a little jab of feminine malice.

'Can't say that I noticed the eyebrows, but she always tried to copy your hair-do. Whichever way you did it one day, she'd do it the next.'

'True, true,' agreed Tatyana. 'All the girls used to laugh at her about that. But you boys didn't understand a thing in those days.'

She bowed her head and sighed lightly as though she, too, were regretting the opportunities lost.

Nikolin leaned back and studied her admiringly. She was damned good!

'And now, perhaps you wouldn't mind telling me who you really are and what's your real name?' he asked bitingly.

'*What?*'

She rose, eyes narrowed threateningly.

'Because', he continued inexorably, 'there never was any Natka Davydova in our school. I made her up, just for your benefit, milady. And you, it appears, even remember her eyebrows . . .'

They were both on their feet now, facing each other, and had Nikolin not been so carried away by his own victory, he would have been transfixed by her unmoving, feral stare. She was like a wild cat ready to spring, hackles up and ears pulled back.

'. . . And how do they pay you for your work?' Nikolin pressed on. 'With roubles, or with currency vouchers for the Beriozka?'

Thwack!

In one flashing movement she tore the beads from her neck and slashed Nikolin across the face with them as hard as she could. Blood spurted from his temple and flooded one eye.

He fled down the stairs, clutching the side of his face.

'You bastard!' she screamed after him at the top of her lungs, following up with a choice assortment of curses. 'I'll sue you for maintenance!'

'Fight, eh?' asked the bearded driver of the car he flagged down, sympathetically.

Nikolin nodded mutely. He fished out his handkerchief and pressed it to the raw wound.

'Hang on, you need to wet that,' said the driver, stopping his car. He pulled a bottle of mineral water out of a bag, switched on the light, and proceeded to pour some on to Nikolin's handkerchief.

'Give us a look, now. No, your eye's still there. What did they do that with?'

'A necklace,' grimaced Nikolin sourly. 'Czech glass. Straight in the face.'

'That must be some dame!' marvelled the other. 'Where'd you find a viper like that?'

'You have to know the right places.'

The bearded driver was so impressed that he refused to take Nikolin's money.

'We blokes have got to stick together, mate,' he said.

Nikolin studied himself in the mirror. He certainly looked a sight. He'd underestimated her, no doubt about it. He washed the gash as best he could, pulled the edges of the broken skin together and smeared them with BF-6 glue. He'd probably have a scar across his eyebrow for ever now, but the cut on his cheek would heal and disappear in time.

Not that he cared. At that moment he didn't even care that he now knew for certain that he was under surveillance. The worry that had plagued him most was gone: she had made up that business about being pregnant, it had all been done to blackmail him. Yes, you can always catch a conscientious intellectual 'on the hook of a child's tear'. You only had to think of just one of the possible outcomes – handing over the newborn baby to a state orphanage. Few knew for certain what it was they did to babies there, but it was well known that by the time they're three years old they're still unable to talk or communicate in any way beyond crying and making disjointed sounds. Nikolin would not have been able to take the child, because only families are allowed to adopt.

Well, you can claw the walls as much as you like, now, you bitch. You'll probably get it in the neck, too, for letting the fish off the hook!

Nikolin was very pleased with the neat way he had managed the whole business.

Chapter Nineteen

VIKTOR STEPANYCH WAS preparing to settle down to an agreeable evening. The lady was giggling pleasurably as he stroked her knees. But, just at that moment, a malignant fate decided to intervene and his hot line rang. Had Viktor Stepanych been a shade less conscientious about his duties, he would have unplugged it now and then. But Viktor Stepanych was not like that.

'Viktor Stepanych? It's me, Forget-me-not.'

'Something wrong?'

'Yes.'

'Can it wait until tomorrow?'

'That's for you to decide. My job's to report. I'm at the Kachalov flat.'

'On my way.'

Viktor Stepanych's companion, duly impressed by the mystery and romance of his occupation, merely looked puzzled: what was she to do now? It was almost midnight . . .

'Stay here, I'll be back in about an hour and a half,' commanded Viktor Stepanych, all business now. 'I'll phone if I'm delayed any longer. I'm sorry, my dear, but duty calls . . . Make yourself at home.'

He dropped a kiss on her ear.

Forget-me-not regained her composure quickly once the Storyteller had gone. She'd failed, and now needed to find a way out for herself. Pity she'd got carried away and yelled all those things in his wake, the whole house would have heard.

She decided that her best course would be to make a clean breast of everything straight away. After all, it hadn't been her idea to pose as a former classmate. Indeed, she had objected to this particular cover-story, and events had proved her right. However, she knew from experience that being right did not necessarily solve a problem; in fact, could well make matters worse.

She switched on the coffee-grinder, making a few rapid calculations in her head. It would take him about twenty minutes to get here, she'd serve him Turkish coffee – say another four minutes . . . She went off to the bathroom to repair her make-up. On the way, she reached for the little glass bottle and shook out one tiny cream-coloured pill.

Viktor Stepanych knew that Forget-me-not would not phone up over a trifle. But what could have happened? Had Nikolin gone and killed himself? Of course, her mission was to reduce his nerves to shreds, but she may have overdone it . . . No, surely it couldn't be that. He distracted himself by studying the back of his driver's head. Usually there's a fold in the flesh where the hairline ends, but this one didn't have it. Funny.

Forget-me-not set two foamy, aromatic cups of coffee on the pol-ished table. Just the thing, working the hours we do, day and night. Viktor Stepanych sipped and listened.

Of course, it was a pity things had worked out that way, but no irreparable harm had been done. Forget-me-not was out of the picture now, of course, because there's only so much mileage to be gained from a faked pregnancy. Now if Nikolin had gone and killed himself – that would have been cause for concern . . .

'And how did you react?'

Forget-me-not, eyes flashing audaciously, gave a graphic description, and even showed him the beads. Yes, a blow across the face with those – wow!

Viktor Stepanych couldn't help laughing uproariously at the picture she conjured up. What a woman! What panache! And why not? She was right, of course – a failure required an immediate termination of contact. No matter the circumstances. But why should a woman like that even need a reason? Look at her now – draped sinuously in that chair, head a little to the side, balancing a shoe precariously on the end of her foot . . . that clod of a Storyteller should be grateful he'd come within hailing distance of her!

Viktor Stepanych was on top of the world. He felt confident, debonair, ready to play the game for any stakes, winner take all – for a winner he knew with joyous certainty he was: in anything and everything. He was gripped by an elated aggression: hey, everybody, out of my way, or I'll trample you underfoot! Forget-me-not looked at him with eyes which shone with unconcealed admiration: yes, real women recognize and feel power. He wanted to seize her fragile shoulders between his hands and squeeze them, not painfully, but masterfully . . .

'Are you satisfied with the special clothes you requested, Forget-me-not?'

'Viktor Stepanych, they're out of this world!'

'Show me.'

Viktor Stepanych set off home not one and a half hours later, but well over two. He was inordinately pleased with himself, and with Forget-me-not, but completely worn out. It was all he could do to stop himself from falling asleep. He really shouldn't go so short of sleep, he had to work tomorrow. The minute he got home he'd crawl into bed, pull the blanket up to his chin and sleep, sleep . . .

Hell, he'd completely forgotten that there would be somebody in that bed waiting for him . . . Of course, he could always apologize, plead exhaustion – and get an inferiority complex in the process.

He searched his pockets feverishly: where was the little white bottle, in this jacket or the other one? Ah, here it was! Viktor Stepanych gulped down one tiny pill. He'd not had a chance to try them out yet, saving them for a suitable occasion. He had no idea how long it would need to take effect.

The pill acted immediately. At once, Viktor Stepanych was filled again with the desire to crush anything that stood in his path: enemies, wild jungles, delicate shoulders, tender spring grasses. He felt angry that the driver was taking so long to get home, hairy idiot that he was, without a crease on the back of his head where everyone else had one! Heaven only knows what he would have done to the driver had they not pulled up outside his block right then. Viktor Stepanych flung himself into the lift.

The lady was crushed, amazed, and reduced to speechless admiration: what men they have working for them in the KGB!

The remaining ninety-eight tablets, issued for use in the operation against the Storyteller, were not required, and were employed in circumstances totally unrelated to the work of the Department.

Around eleven the following evening, Kir turned up at Nikolin's apartment. He wore a suede jacket, sported a foreign tan, and had a bottle of tequila tucked under his arm in the manner of a soldier at attention.

'Hello, old man! Didn't get you out of bed, did I? He-e-e-y! What on earth's happened to you? Had a falling-out with a tram?'

Nikolin's appearance was hard not to notice: the swelling had not yet subsided, and dark blue and purple streaks were already edging the red gash. Especially impressive was the pattern on his forehead, made up as it was of clearly defined little octagons.

'A lady of my acquaintance let me have it in the face with her beads: a little something to remember her by,' explained Nikolin. 'The next time you catch a woman lying, check to see what jewellery she's wearing before you open your mouth.'

'You don't say!' cried Kir with unfeigned delight. 'Introduce me to her, will you?'

'Thank your lucky stars you've never met her. By the way, I hear you've been causing something of a stir yourself.'

'What's that you've heard?' asked Kir, interested.

Nikolin rehearsed the many versions of the story he'd been told. Kir laughed uproariously, waving his long arms, and Nikolin joined in. Good spirits restored, Kir went over the highlights.

'The "village writers" were specially pleased. That's the way, they said: one Russian can account for twelve Georgians any day.'

Kir sighed regretfully.

'I'm sorry now that I didn't. Should've given them a re-run of the battle of Poltava, it wouldn't have affected the outcome, anyway. I've been summoned to the Secretariat tomorrow, they're going to have me jumping through hoops. To cap it all, I was there with another woman, and not Katerina. So they'll add immoral conduct to unbecoming behaviour. You should be grateful that you're not a member of the Secretariat, and, being a friend of mine, won't have to pretend to be sick in order to stay away.'

'Thanks,' said Nikolin sincerely, then added suspiciously:

'What's that white thing in the bottle?'

'That, old man, is a Mexican worm! Tequila with a worm like that is the best there is. Let's try it.'

The fat little worm curled up there filled Nikolin with distaste. He could never bring himself to touch worms: even in childhood, and even with his gloved hands.

'You mean we eat the thing?' he asked cautiously, and tried to substitute a bottle of bourbon for Kir's offering. Kir frowned, offended.

'Why the hell do you think I dragged it all the way from Mexico? The one without a worm is half the price, for your information. Now, don't be afraid, I drank this stuff when I was over there, and I'm still alive, aren't I? All right, we'll start with bourbon to build up our courage, and see how we go.'

They set to, both feeling the need to unwind after their respective tribulations.

Kir described the frescoes of Xicxieros, the character of the Mexican president, the fantastic huge cactus plants – revelling in his recollections. Then, after they had cracked open the tequila, he sank into a depression and began to enumerate his grievances.

'I tell you, old man, I hate Them, really hate Them. They think Kir's been broken? Turned into an obedient lackey?

'What d'you think They'll demand from me tomorrow, eh? That I sign something disgusting about a perfectly decent person? As a "rightful rebuke to enemy wiles"? Write a poem glorifying the Chekists? Crawl on my belly the length of the corridor and back? And what if I do crawl? I love life, I'm not some saintly hermit who's renounced all contact with the world. You're like that, but I'm not. I'm 75 kilograms of living flesh.'

'Eat something,' prompted Nikolin, passing him a ham sandwich.

'And I'll tell Them to go to hell, see if I don't! Let Them put me away. You're lucky you don't get caught up in unpleasant business like this. You seem to get by somehow, and They leave you alone.'

Nikolin smiled bitterly. 'Somehow . . . You don't know what's been happening.'

He told Kir the whole story about Auntie Xenia and Tatyana. And why shouldn't he? If They know that he knows, why make a secret of it? Yes, the writer Nikolin is under surveillance. Let Kir and everyone else know it, too. It could happen to anyone.

Kir's face became grave.

'You say you haven't been involved with any dissidents? And haven't let any work of yours circulate by hand?'

'Of course I haven't – that's the point!'

'It could be that They're after someone you know, and you're of peripheral interest. If that's the case, They'll sniff around a bit and then leave you alone.'

Kir stroked Brysik absent-mindedly, staring off into the middle distance. After a while, he shook his head decisively.

'No, it can't be that. They chopped your book, not someone else's, so it must be you They're after.'

He pointed solemnly at Nikolin, like a Communist League member from a recruitment poster.

Nikolin experienced an unpleasant sinking feeling. It's all very well to call a spade a spade, of course, but to hear it spelt out . . .

Kir, meanwhile, continued to hold forth, all the time nibbling at a slice of lemon.

'All right, let's assume you haven't done anything of the kind yet. But, my friend, you're beginning to emerge from your ecological niche! Children's literature is all very well, a great place of refuge: write your stories and pretend to be some sort of Ivan-the-Fool. But They had grandmothers and grandfathers who used to read Them stories in childhood, too, and They remember full well that there comes a time when Ivan-the-Fool stops fooling around and gets down to business. We all – and that includes Them – have this idea buried in our subconscious. You know, I've read that everything you learn by the age of five remains down there. In the subconscious, I mean. You see what I'm driving at?'

'I do,' muttered Nikolin, 'but you're beginning to lose the point. Any moment now and you're going to start in on all that Freudian stuff.'

'Right, where were we? Ah, yes. You, my friend, have an aura. You have charisma around you. Or is it an aura that people have around them? I always mix them up, but that doesn't matter . . . You've got vision and integrity! Do you think people can't see that? Everyone can! People nod significantly behind your back.'

Nikolin had no idea how he was supposed to react to that, so he looked meaningfully at Kir in the hope that that would pass muster. Kir, however, was in earnest, carried along on a wave of drunken elation, full of revelations and illuminations. Brysik's fur fairly crackled with static electricity under his hand.

'You haven't written your major works yet, my friend. Or maybe you have, eh?' Laughing, Kir wagged a finger at Nikolin, looking at him through glazed eyes. 'Well, if you have, and aren't showing it to your friends, it's not for me to take offence. You'd be quite right. Just look at me – what am I, eh? Can I be trusted? Don't trust me, pal, I'm telling you that as a brother . . .'

Nikolin decided to brew a pot of very strong tea, piling three heaped teaspoons of sugar into each cup. He shooed Brysik away from Kir on to the couch, just in case the poet scalded the kitten with the tea.

It helped. Kir, sipping silently, seemed to sober up visibly, and then said in a normal, everyday voice:

'They're checking you out. It happens often enough. Carry on as normal, so to speak, but don't forget that we're keeping an eye on you. It's inevitable. You know K—? They did that to him, he told me about it himself. And d'you know what he did? Delivered his manuscript There personally: here you are, why bother with intermediaries? You be my first readers. And do you know what They did?'

'Published it?' hazarded Nikolin. He remembered it coming out. There had been an immense hubbub at the time, and an audible gasp of surprise at the fact that it had been passed. Had someone made a gaffe, or been drunk? As far as he knew, nobody could suggest any other explanation.

'Precisely. He couldn't credit the fact that They'd cut hardly anything. If you don't much like K— think of Bulgakov! No objections there, I presume? Right! Well, when They began to push him too far, what did he do? Wrote straight to Stalin: the situation is like this, They're not letting me work. And what did Stalin do? Issued a direct order: let him work wherever he wants.'

Nikolin was familiar with the episode and fidgeted knowingly, but it was impossible to stop Kir when he was in the middle of a good story. Then, in a totally sober voice, he added:

'If you think that everything I've said has been the alcohol talking, I'll tell you what I'll do: I'll brew up some *chifir*, the real thing, the way some old lags taught me. Nothing wrong with your heart? Good. Then, when we've drunk it, I'll repeat everything. So you won't have any doubts.'

For the uninitiated, *chifir* is made as follows: one takes a cupful of tea leaves to a cupful of water, and brings it slowly to the boil, removing it from the hob when it is about to boil over. The more sophisticated then add a pinch of sugar to make it easier to ingest. This was the method favoured by Kir. As he stood over the stove, he continued his philosophical musings:

'Nowadays we all cock a snook at Stalin, but remember when we were kids, how everyone idolized him? Did you?'

'Yes,' admitted Nikolin. He told Kir how, at the age of nine, he had attempted to draw a portrait of Stalin with his coloured pencils. He'd intended taking it to school, but his mother had dissuaded him.

'Your mother was a smart woman,' commented Kir. 'You know what could have been the outcome of a portrait like that?'

Nikolin suspected that childhood recollections would get Kir back on his hobby-horse about the subconscious, but the *chifir* was ready and Kir switched to a lecture on how it must be swallowed and how one should breathe while drinking it.

The effect was powerful. The alcohol fumes dispersed, and were replaced by exhilaration. As he had promised, the now-sober Kir repeated everything about Nikolin's charisma, aura, vision and integrity. Who would have thought that such an impulsive, not to say frivolous personality as Kir would have been gifted with such perception and finesse? He disarmed Nikolin completely by making him a shy offer of money: just to tide him over his present difficulties, he said. It seemed churlish to refuse, but Kir insisted until Nikolin promised him that should the need arise, he would ask Kir himself. Stella had once told Nikolin that Kir was like that: if he had any money, he would invariably help someone on the quiet. But Stella herself was an exalted creature, it was obvious that she didn't lack money, and wouldn't have needed any help from Kir. Nikolin had never heard anyone else say such things about Kir, so he had refrained from comment. Now, seeing Kir's almost childish diffidence – as if he were the one asking and afraid of receiving a refusal – Nikolin realized the truth of Stella's claim; there was evidently a great deal he still had to learn about his friend. To dispel a momentary awkwardness, they exchanged a few jokes together about animals. This led to the subject of cartoon films.

'Look, old man, have you ever thought of writing stories for cartoons? You'd be brilliant at it! D'you want me to introduce you to a couple of people?' said Kir, fired with the idea. They laughed as they envisaged a screen version of the jokes they had just been telling, embroidering the story line and introducing new characters. In fact, they enjoyed themselves hugely. As he saw Kir off, Nikolin suddenly asked:

'Kir, would you have liked to live in the last century, say? Or the one before?'

'The one before, definitely not,' replied Kir at once. 'You know when I'd have liked to live? The end of the last or the beginning of this century, so as to be dead by 1917.'

'Why the end of the last century, exactly?'

'Because there were no anaesthetics before that, you fool!'

The sky was greying when Nikolin accompanied Kir out, and as he returned the streetlights came on. Back in the flat, he started to wash the dishes unhurriedly. He ought to write a story about how to wash dishes once and for all so they would never need to be done again. When the doorbell rang, he flung the tea-towel over his shoulder and went to see who it was.

'May we come in?' asked the comrade in plain clothes politely, holding up an open ID holder with a stamp across his photo. Without waiting for a reply, he eased Nikolin aside and walked in. He was followed immediately by a major of the militia in full uniform, two men in greatcoats, and another two in ordinary civilian overcoats. Looking at these last two Nikolin somehow realized that they had been drafted in as witnesses.

Chapter Twenty

THE MEETING OF the Secretariat was not an ordinary one but an extended general session, which meant that Belokon was invited to attend. He was known as reliable, and not inclined to flirting with liberal tendencies. Alas, Belokon – terribly sorry, comrades! – was unwell. Blood pressure. He was in bed. Olga had called a doctor, who ordered peace and quiet, peace and quiet, and yet more peace and quiet.

So Belokon relaxed at home enjoying his peace and quiet. Kir was no longer formally a relative, but he *was* Denis's father. Family relationships were sacrosanct, and should be treated so. Publicly, at least. In any case, he had no desire to attend: let them manage without him for once.

Belokon lay in bed leafing through *America* magazine. This publication is not available to just anybody, the subscription list is compiled by those in the know. He recalled the hopes he had had for Kir, but without rancour. You couldn't win them all, and it was still possible that he would scale the heights.

What had Belokon wanted? He had seen that Kir was a young man who, typically, wanted the world. That was why he'd fooled around and run risks – he felt himself underestimated. Olga had fallen for him straight away: all that intensity, all that fly-away light brown hair, burning eyes, sunken cheeks, the hordes of twittering fans – no wonder she'd lost her head. It was then that Belokon conceived the idea of using Kir to squeeze out the fashionable Yevtushenkos, Voznesenskys and the rest of that crowd – Belokon allowed himself the luxury of not

203

distinguishing between them, if only because they all treated him, Belokon, the same way. They despised him. But this one, if handled properly, cultivated, petted, accepted into the Union – this one would be ours. If the state needed an avant-garde poet for export, Kir should be the one.

Filipp Savich had seemed to approve at the time: why not give it a try? Belokon still could not understand why it had all fallen through. Kir had been broken to bridle after his first trip abroad, so there was no reason why he shouldn't have been allowed to continue. Moreover, he'd been well received by the West, very well, if with something less than the usual fanfare. He seemed to lack that certain ingredient necessary to become a Leading Export Item, but it was impossible to determine what. He could hold his liquor, had charm and a gift for languages, read his poetry in the requisite emotional manner. He even wore a suitably avant-garde jacket at his readings . . . What more could anyone want?

But something was missing. Maybe it was simply the whiff of scandal, like the one that had just occurred? Maybe that would stimulate him, give him a new slant? Make him seem daring and dangerous once more? Export goods always have to have special packaging. On the other hand, what if this were to break him? In that case – to hell with him. Or if he slips the leash . . .? No, not this one. He, Belokon, knew people well enough to be sure of that. It was his profession, after all – to be an engineer of human souls.

Nikolin, pale but composed, invited his unexpected visitors to take a seat. For some reason, he was at his most urbane, playing the old-fashioned gentleman like some forgotten remnant of the old bourgeoisie.

'To what do I owe the pleasure?'

The one in civvies with the ID answered in kind, extending his search warrant with impeccable courtesy. Confiscation . . . of *what*? Nikolin couldn't understand what it was all about, and asked for an explanation. The explanation was furnished forthwith, in clear and concise terms.

Nikolin's visitors were very sorry to intrude upon the prominent writer's time, but they had a problem: for three months now they had been engaged in a fruitless search and felt as though they had reached a dead end. There had been this academician in Leningrad, S—; maybe Nikolin knew him? Why 'had been'? Because he'd died three months ago, there had been an obituary in the papers . . . Oh, you missed it? Yes, very sad. They say he's a great loss to the intellectual world. Academician S—, it appears, had an innocent passion: collecting antiques. A marvellous, priceless collection! It was frightening to think that such treasures of culture were kept in an ordinary apartment, where any petty thief could pick the lock with a fork. Actually, academician S— had been smart, and willed his entire collection to the Hermitage museum. He realized that it should belong to the people. But while he was alive, he wanted to enjoy it himself. Never mind. Nothing wrong with that.

The academician had died suddenly: came home, sat down to dinner, didn't even fall off his chair, his widow said. Naturally, the house was in an uproar, relatives, friends, casual acquaintances, all in and out . . . Anyway, when the family got around to passing over the collection to the Hermitage, they realized that one of the icons had disappeared. And what an icon! The pearl of the collection! St Nicholas the Miracle Worker, sixteenth century! So there was nothing to do but institute a search, seeing the icon was now state property. Legally and irrevocably. It was a well-known fact that the intelligentsia these days is very keen on icons. It seemed that Nikolin had known S—, met him a few times at least at banquets and similar gatherings . . . In short, the suggestion was that Nikolin should voluntarily show all the icons he had in his apartment, help the investigation along. Nikolin shrugged: yes, he had a few. One his mother had left him, a little one, no larger than the palm of his hand on a convex board. The second was the one Nastenka had left for safe-keeping. He hadn't got round to taking it out of the plastic bag, but pulled it out now. It would be stupid to conceal anything – what if they started digging around and found his hidden manuscript? As for the third icon – he couldn't even remember where it was from, it dated back to Lucia's time. He placed all three on the table without a word. He added a booklet on Russian icon painting for good measure.

'That's all I've got.'

The investigator studied them attentively, smiled slightly at the sight of the booklet and moved it aside. The same with the Virgin and Child. Lucia's icon was of someone dressed in white, kneeling in the middle of a forest, and a bear standing by him. May we measure it? No, different size . . . put that aside. The stern eyes of the third icon were already looking at Nikolin, but showing no great interest in the proceedings. This one he recognized – who in Russia would not recognize St Nicholas the Miracle Worker?

The investigator, however, applied his ruler scrupulously.

'May I? . . . Ah, this one's the right size . . . how did you come by it?'

Nikolin, although surprised by this unexpected turn of events, resisted mentioning Nastenka.

'This is a search, not an interrogation, isn't it?'

'Of course, I just thought you might . . . if you felt so inclined . . . With your permission, we'll take this one to be looked at by experts. If it's not the one we're after, we'll return it with apologies. Please sign the form here . . . you see where it says: "surrendered the item voluntarily". Fine. I would have hated to have to poke around . . . Apologies again for disturbing you. My son is a great fan of yours . . . I brought one of them with me hoping that you wouldn't mind signing it? His name's Maxim . . . Thank you so much, he'll be over the moon! Goodbye, comrade Nikolin, we won't take up any more of your time . . .'

Nikolin was left alone to make what he could of the proceedings. The easiest thing would have been to phone Nastenka, but she was in the Crimea . . . He tried to convince himself that a week or so would pass, and then they would be returning the icon with apologies. She'd said she had bought it from some old man and had spent a long time talking him into parting with it. This couldn't possibly be the icon that was under investigation. And then, look at how far Leningrad was from Moscow! As for icons, every third one would be of St Nicholas, and they come in all sizes, so this could be sheer coincidence. So academician S— had died, had he? Nikolin did remember him: a lively old fellow, always full of anecdotes. They had met a couple of times. People seemed to be dying all around him lately. Except those who survived.

Well, praise be to St Nicholas for averting a proper house search! Now that would have been something . . . It was not as though the thought didn't gnaw at the back of his mind that this icon might turn out to be the one they were after. But Nikolin quashed it mercilessly. Nastenka hadn't cheated on him. Not once.

I cannot say which of Moscow's numerous official buildings the special session of the Secretariat of the Union of Writers took place in, and won't pretend that I know. Those who have attended such meetings know anyway, and those who haven't are too late now. They say that there's this huge oval table there.

For the same reason there are no details about the drubbing given to Kir, but the process of execution lasted one hour and fifty-two minutes. So it is hardly surprising that he walked out with flaming cheeks and not in the best of tempers.

If you break someone's backbone with a shovel or a similar instrument, he will never get up and walk again. If the instrument employed is a collective of his peers, he will toddle out on his own two feet, alone and unaided. There had been times when nobody came out again, especially in the good old days.

In that case, an ambulance would be summoned. But there was nothing wrong with Kir's heart, and the good old days had coincided with his childhood and adolescence, when he was more absorbed with the problems of growing up than with the paternal care of the Leader. So Kir walked out on his own two feet, wanting only to get out and gulp a breath of fresh air.

But it was not to be: he was still making his way along the carpeted corridors when he suddenly encountered the lady of the mothballs with her clip of medals and a cardboard file tucked under her arm. Her sharp face broke into a welcoming smile, as she hurried towards him.

'Ah, Kirill Sergeich! Just the man I need – what luck that you're here! We have this plan on the stocks: we want all the leading Soviet writers to come out in condemnation of the anti-Soviet antics of –'

Kir didn't listen any further, he could guess whose name she was about to utter. Solzhenitsyn, who else? Wasn't it enough for them to throw him out of the Union of Writers, damn them all to hell! Did they want to put him behind bars now, or what? He stared at her with helpless hatred, fearing that any minute, broken-backed as he was, he might sign – what else could he do . . . She'd trap him like a spider traps a fly, drag him off into a corner, give him the text and point out with an arthritic finger just where to put his name. He wailed inwardly, reciting every imprecation remaining in an atheistic society: please, God, anything but this! Not this ultimate disgrace in the face of the whole world!

Once again, the inevitable was not to be. Three colleagues appeared at the end of the corridor, laughing about something. They spotted Kir and headed for him immediately.

'Well, how did it go?'

Whatever you chose to call these disciplinary sessions – a Calvary, a public whipping (the terms were variously favoured) – everybody knew that Kir would be put through the wringer today, and why. Naturally, they were curious to take a look at the victim. There was sympathy in their eyes, certainly, but also an avid curiosity tinged with a desire to assess the damage.

Kir, however, possessed an unexpected trait: if his opponent got him up against the ropes face to face and alone, he could put up no resistance and would sink as low as you like. But in front of witnesses he felt obliged to hold his own. Even if he knew that he would regret it later, when faced with an audience he would be fearless and devil-may-care, while at the same time cursing his theatrical nature.

'I'll tell you everything in a moment, but Marfa Nikitichna here has just been telling me about a very interesting proposal. Marfa Nikitichna, why don't you tell our comrades what they've missed. They're some of our leading writers, too.'

For some reason, Marfa Nikitichna was reluctant to do so, and grimaced with offence. And while she searched for a suitable excuse for declining, Kir bent his gaze on her and asked deferentially.

'Marfa Nikitichna, is it really true that you met Lenin? Tell us about it!'

The three others erupted with laughter, abruptly stifled with coughs, snorts and sneezes.

Marfa Nikitichna drew herself up angrily.

'Are you making fun of me?'

'As if we would! I only wanted to ask about Le –'

'Kirill Sergeich, how old do you think I am?'

'What's that got to do with it, Marfa Nikitichna?' Kir pulled a grotesque face. 'We're not talking about years, but epochs!'

'Well! You . . . you . . . I've nothing to say to you, d'you understand?'

She took off at speed.

'Just as well you've understood,' called Kir in her wake.

His colleagues were laughing and slapping him on the back: should have asked her if she'd known Rameses II! That evening it would be all over town: did you hear about Kir? What a fellow! He's heading for a showdown! They dragged him off to the Writers' Club restaurant to mark the occasion.

'I'm all for it – why not? Only in the presence of witnesses, though! And don't let any Georgians in, boys, must keep my high moral profile intact,' joked Kir. He went over the story again of Marfa Nikitichna's petition.

'They haven't canvassed you yet? Must have decided to start with me. But me – I'm a Russian poet! Let the world know: Russian! A poet!'

He repeated the same story to the long-suffering Katerina when he returned home well after midnight and was struggling to pull off his lilac tie over his tousled head.

'Poet. Russian. Understand, woman?'

In the morning Kir wanted to be anywhere but at home: what if the phone should ring? He went off to see Nikolin, who had already heard from other sources of the previous day's events. Good for Kir! How he'd needled that old hag about Lenin! What greater insult can there be to a woman than to exaggerate her age?

'So you didn't sign?'

'Look, old man, what do you take me for? Yes, I signed in '68, so remind me of that as often as you like. I don't have much resistance. I'm like one of those toys that you push over, and they straighten up again, while everyone around laughs . . . Serves me right.

'So I'm telling you: I've had enough, they won't push me over again. Ah, I bet you're thinking, how can he be so sure? You know how I managed to hold out yesterday? I imagined you refusing to shake me by the hand. And that's the reason, I swear it. Oh, they'll make a meal of me now. Devour me with my boot-laces. I think I'll go into samizdat. I didn't value it properly, more's the pity. I'll write real stuff and send it abroad . . . That's all that's left for me to do after all this. Until the militia gets to me. Come on, let's go somewhere, eh? The Sanduny, for instance . . . Even death has its attractions if it's public enough.'

'Wait,' countered Nikolin. 'How are you fixed for time?'

'As much as you like. Why? Are you thinking of going out of town?'

'No. Here's some cash, hop out and buy us something to eat and drink. I haven't a thing in the house, so bear that in mind.'

Kir, surprised by Nikolin's unexpectedly commanding tone, went off without further question. When he returned clutching bulging string bags and prancing around like a delivery boy, Nikolin steered him to the sofa and handed him his precious manuscript.

'Are you a fast reader? I'm not letting this out of the house, so if you want to read it, you'll have to read it here. And I'll get us something to keep us going.'

He went out into the kitchen.

That was how they spent the rest of the day: Kir read, turning the pages greedily, exclaiming or groaning from time to time, laughing occasionally. Nikolin brewed up coffee, served Kir and himself. Emptied the ashtrays. He even fried up some potatoes and sausage, but Kir waved them impatiently aside: later! He read quickly, while Nikolin watched covertly: what was it that Kir was muttering at, what caused him to grunt 'not bad'?

He felt annoyed with himself for worrying, but the fewer pages remained unread, the more Nikolin hungered for and feared praise. We're all human . . . He had a better understanding of the late Pavel now. Under the circumstances, it didn't seem wrong to allow the manuscript to circulate: he was under surveillance, so he had to change tactics!

Kir finished reading, got up and stared at Nikolin with a kind of mystic awe. Finally, he seemed to realize that he was expected to speak. He collapsed back on the sofa and said, quietly and with total conviction:

'That, old man, is a masterpiece!'

Chapter Twenty-one

KIR PACED AROUND the room, waving his arms.

'I have always had faith in you, old man, I always knew you were a bloody genius! But I never expected anything this good. If I had – I'd have written it myself . . .'

Nikolin perched on the edge of the table, sipped his remaining coffee, and gave himself over to a full enjoyment of the moment. He was a little tired – just a little. He did not overestimate Kir's taste: his poems spoke for themselves, and in recent years spoke too much. But – a writer and a reader are two different things, are they not? Even a middling poet may be able to tell good from bad in literature. Finally, didn't Nikolin have the right to share the pleasure of the only friend whom it didn't turn his stomach to share a drink with lately? And, in any case, to hell with all 'buts'! There was no denying the pleasure it gave him – Kir's sincerity was patent. Who could fail to be pleased that his first reader was in this state of elation?

'So what are you going to do with it?' asked Kir when he'd finished walking around in circles and waving his arms in the air.

'I've no idea. I'm still thinking about that myself.'

'Are you sure that it wouldn't be published?'

Nikolin gave a brief, mirthless laugh and hung his head, like an old man regretting the rapid passage of the years.

'I didn't get that feeling. After all, you're the author, you see a whole lot of things in the background that aren't reflected in the text.'

'They see a whole lot, too,' objected Nikolin, almost wishing that Kir would dissuade him.

But Kir refrained. He sat on a stool, rocking it back precariously on two legs, his chin in his hands.

'Look, what have you got to lose? Let someone else read it . . . I could be prejudiced in your favour.'

It was true that Nikolin had nothing to lose. But he only had that one copy available – it was better to forget about the second one for the time being. He could type up another one, and let it circulate around Moscow. It would take a week to do the typing, but the surveillance . . .? They could get wind of it and take steps, so he wouldn't be able to finish it. On the other hand, maybe audacity would do the trick: just take the manuscript and openly do the rounds of the publishing houses? He'd not thought the work stood a chance of publication while he was writing it, but what if he was wrong? Every so often something would appear that would have everyone gasping with amazement. Maybe he'd lost his sense of objectivity, the novel hadn't lain untouched the requisite amount of time . . . Maybe Kir was allowing his judgement to be swayed by his enthusiasm, he was always getting worked up about something . . . Who else could be trusted to read it who wouldn't open his mouth before time?

He put this question to Kir, then added severely:

'I'm not letting it out of the house, mind. For the time being.'

Kir sat there thinking: a good question. Then he brightened.

'Mitri! Look, I'll bring him here! Now, what are you looking so down in the mouth about? You simply haven't figured him out yet. Yes, he likes to act the provincial – which isn't the lowest of taste, by the way! He's got two university degrees, even though he's working as a boilerman. I tell you, he conducts these psychic experiments you wouldn't believe. And he knows literature inside-out!'

'He acts the village idiot, not the provincial,' muttered Nikolin unpleasantly.

'Well, that's his way of protecting himself. He is pretty boorish in company, I agree. He'd be run off his legs if he wasn't – you know that he can even cure cancer? So he wears a mask in self-defence. But he's got a very refined soul. It's people like him you're writing for, not the usual *hoi polloi!*'

The following day Mitri was ensconced on Nikolin's sofa, for once not reeking of onions. Nor did he point his little finger when holding his teacup. True, when he came in he looked around for something to cross himself before. Nikolin, being an unbeliever, did not decorate his walls with icons for effect, but kept them in a drawer. Mitri resolved his own dilemma: he blessed the little blue plasticine wolf, and then crossed himself in front of it.

'This object has an excellent energetic field, the child may be an avatar in its next incarnation,' he said in passing, but didn't elaborate.

The subject of the conversation was a common one: emigration. Kir was glad for Kuznetsov: the man had escaped to freedom! A free artist has the right . . .

'Everything in nature is interrelated, what's truth got to do with anything?' said Mitri with a condescending smirk. 'Who does a writer work for? For the reader. Out of the three of us, I'm a reader pure and simple. So may I ask: why should I be grateful? Kuznetsov wants to be at odds with the authorities. He wants to emigrate – and, naturally, with the maximum of fuss. Why should I care? Is he thinking about me, his reader? Graham Greene, being an honourable man, feels obliged to speak out in his defence. The result? They don't publish Graham Greene here now, and won't in future. Kuznetsov will be published in the West, granted. But maybe I'd prefer to read Graham Greene, not Anatoli Kuznetsov!'

Nikolin gestured uncertainly.

'But that seems so . . . utilitarian.'

'So is all this talk about rights,' retorted Mitri, raising an admonishing finger.

For some reason, they all studied that short finger covered with ginger down with great attention.

Mitri eyed Nikolin narrowly.

'I see you're limping. Had an accident?'

'Is it that noticeable?' asked Nikolin, disappointed. 'An accident, yes, but thirty years ago. Sometimes aches because of the weather. Not too often. I'd forgotten all about it for some years, but now here it is again. Been sitting still too long, I expect. Normally I don't limp.'

'Knee?' asked Mitri abruptly.

'Knee,' confirmed Nikolin. He decided to answer, what with Mitri having extra-sensory powers. Who knows, maybe he'd come up with a cure. Nikolin had nothing to lose.

'Pain in the knee, especially the right knee, is a sign of suicidal tendencies. Have you been thinking about doing away with yourself? Or thought about it in the past?'

'Me? Suicide?' repeated Nikolin incredulously. He was surprised and offended. Still, what could one expect from someone like Mitri? The man was out of his mind. And Kir doesn't know what he's talking about, going on about how Mitri could see through anything like an X-ray machine. He's just a nutter. Gone off the rails among his astrals, most likely. Suicide my foot!

Mitri did not press the matter further, and seemed to have lost interest in Nikolin's knee. He asked where he could settle down to read so as not to be in anyone's way. Conscious that they ought not to distract Mitri with their presence, Nikolin and Kir went out to eat, leaving Mitri supplied with food and drink. As they had no way of knowing how long Mitri would be occupied, once their meal was over they drove around the city for a while in Kir's Moskvich. Nikolin was suddenly displeased with himself. Not simply because he couldn't out-argue Mitri, but generally . . . He was condemned to go through life holding up his hands helplessly while others pointed admonishing fingers at him. He wanted to go home. Kir turned back without protest.

When they returned Mitri was fast asleep on the couch. The manuscript lay in a neat stack, so it was impossible to say how much of it he had read. He saved them having to decide whether to wake him or not by waking up of his own accord while they were still hesitating in the doorway. He did not test the author's patience by drawing matters out, but went straight to the point without any yawning or stretching. He ran a hand over his face, shook his fingertips as if dispelling something invisible, and announced thoughtfully:

'I've looked at it. I'm sorry, but I can't give you an answer to the question that interests you most. I'm not qualified to judge what will, or won't, be published. As for the rest – do you want it with or without anaesthetic?'

'Without,' answered Nikolin shortly. In his heart he sent Mitri to the devil, then felt ashamed of himself. After all, who was doing whom a favour?

'This work's full of unexpiated karma. Which, sadly, doesn't measure up to your potential. If I were you, I wouldn't write in this apartment at all. You have a superb aura outside this house, but it is reduced to tatters here. Can you guess to whom you're bound by karma? No, I don't mean your wife, I'm talking about at the planetary level.'

'Can you put it a bit more simply?' asked Nikolin in a more aggressive tone than he had intended. 'In layman's terms, so to speak? On the level of literary criticism, say?'

'If you like,' agreed Mitri indifferently. 'Of course, I'm only your average reader, so I could be wrong. But I don't perceive this work as truly artistic. There are literary pretensions here, and a tendency to modishness. Employment of the method of what could be called meaningful hints. Why, for instance, is that Ignat character an exile? Does the logic of the text call for it? And so on . . . As for that business of people's doubles – that's completely confused, it happens quite differently, you can take my word for it. Or if you don't believe me, at least study the matter thoroughly for yourself. I'm sorry, I can see you're disappointed. Still, I'm certain that your main works are yet to be written. Even this one is no worse than most stuff being published these days.'

Nikolin itched to have Mitri out of his house. If he says one word about Lucia – Nikolin wouldn't hold back, and there'd be a vulgar brawl. Mitri seemed to feel the latent threat hovering in the air and began to say his goodbyes with an elaborate show of manners. He paused in the doorway.

'So that you won't be unduly offended by what I said about karma,' he expanded, 'I can say that it affects more than half the population of this planet. You understand who I mean?'

'Stalin?' blurted Kir on the spur of the moment, just for something to say.

'There,' replied Mitri encouragingly. 'He who has gained awareness is already one sixth of the way to liberation. I had to go through it myself, so you see that it's possible.'

'I suppose we should be grateful he didn't advise us to read the classics,' commented the aggrieved author after the door had closed behind Mitri.

'Look, old fellow, what can I say?' cried Kir guiltily. 'Serve me right if you chuck me out, it was all my fault! I could see you were not on the same wavelength, but arranged this reading and ruined your day. Don't pay any attention to it, eh? Sometimes he comes out with things nobody can make head or tail of. Anyway, I think he was just bolstering his own ego at your expense. He realizes you're someone to be reckoned with –'

'Now don't start that all over again,' begged Nikolin. 'How about a glass of sherry?'

'Why not?'

*

217

Viktor Stepanych listened to the recording, positively humming with pleasure and ticking away furiously on a piece of paper. Agent of influence Kuzma, ESP buff Mitri, was wiping the floor with the Storyteller, not suspecting what enjoyment he was providing for an up-and-coming officer of the Committee. The ticks came to a total of eighteen, no less, after which Viktor Stepanych switched to exclamation marks.

Once the tape had finished he stretched himself out lazily, and clasped his hands above his head. Well, that had been fun, but now – to business: the situation had to be analysed.

Kuzma must be looked after, that much was clear. Every word was pure gold, and a lot of people paid attention to him. The financial inspectors had been on to him recently, and not without cause. That would have to be stopped: let the man cure his nearest and dearest of cancer in his leisure time.

Buttercup – Nastenka, that is – could stay in the Crimea, there was no need for her to encounter the Storyteller until the end of the operation. They would find employment enough for her talents down there come the spring, when the cream of the anti-Soviet scum headed there in droves.

Bugging of the Storyteller's apartment was to be maintained around the clock. It was hard to say what Arseni – Kir, that is – was playing at. On one hand he seemed to have run amok and had the effrontery not to turn up to meet his controller. On the other hand he was observing his obligation of silence, even while pouring out his heart to the Storyteller. In any case, what orders should Viktor Stepanych give him right now, and would he obey them? The orders would have been to do exactly as he was already doing off his own bat . . . Still, what was to be done with him if he did get out of control? The only solution that occurred to Viktor Stepanych was that he would have to start a rumour that Kir was a KGB agent. Ruin his reputation beyond repair. Let his colleagues show him what they thought of him then. Giving him the cold shoulder. Avoiding sitting next to him at sectional meetings of the union. And to tip foreign correspondents the wink, so that word would filter out abroad. So you want to be squeaky clean, you bastard? We'll clean you up, see if we don't!

Admittedly, the idea was not a new one. And not all that fancy. In the eyes of the bosses it would not suffice by itself.

Viktor Stepanych sighed: should he go to Filipp Savich for advice? Even if he got it in the neck for lack of initiative, he would still receive a few clues about what to do with an unruly agent. With regard to the Storyteller, Viktor Stepanych had no qualms – he knew, he felt that the time had come!

He went off and got his advice.

Kir unburdened himself frankly to Nikolin: how he'd married Olga, how he'd stifled his better instincts because of his family – at least, not stifled, but put them on the back burner for a while. And Olga, instead of understanding, kept egging him on to take part in protests and demonstrations, then began to despise him, claiming that he had been 'bought'. In short, she had turned out to be one of those bitches who place greater value on principles than people's lives. In any case, what had being 'bought' to do with anything, when all he wanted was to work in his chosen field? He wanted to see the world, too, and refused to accept the old saw that you can't have your cake and eat it also. At that age . . .

'If you have position, a name at least – it's easier to fight,' he assured Nikolin.

Without looking at what he was doing, Kir lit the filter end of a cigarette, and began to splutter. Cursing, he went over and opened the small pane at the top of the window.

The spasm passed, and he continued. He didn't gloss over his first overseas trip, how humiliating it was to have to go around everywhere in threes, and have to keep up with the group. How he'd received a hint before he left the country that one of the chain of visa officials was very fond of pornography. And how he'd been caught by customs with a couple of pornographic magazines on his return to Moscow . . .

He got as far as this, but, try as he might, he could not bring himself to admit that this was the hook on which he had been caught and recruited. He couldn't admit it to a single soul, and would have been glad to forget all about it himself. It was easy enough to express remorse about '68, because everyone knew about it anyway. Olga, as might have been expected, had slapped his face and tossed his things out of their apartment.

Little did she know that if she hadn't been so inflexible, he wouldn't have had to beg and plead for the story of the porn magazines to be hushed up, and would never have signed that undertaking to cooperate. What had he feared most? That Olga would find out that her beloved husband – and he was still beloved at that time – had bought pornography while abroad? Would someone like that have understood?

But that was not to be told, never, never, no matter how much had been drunk. He would have died of shame, he would have – something worse than death. In order to calm himself down he swore inwardly that this was all in the past, that he would never do anything like it again. Even if they ran him down with a truck in the middle of the street.

Had it entered Kir's head that Nikolin's flat might be bugged he would have certainly warned his friend. But it didn't: there are no grounds to assume that the Department's agents are on all matters better informed than your average citizen. Why burden an agent with extra knowledge? The idea is to make him think that he is the sole source of information. That makes it easier to keep tabs on him.

No such possibility occurred to Nikolin, either – though in his case out of ignorance. He never shoved pencils in the dial of his telephone, because there was no reason to do so. As for bugging through window glass, he'd never even heard of it: as though he were living in the Stone Age, and not in a civilized country.

Kir's outpourings did not annoy Nikolin: they distracted him from dwelling on the brutal affront to his professional pride. Still, he had been hit hard, and to his shame he kept wanting to find justifications . . . Listening to Kir gave him a pleasant conviction of his own good nature, and anyway, how could one refuse a little support in such a situation? Kir was afraid, and not without reason.

'You know, Kir, why they push us so hard? To supply us with a creative stimulus – fear. Whatever we write, that atmosphere is an invisible element that communicates itself to every reader . . . And if you say another word about the subconscious, I swear I'll strangle you with my own hands.'

Kir clapped a hand over his mouth in mock terror: not a sound! Nikolin drew a breath and went on:

'So we in turn become vectors of fear. We spread it the way rats spread the plague. That's why they keep us in the Union, build us housing, keep us supplied with carbon paper. They don't ask for anything in return, only that we should be afraid! Apart from that, you can write about the weather, if you like, and nobody will say a word.'

Let God be Nikolin's judge if there was anything new in his words, or indeed any truth. They'd both had a bit too much to drink, and, in light of recent events, wanted to discuss that matter of concern to them both: fear. Philosophically, at arm's length, as if they were on one side of the question, and fear on the other: a completely separate entity. Like a sample under a microscope.

After he had seen Kir off and dropped on to the sofa hugging Brysik to him, Nikolin made a final effort, before succumbing to sleep, to recall who else he had seen with such powerful fingers, covered with ginger fuzz . . .

But sleep overcame him before he could find the answer.

Chapter Twenty-two

THE RING ON Nikolin's doorbell came at a perfectly reasonable hour: nine o'clock in the morning. A time when most people would be up and about.

'Sign the receipt here, please.'

Nikolin signed and stared at the piece of paper half-awake: what on earth could this mean?

He was ordered to report to his local militia station to see investigator so-and-so . . . Today, at 11 a.m. He was required to bring his passport with him. That was enough to wake anyone up.

Nikolin had time to shower, shave and feed the kitten. There was no likelihood now of following his plan to do a five-copy retype of his manuscript, of course: he had to be on his way . . .

He was received politely and directed to one of the offices. Criminal investigator Malotin was an amiable man, reminiscent of a good-natured bear with intelligent eyes under bushy brows. The icon lay in the middle of the table, and Nikolin was asked to confirm or deny, in the presence of witnesses, that it was the one taken from his apartment.

Nikolin made no attempt to lie, but admitted that it was. The witnesses signed, and were immediately dismissed. Major Malotin inclined his head thoughtfully.

'So what are we to do, Anton Semyonych? This is it, the icon that was stolen.'

Nikolin could not think of a single thing to say. He sat there, breathing heavily and trying to recover his composure. The investigator quite understood: the man was bowled over by the unexpectedness of it all. He gave Nikolin time for a breather, then went on to explain: the theft had occurred after the academician's will had come into legal effect. It was therefore a case of theft of state property. Criminal proceedings had had to be initiated and he, Nikolin, was a material witness. That's how matters stood. Now let's draw up your statement. The penalty for giving false information comes under article such-and-such and carries three years' imprisonment. No, we don't for a moment think that a Soviet writer would lie . . . this is just a formality we have to observe in all cases.

Nikolin read out his passport details – another obligatory formality. Malotin pounded them out on a typewriter. Then he asked his first question: had Nikolin been aware that the icon in his apartment had been stolen from the Hermitage collection?

'No.'

'How did you come by it? Who gave it you?'

Nikolin remained silent for a moment, then gestured dismissively.

'I can't tell you that.'

'What, you can't remember?' asked the investigator as if to assist him.

'I do remember, but I can't tell you,' responded Nikolin with genuine desperation.

'Well, can you at least tell me how long you've had it?'

Nikolin thought, and gave him an approximate date.

To give the investigator his due, he never raised his voice at Nikolin; he uttered no threats, remained perfectly polite. Indeed, he was openly sympathetic: fancy, a reputable man like Nikolin getting involved in an affair like this. Nonetheless, Malotin could do no more: Nikolin, after all, was refusing to cooperate. All right, he was free to go for the present. He had plenty to think about, so did the investigator. There was no need at this stage to take a written undertaking from him not to leave town. He'd be summoned if and when necessary. Sign the record here, please . . .

Nikolin walked down the street sunk in thought. It was grey, flat and dry. The snow was gone, but it was still too early for the buds to be opening. The anniversary placards and portraits made bright splashes of red, though liberally marked here and there by the attentions of the city's pigeons. Still, the celebrations were three weeks away, so they'd hang up new ones if need be. Nikolin, it seemed, was the only person paying any attention to the decorations, the rest of the world hurried by or stood around in queues. Got on with the business of everyday life, in other words. Only Nikolin was out of step. He walked with a measured tread, beating a rhythm to his thoughts.

What were the possibilities? That he'd be put away? What would happen to his manuscript then? Maybe he should make as many copies as he could and get them circulating in samizdat? Then, whatever charges they brought, the real reason would be obvious. But could he rely on it? When that kid – what's his name? – was arrested for selling medals on the black market, no one thought this was only a pretext. Except for Stella. Had Nikolin believed her? No, he had turned his back on her and hurried away, turning his back on the boy at the same time. No sense in fooling himself: he'd be in just the same position. How did the joke put it? – 'I don't know whether someone stole his coat, or he stole someone else's, but he's involved in something fishy.'

He could end up in the camps. He'd have to check the Criminal Code and find out what sort of sentence he could expect over this business with the icon. But where could he lay hands on a copy of the Criminal Code? You can't buy it in the shops. He'd have to phone Alexei Vanych: he was a thriller writer, he'd know what articles apply to what crimes. But what if he were to circulate his novel in samizdat? – wouldn't They lock him up in an asylum? Well, at least that would take care of his present dilemma over the icon. But what if all this was simply an act of provocation? To set him going, so he began to relax his precautions over the manuscript? Idiot. When has the KGB ever made it its business to promote the circulation of samizdat? If They know about the manuscript . . . No, his mind refused to think logically.

One of his shoelaces had come undone, and Nikolin stooped to retie it. They say that psychiatric patients' shoelaces are taken from them. To avoid the possibility of them strangling themselves while undergoing treatment. Nikolin felt an urge to go home, to surround himself with the illusory protection of four walls. If only there was a shoulder on which he could lean and howl his heart out. For pity. For protection. Stop, he told himself, you're getting hysterical. Breathe deeply: in–out–in–out . . . Throat's eased. That's better. Lenin gazed down at him from a huge billboard, cap in hand and smiling benevolently.

Nikolin tried to phone Nastenka from a call-box, but nobody answered. Clearly, she was still away: he had no way of knowing when she would be back.

Once home, he got a grip on himself. The fear that had seized him outside receded, leaving him feeling dull and limp, as if his brain had released some kind of narcotic into his system. Listlessly, he loaded his typewriter, vaguely surprised at how calm were his movements and thoughts. When you don't know what to do, the best thing is to occupy yourself with the obvious. Let events take their own course.

He was on to page four when the phone rang. It was Lidia Petrovna, Pavel's widow. She entreated him to come around straight away.

Lidia Petrovna was highly agitated. Let me introduce you: Signor Poggi from Italy – the writer Anton Nikolin, a good friend of Pavel's.

Signor Poggi, a dark-eyed, black-haired young man of less than average height, bore a slight resemblance to Napoleon, down to the tuft of hair on his forehead. He was clearly ill-at-ease, and equally clearly, Lidia Petrovna had no idea what to do with him. She gazed wistfully at Nikolin in hope of a solution to the problem.

Lidia Petrovna plunged into explanations.

'Signor Poggi wanted to see Pavel, he hadn't known that Pavel . . . was no longer . . .' She dabbed at her eyes with a small handkerchief. Both men lowered their heads and stared at the floor. The widow recovered herself and continued.

'Signor Poggi came for a manuscript. He says Pavel promised him some manuscript at the end of March – beginning of April. He's a friend of a Swedish gentleman . . . Signor Poggi, I'm sorry, but I've forgotten his name?'

'Hans Bjerkegren,' supplied Poggi obligingly. 'You know who is he?'

Oh, yes. Even Nikolin knew that name, as did most of his colleagues, although the gentleman regrettably was no longer permitted into the Soviet Union. Bjerkegren was a Contact with a capital 'C' for those who had published or nourished dreams of publication in the West.

Certainly, Nikolin said, he knew of him, and looked at the Italian inquiringly to see if he understood. The Italian did – with Russian language no problem.

Lidia Petrovna brightened: at least something was becoming clear.

'I was completely at sea,' she exclaimed. 'I don't know anything of such a manuscript. Signor Poggi suggested that maybe some of Pavel's friends could help? So I phoned Andrei Mikhalych . . .'

'Andrei Mikhalych?' asked Nikolin, not understanding.

'Belokon, of course! It was he who helped me hand over Pavel's papers to the Central Literary Archive . . .'

Idiot, idiot, idiot, thrice idiot of a woman! Nikolin groaned inwardly. Of all the people to turn to! Everyone but this asinine female knew that Belokon works for the KGB. She might just as well phone the KGB direct and say: Pavel had this manuscript he wanted to send abroad, and now someone's come for it. Signor Poggi's here, and waiting for further instructions. However, his face remained impassive and Lidia Petrovna rattled on serenely.

'But there was nobody home, so then I called you . . .'

Thank heavens for that, at least. Plainly, the Italian had to be got out of here before this fool of a woman took some other idea into her head. But Lidia Petrovna continued chattering away merrily to her guest: had he been to the Milan opera? Yes, she realized he was not a singer, but had he been there? She'd heard it was magnificent! And where was Signor Poggi himself from? Rome? Ah, Riva Trigoso? How lovely that sounds, how musical. It was probably a very large town . . .?

Signor Poggi and Nikolin exchanged glances, equally expressive of a desire to flee. Which they did, politely declining the offer of a cup of tea. Lidia Petrovna didn't mind. She wasn't sure whether she should offer them just tea, or something more substantial. What do Italians eat? As it happened, she didn't have so much as a stick of macaroni in the house.

Out in the street, Nikolin told Poggi what little he knew of Pavel's manuscript. He also explained why there was no point in applying to Belokon. The Italian was visibly upset: so the work was lost? Hans would be so disappointed! It was such a shame, given the opportunity . . . He was leaving tomorrow and could have taken it with him. He was a great fan of Russian literature, he confided to Nikolin. Ah, Madonna, these were very difficult times! He was ashamed to be able to do so little to help, and even this chance was now lost . . .

Crazy technicolor zig-zags flashed across Nikolin's brain. It was now or never, that much was certain. If only it weren't for that wretched business with the icon, which would end God knows how – or, rather, it was painfully obvious how it would end. After all, he was already under surveillance. Was there any justification for him to procrastinate further? Was he always going to be dithering around, letting every opportunity pass him by? Sitting at the kitchen table discoursing on the nature of fear . . . Or do the same thing in a prison cell?

So, not wishing to appear too thrusting, he asked idly, in the course of conversation, whether Mr Bjerkegren might be interested in a work by an unknown author, a first novel?

Poggi beamed like a child on Christmas morning. Or like Napoleon at Josephine.

'Yes, for certain! In Russia always there is new writings! Russia it is wonderful! Signor knows this new writer?'

'Why don't we go to my place, Signor Poggi? Do you have an hour or so?'

'*Sí, sí!*'

Nikolin ushered the Italian to the street door. Oh, please no trouble more, he know Moscow well, second visit and no problem. Then he sank into his armchair and began to gather his thoughts. No need for retyping now, especially as the manuscript was gone. Maybe he should have kept his pencilled original after all, and not burned it? Too late for any regrets about that. He had decided a month ago that he would make two typed copies, and no more. He'd given Poggi his copy, and the second one was to stay untouched at Klim's, where he would leave it for the present.

Methodically he destroyed all copies of the four pages he had retyped, and shredded the carbon paper as well. That was that.

What a relief! The hidey-hole was empty, anyone could search the place now if they wanted. Whatever became of him, the manuscript was safe and would be published. He had no doubt that it would be published. Only now, having let the book out of his hands, did he realize how good it was; it needed no changes. His life was justified. He could do whatever he wanted, he was completely and utterly free. There was no need to hurry any more: the race was over. Strangely enough, indeed, there was nothing he wanted to do. Just sit there and smoke, tunes of glory echoing faintly through his head.

Inevitably, the next day he was summoned round to the station again. Setting off for the now familiar destination Nikolin marvelled at how calm and self-possessed he was. Let the stupid situation resolve itself how it would! The fact that he was not the thief could be easily proved: he hadn't been to Leningrad in two years.

His view of Nastenka had clarified a little, too. He didn't believe, didn't want to believe, that this was a deliberate set-up and that she was involved. Yet he realized the childishness of pushing the thought aside. And now the thought had occurred, he decided to follow it through. If he had been deliberately framed, they would put him away whatever he said. So unless he was provoked, why give Nastenka away . . .?

Come what may, he'd no need to name the person who had given him the icon. And he would say so: that he was refusing to speak on ethical grounds. He'd had no idea that the icon was stolen. He had surrendered it voluntarily. So do your worst. You do your business, and the Swedes would do theirs.

He cut an odd figure: an awkward sort of fellow, bare-headed, smiling as he squinted in the spring sunshine. Evidently in harmony with the world at large, enjoying the sight of birds fluttering down and the clouds floating by. Not even the cars belching fumes and the overcrowded trolley-buses brought a frown to his face, as he strolled along, swinging his attaché case. Where could he be going? To meet a girl-friend? Unlikely – he'd move faster than that.

No, he's off to keep an appointment with a criminal investigator. His attaché case contains a toothbrush, spare socks and a change of underwear, in case they arrest him on the spot. He had given Kir his spare key, and told him the story of the icon, naming no names. Should anything happen, Kir would make sure Brysik wasn't left alone in an empty flat. So why should Nikolin worry?

This time, they did not take him to the same office, but conducted him to a black Volga, saying he was expected elsewhere. The investigator sat in the front with the driver, while Nikolin was placed in the back between two guards. They drove off. It was only when Nikolin saw the familiar square with the monstrous monument rearing up in the middle that he realized where they were heading.

He was told to leave his case in the vestibule, with assurances that it would be safe, then led through a maze of corridors and winding passages. Finally, he was ushered through a heavily padded leather door, into an office filled with sunlight. Gold framed portraits of Lenin and Dzerzhinsky stared down from the walls: a little reminder of where he was. The young man who confronted him across the desk, a round-faced Committee official in a grey suit, seemed barely past his student days. He looked at Nikolin with unconcealed triumph. Propped up on the desk, St Nicholas gazed out at him and his surroundings. And there was something else on the table, too . . . Ace of trumps!

The manuscript. The one from his apartment. The one that was meant to be in Sweden.

Viktor Stepanych (inevitably, it was he) motioned investigator Malotin out of the room. They were left tête-à-tête.

'Well, Anton Semyonych, time to get acquainted!'

He proceeded to introduce himself formally. Then, without wasting more time, went straight to the point.

'Really, citizen Nikolin, what did you think you were doing? It's bad enough trafficking in icons, but now you go and get yourself involved with the foreign secret services. Have you any idea who that Italian is?'

Nikolin thought it best not to answer. Anyway, the question

was purely rhetorical for the young officer was fairly bursting with righteous indignation.

'A member of the Union of Writers! A fighter on the ideological front, one could say, and what do you go and write? And whom do you write to?'

Distastefully, Viktor Stepanych picked up the note Nikolin had scribbled to Bjerkegren, and held it at arm's length with the tips of his fingers.

'Gone over to the other side of the barricades, Nikolin? Soviet royalties aren't enough for you, it pays better to publish anti-Soviet propaganda abroad? Send it illegally out of the country with some Italian spy? Sell your country for a few dollars?'

Viktor Stepanych fairly choked with rage.

'You, a Russian through and through! What was it you wanted, eh? What?'

All these questions thundered down on Nikolin, every one to be recorded. Nikolin sat immobile, as though anaesthetized. Lost. Everything was lost. Everything.

'Come. Why don't you answer? How many copies of this junk did you make?'

Again, Nikolin didn't answer, but sat still as a corpse.

'What did you do with the other copies? Think you can get away playing dumb?'

Viktor Stepanych slammed his fist down on the table.

'You answer when you're spoken to! Or we'll find a way to make you talk!'

There was nothing heroic in Nikolin's silence; this was no partisan defying enemy interrogation. He was simply paralysed with despair, he didn't care any more. It is doubtful if he could have managed so much as to repeat the questions that were flung at him.

Viktor Stepanych leaned back in his chair, pondering him through narrowed eyes.

'Decided to play Simple Simon? Well, we can arrange a psychiatric examination for you. I'm giving you exactly one minute to make up your mind whether you're going to answer or not.'

He pulled back his cuff and looked ostentatiously at his watch.

Evidently, not everything in Nikolin had died of despair. There was still room for more fear. The seconds separating him from a lunatic asylum ticked by, hurrying themselves out of this inhospitable world. But Nikolin himself had nowhere to go.

Suddenly, one of the two telephones on the desk rang, and the irate officer before him sprang to his feet and stood to attention as he listened to the voice at the other end.

'Yes sir. Of course. Yes. Now? Right away!'

He put down the phone reverently and addressed Nikolin with sudden politeness.

'There is someone who wants to speak to you. This minute.'

He pressed a button on the other phone, and two uniformed men conducted Nikolin to another floor and another office. A third followed behind, carrying the icon.

Chapter Twenty-three

IN THE MEANTIME, other people were getting on with their lives. Everyone, after all, has their own affairs to attend to.

Kir remained by the phone: how were things with Nikolin? Would he ring? Perhaps not. Kir was in a state of heroic euphoria: he'd severed all ties, burnt all his boats. He was no longer their agent, he was no longer Arseni. Perhaps he'd be packed off to Siberia? So what! He'd been in Siberia as a child, he knew that people can live there. A camp? People survive in the camps, too; he could take them in his stride. He was known for his easy ways, after all. A looney-bin? To hell with it! He knew, he sensed that his fellow-writers despised him a little. Well, they'd have to think again now, wouldn't they?

Nikolin didn't despise him. He had become his friend, friend to a low-down informer. He'd trusted Kir with what was most precious to him, and fallen foul of a crude deception, with his sad eyes, the greying lock of hair forever falling over his forehead, his talent and his solitude. Kir had burst in on that solitude uninvited. And found himself unable to do the deed. Anywhere, but not here. How lonely Anton Nikolin must have been if he was glad to be befriended by Kir. He can't have been ignorant of the rumours that went around about him. But he overlooked them. Treated him as a human being.

But Katerina was another story: he felt sorry for her. Whichever way you looked at it, she was not likely to get any more Mexican ponchos. Tough times ahead, eh Katy?

But the splendid Katerina continued to busy herself in the

kitchen: if one's husband is worried and doesn't answer questions, it's best to leave him alone. Better cook up something nice. Such is the received wisdom, which has stood the test of time through all ages and dispensations.

Olga had put everything else aside. Denis had the measles and was running a fever.

Belokon was run off his legs. He had to get the best possible doctor to come and see Denis, and that meant pulling every string. Then he had to tell him stories, stroking his hot little face. Olga had to be bullied into snatching at least a couple of hours' sleep, she was on the verge of collapse. What can Grandpa get you, Denny? Now, there must be something you'd like! Finally, he put his Order of the Red Banner into Denis's sweaty hands, a treat previously denied – play with it, go on!

There was food to be obtained, too: Olga had refused to accept any 'privileged' goods before, wouldn't hear of it, but she kept quiet now. The child was ill, and needed proper nourishment: caviare, pineapple, all that sort of thing. Vitamins and more vitamins.

On top of that, Belokon had to prepare for the Lenin centenary: a speech at the official assembly, articles in the press, this and that. Then there was his fiftieth birthday in May. That needed preparation, too. Fortunately, he wasn't one of those whose congratulations were published in *Pravda* without an accompanying photograph. He didn't have to worry about that, at least. But there was a complex hierarchy of other honours, and this was no joke.

Why, there had been that academician who had been certain that he would be awarded the Order of Lenin on his seventieth birthday, but all he got was an Order of the Red Banner for Labour. He collapsed and died on the spot when he found out – just like that, still clutching the telephone in his hand. The blow was too much. Belokon had received hints about an Order of

Lenin, but it was still wise to take steps to ensure that he wasn't forgotten.

Dima sat in prison awaiting trial and still hoping to get off with a light sentence. His mother had finally brought him his slippers.

Stella drank. With friends and alone. Drunk, she would recite Dima's poems to the ceiling. She pestered the investigator to grant her a meeting with Dima after the trial. What is your relationship to the accused? A woman who loves him, that's what! Well – after the trial – that wasn't up to the investigator. Yes, it's permitted sometimes.

Petya was wilting from the heat at the Equator, but working away dutifully. He enjoyed everything about the expedition. Wrote regularly to his mother. Prayed the way the priest had taught him, watching the dawn over the ocean and the stars at night. And standing before the little icon the priest had blessed him with. Petya was happy. He immersed himself in this happiness, as one born anew. All his past life seemed inconsequential: how could he have got by without *this*?

Signor Poggi, the Italian, who was no Italian but a young graduate from the Institute of Foreign Relations, Misha Drykin, was commended on a highly successful operation, and was preparing for his first trip overseas. To Italy, which he had dreamed of all his life. Misha's mother packed his case while Misha sat in a youth café, teaching a young American tourist to speak Russian. It was very easy: all you need to know, Cathy, is a single sentence, and you can use it in all situations, even in answer to a question. Everyone will be thrilled.

'Now, Cathy, repeat after me: "Th-a-t's . . . ve-ry . . . se-xy."'

*

Lyokha and Mikha were fussing around the river bank, soaked to the skin: the ice had broken, and a huge floe with pages of the Bible stuck to it had come adrift. Nothing happens to photographic paper in water, and it floats to the top. The floe started to drift, with stacks of Luke's Gospel stuck to it. And Matthew. Lyokha and Mikha tried to pull the floe back to the bank – someone was bound to see it, and track down those responsible! Their efforts proved fruitless, and Lyokha slipped and ended up waist-deep in freezing water. They tried to race the floe and catch it further downstream, where there was a little wooden bridge, but the bridge had been washed away and the current bore the floe out of reach. Carrying Mark with it. And John. Other floes hurried it along, ice cracking everywhere and people standing on bridges watching it pass by.

It was Auntie Xenia's day of triumph: she had been elected head of the tenants' committee. Unanimously. Her Cleopatra, realizing the honour accorded her mistress, showed her respect by purring and rubbing against her legs. Clever, for all she was an animal.

Brysik slept blissfully on the couch: he was used to Nikolin's frequent absences. His stomach was so full he couldn't curl up, so he lay on his side, like the hare in a famous still-life painting of 'Game' by one of the Dutch masters.

Forget-me-not, whose name had never been Tatyana Kuzina and who had no daughter Alisa, was on her way to their dacha with her husband. It was a sunny day, and she hoped to gather a bunch of snowdrops. She was wearing none of her special clothing: it was back to East German undies and an unremarkable pair of stretch slacks, suitable for a day in the country.

Buttercup, however, also known as Nastenka, was got up in special clothes from early morning. There are many friendly foreigners recouping forces in sanatoria on the Crimea. Nastenka ran along a deserted shoreline in something white and flimsy, testing the tide with a delicate foot. The nearby camera whirred busily. Stop! Another take! The guests of the sanatorium above the beach watched from their balconies. The Russians are making a film down there; the girl in white, they say, is a leading actress. A rising star.

Nikolin was ascending in a lift with a panelled mirror in which he could see his grey eyes and impressive pallor. As he is at the centre of events, we shall remain with him.

Filipp Savich sat waiting for Nikolin to be brought in. When the writer appeared, he moved forward, hand outstretched.

'How d'you do, Anton Semyonych! I'm Filipp Savich. This is long overdue.'

Nikolin accepted the outstretched hand automatically, waiting to see what would happen next. Filipp Savich began setting things in order: he laid the icon on a side table, but moved the manuscript towards him.

'Please sit down.' He waved him to a seat. 'Why, Anton Semyonych, there's no need to look as though you've been thrown into the lion's den! Has someone upset you? Viktor Stepanych, no doubt? He's young and hot-headed, I'm afraid, so his manners can be – in short, he doesn't know how to deal with writers. Do you wish to lodge a complaint against him? No? Well, that's fine.'

He pushed a button and coffee was brought in on a tray. Filipp Savich was sorry that they had to meet under such disagreeable circumstances. Still, we're not monsters here, surely everything can be resolved. He hoped Anton Semyonych had no special prejudice against members of the Department? Unfortunately, there were those who were prone to blame the Committee for everything ever since Stalin's day. He was glad to hear that Nikolin wasn't one of them. After all, Anton Semyonych is no enemy of the Motherland, but a good Soviet citizen, isn't he?

There was nothing Nikolin could do but agree.

Now, let's sort things out, shall we? Reasonable people can always find a reasonable solution. With regard to the icon – Filipp Savich could only wonder at the criminal investigation department: what could be more open and shut? The icon had been recovered, Nikolin was not the thief, but had become involved purely by chance, and the reason why he refused to talk was plain to anyone with a modicum of intelligence: he was protecting a lady of whom he was fond. The authorities had tabs on most of those caught up in the collecting of icons, so they would have no trouble establishing the guilty parties without Nikolin's help.

Let's forget about the icon once and for all. If by any chance the criminal investigation people bothered Nikolin about it again, he should contact Filipp Savich directly.

The business with the Italian – yes, that didn't look too good. Why on earth had Nikolin taken such a step? Had he been somehow slighted or passed over at home? Yes, he'd heard about that business with the children's book. There are too many people who tend to be cautious to the point of paranoia, suspect their own shadows of subversion! They do more harm than good, and we're left to pick up the pieces. When it's too late.

'And it is too late,' he said looking at Nikolin with sudden dismay. 'We missed our chance. I blame myself: we should have met earlier, before all this. But now everything's on record – in customs, all that sort of thing. And that note in your own hand – to someone who's an enemy of the state, when all's said and done. Just at a time when They' – Filipp Savich jabbed a finger upward – 'have decided to tighten the screws in matters like this. And tighten them very much. So what should we do, Anton Semyonych, eh?'

Nikolin had no idea, and Filipp Savich went on mouthing regrets. The main thing, he lamented, was that the novel was superb: he, Filipp Savich, hadn't slept a wink all night, couldn't put it down. Frankly speaking, there was no chance of publication in the present climate. It was too bold. But times change! And the work went only slightly beyond the bounds of what was permissible, so the chances were that in two or three years' time there wouldn't be a problem. Filipp Savich was extremely hopeful that there were great changes afoot. Just take a look at the Committee, as a case in point – there was no comparison with what it had been like in the days of the personality cult. New attitudes, new people. Moreover, people who appreciated culture. If only Nikolin had waited, instead of jumping the gun . . .

Nikolin wished he had waited, too. And how.

'And so, Anton Semyonych,' concluded Filipp Savich, 'I won't conceal from you that the matter is a serious one. And the decision taken higher up has been not to imprison people in such cases, but order medical treatment.'

Nikolin could not repress a shudder. Not a very noticeable one, but he blinked nervously. Filipp Savich could only agree.

'Yes, it's six of one, and half a dozen of the other. I must admit that it's not my decision alone. I have superiors, too. I can come under fire myself. The only way is for me to be able to prove that I am defending one of our own. That's an accepted tradition which the Central Committee respects. The Committee always takes care of its own people. Now, I'm an admirer of your talent, so I'm prepared to stick my neck out for you. Tell me in all honesty – can you give me some ammunition to protect you? Something, at least?'

Nikolin was silent for a few moments, then asked quietly:

'What do I have to do?'

'Nothing public! I understand and – between ourselves – respect your position. Perhaps you could write me a note – shorter than the one to the Swede! Just so that I would be able

239

to produce it higher up if necessary, to prove that you're our man. Ours.'

'You mean, an undertaking to cooperate?'

'Yes,' agreed Filipp Savich baldly. 'Believe me, I know how such undertakings are regarded in your circles. However, let me assure you that if all your colleagues who have signed such undertakings did in fact work for us, we'd have to increase the Committee ten times over, if only to work through all their reports.'

He grimaced comically and waved a hand to indicate the extra floors that would have to be built.

'We have enough to do analysing our own information. I assure you that in ninety per cent of cases this is a protective measure, no more. I can't name names for ethical reasons, as I'm sure you'll appreciate. But let me put it another way: have you ever heard of any such undertaking leaking out? Under any circumstances whatsoever? You see!'

Their talk ranged over many other matters, but nothing important. Nikolin had been hooked from the words 'I'll stick my neck out for you'. It's a real art, knowing what to say to someone. If that person has a penchant for gentlemanly behaviour, why not accommodate this quirk?

There was nothing particularly interesting about the moment of signature. It needs no amplification, if only out of consideration for those concerned.

Their business concluded, Filipp Savich reached for the present he had prepared for Nikolin. There it was: the book about the royal blue mouse and the wily old man.

'It's excellent,' he enthused. 'I'm a great admirer of yours! You thought the print-run had been scrapped? In fact, all that happened – I give you my word – was that someone, literally at the last moment, expressed qualms about the king being such a sympathetic character.'

Filipp Savich laughed heartily at such a want of literary judgement.

'Anyway,' he continued, 'we managed to save the situation, even at some cost to ourselves. Sorry about that. This book will bring you a host of surprises yet, I shouldn't wonder. As for *this* manuscript – I'm going to have to keep it, I'm afraid. It'll be safer. And I should imagine it's not your only copy, eh?'

He laughed, wagging a cautionary finger: you're a crafty lot, you writers.

They shook hands and parted, mutually satisfied. Nikolin's attaché case was returned, safe and sound, although its contents were no longer necessary. It was only when he went to phone Kir to say that he was on his way home that Nikolin suddenly felt cold all over.

What had he done?

Now, and forever after, he realized, there was something in his life that had to be kept secret from everyone. There was not a single soul he could tell about it. Not even on his death-bed. He felt vaguely surprised that Filipp Savich hadn't warned him about that.

There was nothing for it but to lie to Kir. Yes, the investigation had been a pain in the neck but he, Nikolin, had maintained his position, and that was that for the moment.

Viktor Stepanych spent a lot of time listening to the tape made especially for his edification, and had to hand it to Filipp Savich's genius. Filipp Savich appended a few further observations: words are not the most important thing. They're simply a channel, along which an impulse of will is projected by one person on to another. Of course, the channel must be without its weak spots, in case the subject is particularly resistant. The channel doesn't function by itself. It's other things that work. It may not even be necessary to use a lot of words; facial expression, gesture, can all be employed according to personal preference. So work on developing the impulse, Vitya. Learn to be convincing.

Chapter Twenty-four

A DAY LATER Nikolin's book went on sale, as though nothing had happened. All sixty thousand copies lay on the counters of bookshops and kiosks: good cover, bright and attractive illustrations, an intriguing title. They beckoned invitingly through shop windows and gladdened the heart – Nikolin's, at least.

The occasion called for celebration; and a dinner was held in a restaurant, to which many were invited. The occasion was duly celebrated, the usual toasts were drunk and new ones proposed. Nikolin felt strange as he looked at his guests.

Here he was, a man who had signed an agreement to cooperate with the KGB, talking with them as easily as you please, and they don't even suspect. So what? He was not an informer, after all. He had not been ordered to keep the supply of reports flowing in. Anyway, that entire episode was best forgotten: he had done nothing wrong. Nor would he. Who could say how often such idiotic formalities took place? Maybe every person present had signed just such an undertaking, but were keeping quiet about it? That would be a laugh!

It was time to raise a toast to the artist and Olga, clad in a functional 'little black dress', stood up to be applauded. Kir, seated at the other end of the table, joined the applause. They had both had to be invited, divorce or no divorce. The previous evening Kir had asked Nikolin to find out how Denis was doing, as Olga still refused to speak to him. Still, if she were there, it meant that the little one was all right. Nikolin, of course, talked to her and autographed a copy of the book for Denis, who had spilled cherry juice all over Olga's presentation copy.

Yes, she'd said, he was on the mend . . . you wouldn't believe how much food that child manages to put away.

Olga and Nikolin entertained the company with a barrage of extravagant compliments, each vying to outdo the other.

His cat, Nikolin said, a marvellously clever creature who doubles as his consultant on Russian grammar, spent a whole day trying to trap Olga's blue mouse, which evaded all attempts at capture.

If Nikolin switched to adult literature, Olga countered, schools all over the country would grind to a halt, the children would declare a general strike and an entire generation of schoolchildren would have to be kept down an extra year. And no doubt their younger colleagues would boycott kindergarten-issue porridge.

Their sallies became increasingly outrageous, and had their guests rolling with laughter and calling for more. And all the time Nikolin knew with unshakeable certainty that Olga would never, in any circumstances, have signed that wretched under-taking. Someone else might, but not her.

Damn it, he thought irritably, why couldn't he push that out of his mind? He decided to get well and truly drunk, and experienced a curious sensation. Suddenly he seemed to split into two distinct persons: while the one laughed and enjoyed himself, becoming unusually gregarious under the influence of drink, the other Nikolin remained stone-cold sober, keeping a watchful eye on his twin. What are you making that sour face for, you killjoy?

The next day Nikolin had a phone call from the film director L—. Yes, the very same. Amazing! You'd think they had known each other for ever, the way L— went straight to business, suggesting they work together on a film. It'll be great, we'll make it subtle, multi-layered. A sort of watercolour masterpiece, eh?

243

Nikolin returned from his meeting with L— on a cloud of inspiration. Yes, yes, it was a fantastic idea. Who would have thought that one day he would work with the famous L— himself? He had never attempted a screenplay, but it was already taking shape in his head, all the various aspects intertwined. One line would be a fairy tale – the story of the blue mouse. The other would be about children, today's ten year olds: how they grow out of fairy tales. Some leave them behind for ever, while others retain the ability to fly in their dreams, and yet others . . . It would be set in a small southern town – where everything is transformed . . . When it rains, the children long for a miracle, and – sure enough, snow starts to fall from the sky, covering the roofs and streets . . .

It was just what he needed now – the chance to immerse himself in something worth while. So that is what he did, shutting himself off from the world, paying no heed to events, not even listening to the BBC. Spring was out on the streets of Moscow, but he didn't see it, not even when he popped out for food and cigarettes. His whole being was consumed by that small town, its streets made up of steep steps winding down to the sea, tufts of grass sprouting from its stone walls. He cancelled all appointments and didn't even bother attending the anniversary session of the Moscow prose writers' chapter of the Union of Writers. The only person with whom he had any contact was L—, whom he'd phone once in a while to discuss or clarify some point concerning the scenario. They seemed to understand each other immediately, without any need to get accustomed to each other's working methods first.

Kir phoned to say that he was off to Arkhangelsk for a month: a special 'creative assignment' he called it, and well overdue. He'd been hard pressed on all sides since that Secretariat meeting. He laughed about it and said he was considering becoming an 'fsi'.

'But how are you getting on? Still writing away and smoking? You're really coming up in the world, old man, no doubt about

it! I'll have to start addressing you more formally soon . . . no, of
course I'm only joking . . . Make sure you don't lose touch with
civilization, there in your retreat.'

A man who shaves daily, however, is in no danger of losing
touch with civilization, so Nikolin remembered to shave while
laying down episode upon episode: episodes that would
overlap beyond the boundaries of logic, while that very illog-
icality would create the illusion of flight or the disquieting
apprehension of adulthood. Nobody disturbed him, and his
only chore was to make certain that Brysik wouldn't take it into
his head to try to jump off the balcony. There may or may not
have been happier times in Nikolin's life: on the whole, the
present period might best be described as an escape from reality.

May rolled by, together with two public parades and several
firework displays, one very significant arrest – or, rather,
hospitalization, in line with current policy. There were also a
number of further arrests and hospitalizations which attracted
less notice. A rise in marriages and divorces kept the registry
offices hard at work – a lively month, the month of May. The
nightingales sang their heads off, coming as far into town as
Moscow's Garden Ring. All those Muscovites who were in a
position to do so were leaving for the country, while people from
out of town crowded in. A special ventilation system was
installed in the Mausoleum. Skirts were worn with an eye to the
pleasure of one's neighbour, while newspapers were printed
with an eye to those further afield. Lilac, tulips, spring storms –
everything passed Nikolin by. His whole being existed in
another time and place.

He deposited the completed screenplay in L—'s hairy hands in
June. Now it was his job to take matters on.

Nikolin heard out the praise heaped upon his efforts with
unconcealed delight, then looked about him with a fresh eye:
yes, life could go on. His first step was to go out and buy a new

pair of trousers: his old ones wouldn't stay up. While he'd been working on his novel there had been Auntie Xenia to keep him in line and make sure that he ate every day. But while working on the screenplay he had only had Brysik, who had adopted the pragmatic approach that so long as he was fed, his owner could look out for himself. It wasn't Brysik's fault that there were no mice in the house.

For the past few nights, however, Nikolin had been having bad dreams: the same dream, actually, going back to his child-hood in Lipetsk. In this dream one of his childhood friends, Vova, was telling him all over again that if you cut a worm in half, it becomes two separate worms, which would crawl off in different directions.

'You don't believe me? Look, I'll show you!'

It was a bright sunny day, the sunlight gilding Vova's closely cropped hair. Holding a blue shovel in his hands, he used it to prise a broken brick out of the ground, uncovering a fat, pink worm.

Little Nikolin was screaming a silent 'Don't!' as Vova slowly raised the shovel . . .

He needed to take a break, he realized, go away somewhere for a week or so. He could ask the neighbour from downstairs to see to Brysik, she wouldn't mind. What Nikolin forgot was that when you decide to take a break, the first thing you do is switch off the phone. So he didn't, and was asked to drop into the house administration office for a few minutes.

The person occupying the manager's office was none other than Viktor Stepanych – clad this time, because of the heat, not in his usual grey suit, but in a lightweight white shirt with a tie covered with a fussy granny-style print. People deserved to be shot for wearing ties like that, never mind anything else.

Smiling affably, Viktor Stepanych informed Nikolin that he was now his controller. Nikolin's code-name, he added, was Storyteller, and it was time Nikolin got to work. Present events made Nikolin's assistance vital to the Committee. Not waiting for Nikolin's reaction (which, in any case, consisted solely of incredulous, open-mouthed astonishment), he proceeded to issue instructions. This was the phone number Nikolin was to call in case of need. He was also to report every Thursday without fail at 11.20 a.m., by presenting himself at a certain street corner where a certain Zhiguli saloon would pick him up.

His assignment was to keep an eye on the poet Kir Usmanov, who had been behaving strangely of late. It was these irregularities of behaviour that Nikolin had to note, including Kir's contacts and actions generally. Usmanov was due back in Moscow tomorrow. Nikolin was to report in writing and sign his reports 'Storyteller'. Money for expenses – within reason, naturally – would be issued commencing with Nikolin's first report. Further instructions would be issued as and when necessary.

'Is that all clear, Storyteller? What are you looking at me like that for? You're free to leave. Go on, don't just stand there! Oh, before you go, sign this undertaking as to confidentiality. The activities of the Committee are a state secret, and any breach of security is a punishable offence. Sign here, and go.'

The monologue allowed of no interruptions. The shattered Nikolin could do nothing but obey. He signed and left.

Nikolin spent a bad night. His knee ached fiercely, and his mind went back remorselessly to Mitri and his crazy diagnosis. The sight of Mitri's thick, admonitory finger swam before his eyes. Then suddenly before him he saw Lucia and Dasha – who, for all she was so small, seemed able to swim – splashing among the green waves, laughing and calling to him: come and join us, come and join us! He ran towards them over the firm, wet sand, lightly, gladly – longing to be with them, throwing off the cling- ing beach-towel and getting entangled in its folds . . .

He awoke at this point with a feeling of incredible happiness.

He was sprawled uncovered on the divan, the ashtray beside him full of yellowing cigarette butts: he must have chain-smoked his way through at least one and a half packets. The room reeked of stale tobacco. Nikolin emptied the ashtray, aired the room, and tried to gather his thoughts at the point where he'd fallen asleep. He reached three quick decisions which he intended to implement one after another.

When Kir phoned, Nikolin excused himself, saying he was already taken up for the whole day. How about the evening, though, at the Writers' Club? They could have a bite of dinner there and catch up. Fine? Fine.

When Nikolin arrived, Kir was already in the vestibule, and in high spirits. His face was wind-burnt, he had grown a dashing beard, and was surrounded by a crowd whom he was entertaining with accounts of his doings in Arkhangelsk. He was proudly showing off an antique copper cross which someone had given him, almost the size of his palm and richly patina'd, dating back to the period before patriarch Nikon's church reforms.

The moment he spotted Nikolin, he rushed over to greet him.

'Great to see you again, old man! Good Lord, look at you – you're half the man you were, you ascetic old recluse!'

And launched straight into a eulogy of the women, married and otherwise, of Arkhangelsk: breasts like this, sky-blue eyes, very Nordic in their ways – very self-possessed but gentle as doves, for all that they were the size of London bobbies. They're pretty careful of themselves around married men, mind, but it's a paradise for bachelors . . .

'I tell, you, Anton, let's chuck everything and head off to Arkhangelsk! We'll show you around and have you married off in no time, right as rain.'

'A bit less of that,' retorted Nikolin through clenched teeth, but Kir was in full cry.

'Live like a monk, you do! That's being downright disrespect-
ful towards Soviet literature!'

This was Nikolin's chance.

'And you – you foul-mouthed bastard! Can't you keep a clean
tongue in your head?'

Kir stared at him in amazement, and put a hand on his shoulder.

'What's got into you, old fellow?'

'Do I have to punch you in the face before you see sense? You
cheap clown! I don't want to see you again! Stay out of my way
in future!'

He turned away abruptly in order not to see Kir's frightened,
uncomprehending eyes, and strode out, leaving total silence
behind him. What on earth had brought that on?

Nikolin fought off waves of nausea, although he didn't usually
get car-sick. Luckily the taxi driver was a taciturn sort and didn't
make conversation unnecessarily, just listened to his radio and
drove on. Yes, thought Nikolin, he wasn't up to Auntie Xenia's
plain-spokenness. He'd had to find a reason. As a result he'd
inflicted a worse hurt. He'd achieved what he had set out to do
– severed relations publicly with Kir. Now he was left to imagine
how it would be described by those who were present. That
'cheap clown' crack would be repeated, no doubt about it.
Nikolin groaned loudly enough for the driver to glance round.
No, no – it's nothing, drive on.

In the morning, Nikolin went to his local clinic. He complained of general weariness and considerable loss of weight.
Sleep? Constant insomnia. He'd even tried drinking hot milk
with honey, like a small child, but nothing helped. The doctor
advised him to take vitamins and wrote out a prescription for
sleeping tablets.

'Don't get carried away, though. One tablet an hour before
you go to bed, and not more than once in twenty-four hours. As

soon as your sleep's back to normal, stop taking the tablets, or they'll become a habit.'

'Thank you, doctor.'

He heard the phone ringing through his locked door. Three minutes later it rang again.

'Storyteller? What the hell do you think you're doing? You think that'll help? Get to work! I don't advise you to fool around, you're not in kindergarten. You remember the rendezvous? Make sure you're there on the dot, and don't get any fancy ideas!'

Nikolin hung up and decided not to pick up the phone again. That was why L— got no response when he tried to reach Nikolin, and was not best pleased. The screenplay was coming up before the censor, and the author was out – God knows where. But Nikolin was at home, drinking vodka: he'd bought a full case. He reckoned that by Thursday he would be unable to distinguish one day from another.

Mulin had told him that in the West there are telephones with some kind of answering device. You could leave the receiver down, Mulin had said, and still hear the messages being left for you. Nikolin felt profoundly thankful that technical progress of this kind was unlikely to be at the disposal of the average Soviet citizen for many years yet. It would be too much if he not only had to listen to such phone calls, but have Their voices on tape as well. That would really drive him crazy.

He put a pillow on top of the telephone and poured himself another vodka.

It was hard times for poor Brysik again. His master smelled dreadful, so there was no pleasure in cuddling up to his shoulder. Getting a meal entailed long and protracted squalling in the most unpleasant tone he could muster. His toilet tray hadn't been emptied for days. Brysik registered his protest at such neglect by relieving himself on the carpet in the middle of the room, but it went unnoticed. All Nikolin did was to tickle Brysik absently behind the ear when he got underfoot, and that was that. Cats can't sigh, so Brysik mentally gave up the struggle and started using the toilet bowl, even though the seat was made of plastic, not wood. Dark days, dark days.

Approval of a screenplay is preceded by a number of conferences. There is the studio arts council, the Goskino Secretariat, as well as any number of intermediate steps. In addition, the Ministry of Culture have to see it, and – most important of all – the Propaganda division of the Central Committee. There is then a further panel of committees which grants or withholds permission to make a film of the screenplay in question.

There was nothing surprising therefore in the fact that, though holding no official post within Goskino, Belokon was one of the figures on whom the cinema people were dependent. The Ministry of Culture could easily wish to acquaint itself with this or that screenplay. Or Belokon might encounter the film director L— by chance and stop for a chat. Or turn up at the studio while it was still at discussion level: do you mind, comrades, if I sit in? Of course not. Belokon was an old Communist, a people's deputy. As to the faint sound of grinding teeth in the background – well, somebody might be suffering from haemorrhoids . . .

Belokon enjoyed himself hugely. There was a time when all matters pertaining to the cinema were easily decided: by one man. Despite the heaviness of His workload, the Leader had thought nothing of assuming this added burden. He looked at every film himself, and decided its fate. And the fate of the director at the same time.

Everything was so much more complex and fragmented nowadays. But Belokon was not one to shift his responsibilities

251

on to anyone else's shoulders. Rest in peace, Father. We'll win through.

Director L— could grind his snow-white teeth as much as he liked and try to disguise his grimace of long-suffering as a smile – or not, as he chose – it made no difference. Belokon had demolished much tougher texts than this in his time.

Yes, that was one of the major faults of the screenplay – it was too convincing. As for the father who's over-fond of the bottle, one feels too much sympathy for him. Indeed, it seems only natural that the young boy should love him – and the viewer will feel the same. Now, is it permissible, in our society, to sympathize with alcoholics?

The stupid schoolteacher was very realistic, too. This was a downright insult to the Soviet teaching profession. And all that suspiciously symbolic fantasizing . . . For instance, take the scene where the children fly away from their desks right in front of her eyes, and the teacher waves her hands at them helplessly and then takes off her shoes, thinking that if she does so, she'll be able to fly after them . . . Oh, and that business about the blue mouse: is the choice of colour supposed to imply something?

Director L—, the pride of the nation's film industry, could have countered all these objections with the talent and charm for which he was renowned. But what would have come of it, comrades? Nothing good, you can be sure, and it's better to admit this straight away and not squander national resources on the film.

Sadly, Nikolin remained oblivious of the disappointment they'd been dealt, because he was still immersed in carrying out his programme. By the time Thursday came round he was totally incapable of distinguishing it from Friday, or even Saturday. He did not pick up the phone or answer the doorbell. For some reason, when he got drunk, he started to write poetry, which, even in his own opinion, was absolutely lousy: it was full of self-pity, heaped reproaches on the world and a shameless playing to the public. A public – so a contemptible vanity whispered to him – that would discover these works in the fullness of time, and come to understand everything. Then something stopped him in his tracks. Either his body, or some residue of pride, held him back.

At last, the day came when Nikolin, shaved and sober, sat at his table, restoring order from chaos. The poems over which drunken tears had been shed were ruthlessly torn up and flushed down the lavatory. Then he cleaned the apartment and washed out the glasses. Finally, he changed his socks and ironed his trousers. A large piece of white dandelion fluff floated in through the open balcony door. As children, they had called these bits of fluff 'postmen', and tried to catch them: if you caught one, you'd get a letter. Nikolin made no move towards it, but it caught Brysik's attention, and he crouched down, ready to pounce. After a few attempts he succeeded, and rolled over on to his back, clutching his prize.

Someone pounded on the door – no ringing the bell this time, followed by a scrabbling sound and rapid footsteps hurrying away towards the stairs. Nikolin went to the door and listened, without opening it. Then he saw that a card had been pushed under the door. The front of the card proclaimed: 'Congratulations on Soviet Army Day!' The reverse side bore a handwritten message.

My dear Storyteller, where have you disappeared to? Nerves playing up? I know a very good doctor, I can arrange to have him treat you if you like. Come round on Thursday, there's a dear. I miss you.

Lots of love,
Sophy

So that was the way it was, was it? Nikolin fairly shook with rage. For some reason, it was the 'Sophy' that infuriated him most. You cling to life, and this is the kind of life that's been planned for you. With Sophy. Let's not fool ourselves and try to avoid facing facts any longer. The third decision must be implemented without delay. Or it will be too late.

He picked up Brysik and stroked the little round head. Then marched across the landing and rang Auntie Xenia's bell. Luckily, she was at home. She opened the door clad in an enormous dark red candlewick dressing-gown. She was so surprised to see Nikolin that she couldn't say a word. He hastened to speak before she could slam the door in his face.

'Auntie Xenia, I have to go away for a very long time. For ever. Please try to find Brysik a home, you're a good-hearted woman, I know that. And – thank you.'

He shoved the kitten into her unresisting arms and fled back to his own apartment.

Chapter Twenty-five

SOMETHING STILL REMAINED to be done, but Nikolin couldn't think what. Write a note saying 'my death is not to be blamed on anyone' the way they did in novels?

No, damn it, why should he? He took a clean sheet of paper, and, choosing his thickest felt pen, wrote across it:

'I WILL NOT work for you!'

That, too, was a childish gesture, but it gave him a feeling of satisfaction. He had heard that once the KGB started a file on someone it would be marked 'For permanent retention'. Well, they could add this sheet to his file, too. When a writer dies, members of the KGB appear on the scene even before workers from the morgue.

He pulled out the phial of sleeping tablets. He'd been saving them for just such a moment. All his emotions had cancelled and burned each other out, so he swallowed the lot quite calmly, rinsing them down with sips of water. Then he sank into his armchair, facing the balcony. A sparrow hopped around on the railing, turning its head this way and that. Nikolin hoped the sparrow would stay. He enjoyed watching it, it was such a happy, speckled little creature . . .

Someone rang the doorbell. Either Auntie Xenia had recovered from her surprise, or it was Them again. The sparrow was still hopping around, and Nikolin stayed immobile so as not to scare it away.

Then he heard the sounds of a key in the lock. Well, everyone knew They had keys that would open any door . . . Too late, comrades, the train's gone. Pity about the sparrow, though – they'd be bound to frighten it off, the bastards. At least They'd manage that.

Kir catapulted through the door, hair on end, eyes wide.

'Anton, I'm sorry to burst in like this, but I've been very worried. I thought maybe something . . . And I had your spare key . . . Are you all right?'

Nikolin smiled at him without rising. The world was beginning to spin and he felt extraordinarily light-headed. If someone had insulted him the way he'd insulted Kir, he wouldn't have cared what happened to them. But Kir had set aside his own hurt feelings and come, at the risk of having the door slammed in his face.

Kir put the key on the table and stood there, looking at Nikolin with concern. Are you all right? You're sure?

'Yes, I'm sure, Kir. Thank you for coming. Forgive me for what I said. I had no choice. It . . . had to . . . be done. It . . . wasn't your fault, it . . . wasn't . . . my . . . fault . . .'

Nikolin suddenly felt violently ill, which stopped him from drifting off. He must have looked very strange, because Kir leapt over to him, seized him by the shoulders and stared intently into his face. His first thought was to get some water, and he grabbed a glass which stood on the table. And saw the note.

Nikolin made no effort to stop Kir from calling an ambulance. He had no idea of the dosage, he was vomiting violently and was in no state to be coherent about anything.

He returned to his senses two days later. The first thing he saw was a maze of transparent plastic tubing, then a white ceiling. He felt flat and depleted, and very, very cold. The tubes reminded him of something: he knew they had to be torn down, but not why. He moved his hand weakly, and remembered. Dasha's tiny, bruised hands. Not tied down, no. Bandaged into place. They would bandage him down here, of that he had no doubt. Was he already in a psychiatric hospital? He considered the question with no particular interest. For some obscure reason he suddenly wanted to know what kind of floor was under his bed: parquet, linoleum, or maybe cement. But he couldn't raise his head to look.

A day later, when they had put him into an ordinary hospital bed, he learned that he was in one of the best hospitals in Moscow. The revolting tubing was taken away by a young nurse with a sweet smile. The floor was parquet. By that time, Nikolin began to feel the first stirrings of emotion. Actually, one emotion. Unreasoning shame. It was the only thing he had brought back with him from the realms of unconsciousness. As though someone had given him an almighty slap in the face, and flung him down here. He lay there, wondering quietly: why?

They admitted Kir, dressed in a white coat and clutching a bunch of flowers. He bent over Nikolin, gave him an awkward hug and whispered:

'Keep quiet for now, I've fixed everything.'

What had he fixed?

The nurse went out, leaving them alone. Nikolin was considered to be out of danger. Convalescing. This meant he could have visitors.

Still whispering, Kir informed him that he had pocketed the piece of paper; nobody else had seen it. So the whole incident could be treated as an unfortunate accident: anyone could mistake one medicine bottle for another. Maybe all Nikolin had wanted to do was take a couple of aspirins.

Kir had acted with good reason: a suicide attempt meant compulsory listing at a psychiatric clinic at the very least. As a rule, it involved having to go through a whole battery of tests. Well, thank you friend for your trouble. Either way, Nikolin knew that he was unlikely to escape a psychiatric ward. Yet he was still grateful. Kir was doing all he could to protect him. That was the second emotion Nikolin felt. It was pleasant to feel Kir's concern. It was good to see Kir, too. The shame was not lessened by this; on the contrary, it increased, and brought under-standing: you thought, friend, that you had paid up and closed all your accounts? Weakly and meekly, Nikolin acknowledged that he hadn't, not all of them. He still had accounts to settle once he was back on his feet, and settle them he would. But while he was flat on his back, he had a temporary reprieve. Because he was so weak. A blessing in disguise. The ceiling above his head was white. Kir's hand was warm. He lay there, smiling. His lips trembled a bit, but it passed.

Kir, too, smiled happily, even though he was clearly ill-at-ease in the hospital atmosphere and didn't know what to talk about. Surely not about the weather. But for some reason that was all he could find to rattle on about.

'It's nice and cool here. You wouldn't believe how hot it is out in the streets, old man, not a breath of air, all the asphalt's melting. You get into the car and it burns your backside. They say there's going to be a terrible drought . . .'

Auntie Xenia came next, also with flowers and a bag of home-baked jam biscuits – as much at her ease here as she was every-where else. She talked to Nikolin as though nothing had happened, as if there had been no strain in their relations, nothing untoward . . .

'How thin you've grown, Anton Semyonych! I'll bring you some broth tomorrow, the stuff they give you in hospitals isn't food. And don't you worry about Brysik, I'm looking after him. He's grown so big, it's amazing. Would you believe it, he had my Cleopatra hiding on top of the cupboard, the little terrorist. I've divided up their territory for the time being: Cleopatra's inside with me, and he's in the kitchen. They hiss at each other, but that's all.'

'Thank you so much, Auntie Xenia! I'll ask my friend to give you the spare key to my flat, all right?'

'Yes, that'll probably be better. And the kitten'll be better off. I'll keep him fed and clean, and I'll do out the apartment for when you come home. When will they discharge you?'

'I've asked them to let me go as soon as possible.'

'Now, I'm not sure that's wise. The doctors know best. What would you like me to bring you?'

To Nikolin's genuine surprise, he had lots of visitors: the whole ward was filled with flowers, like a funeral parlour.

Somehow, the word had got around that They had tried to recruit Nikolin, and he had told Them to go to hell. So They'd tried to pressure him and nearly driven him over the edge. Food poisoning, indeed! Everyone knows what *that* kind of food poisoning really means . . . It was a miracle he was still alive . . .

So visitors trooped to the hospital with a demonstrative air, as if to say: we respect *you*, and we despise *Them*. Who could object to people paying a visit to a sick man in hospital and cheering him up with a bunch of flowers?

Olga came running round and looked at Nikolin with comical admiration, as if he were some kind of hero. Nikolin squirmed uneasily, but what could he say to her, how could he explain? As was to be expected, Stella turned up; so did Mulin, and a whole host of others.

Director L— flashed his white teeth at him.

'Get better quickly, and don't worry about a thing, my dear fellow. We'll show them yet!' He pressed Nikolin's hand meaningfully.

Nikolin found all this amazing. Arising unprompted, such a wave of human kindness and sympathy. In his opinion, the only thing that could have warranted such interest, the only worthwhile accomplishment of his life, as he saw it, was now never to be realized: his novel was gone. Yet people kept coming, bringing bags of fruit and endless bunches of flowers, and all the latest journals. Translator S— went so far as to present Nikolin with a volume of Akhmatova's poems, a bibliographical rarity and a great sacrifice on his part.

Nikolin was sincerely glad when he was finally discharged and Kir drove him home. He had no idea what would happen now, and didn't want to think about it. Certainly there would be no second attempt with the tablets – of that he was sure. His shame had tormented him, and then all those flowers . . .

His apartment shone from top to bottom, Auntie Xenia had even washed all the windows. A pie sat on the table, covered with a clean cloth. Brysik, purring at full volume, climbed into Nikolin's lap with the air of an abandoned orphan who had suffered the indignity of being locked in a strange kitchen and being menaced by a wild beast.

His letter-box contained an official summons to report to his local army recruitment office tomorrow. Kir was still with him, so Nikolin handed the paper over. Kir's eyes widened.

'You think it could be Them?'

'Maybe They mean to promote me!'

That Kir should have known that the Committee occasionally made use of military premises was not particularly surprising, but it is a measure of how far Nikolin's eyes had been opened that this possibility had already occurred to him of its own accord.

'So what are you going to do?'

'Why, I'll go along since I've been ordered to. Then we'll see. I'll phone you later and let you know.'

Nikolin had decided to live for the present, and not try to anticipate the future. Future prospects looked bleak, while the present moment had nothing disagreeable about it. What could be pleasanter than to sit on the balcony and look down on the blossoming linden trees?

In the evening, however, he did make one concession to the future. He conceived the excellent idea of phoning everybody.

At least, all the people who'd visited him in hospital. They were all friends, they had all realized that he was under fire, and that was why they had come. Why had they understood? Because they all knew what it was like to be under pressure. We're all under pressure to some degree. The System is like an ideal gas out of a textbook on physics: pressure is never null. Yet the people came. If they had been afraid of being associated with him, they would have kept clear. There, in the hospital, he had felt moved to tears, and not only from weakness. He'd had to keep a careful check on himself so as not to give way. So why shouldn't he invite them all round for dinner the following evening? To – ha, ha! – celebrate his promotion: what other reason, after all, could there be for requiring a forty-year-old senior lieutenant of the reserve to report to the army offices? If not that, then simply to celebrate his recovery. He'd ask Kir to come round a bit earlier, get Auntie Xenia to let him in. If Nikolin were held up, Kir could act as host, receive the guests. He'd borrow some chairs from Auntie Xenia – they used to do that with Lucia from time to time. How long ago that had been, Lord, how long ago!

He phoned around, issuing his invitation. Sixteen people expressed their pleasure and accepted, everyone else was off on vacation, it being that time of year. He'd have to borrow some plates. It would be a laugh if the guests were to gather, with no host at the table. Where is he? In the lunatic asylum!

Auntie Xenia agreed to act as hostess and to get everything ready. She took the money to make all the necessary purchases and set to work in a whirlwind of activity.

Preparations laid, Nikolin was able to set off with a light heart for his appointment. He didn't even bother to take any spare clothing. Lunatics are clearly not supposed to have their own clothes. They have regulation-issue straitjackets. Toothbrushes were a moot point, but it seemed fairly safe to assume that they were not supposed to have teeth, either. It was a pity Nikolin had never taken the time to find out what it was really like in there. Study the subject, as Mitri might say. Well, time would show.

Inevitably, Nikolin found himself directed into some office. Equally inevitably, there was someone dressed in civilian clothing behind the desk. Not Viktor Stepanych this time, though.

'You probably know why we've asked you here?'

'I suppose you'll tell me,' replied Nikolin, surprised at his own calm. He knew that at any moment the same numbing, all-pervasive fear could descend on him again. Having experienced this so many times now, he made himself no promises. But for the moment, in the welcoming present, he felt perfectly in control of himself. The office was like a thousand other offices, a light curtain drawn over the window. And the somebody across the desk was just a somebody. The chair was comfortable, with a high back.

'We have a hard and fast rule, Anton Semyonych: if, for some reason, we decide to dispense with the services of one of our agents, we advise them of that fact. Therefore I am informing you officially that we find you unsuitable. Because of your instability and tendency to drink. So we are now breaking all contact with you. Do you have any questions?'

Nikolin had none.

'In that case – goodbye.'

Nikolin walked out without knowing what to think. Was that all there was to it? As simple as that? But then that means . . . just a moment . . . Everyone knows that once They get someone in Their grip, there's no going back. How come everyone knows this, but not that They can also say goodbye – just like that – we're jettisoning you as useless ballast – why doesn't everyone know that? Then the realization came: what was he likely to do – talk about it, or keep quiet? Of course . . . Nor would anyone else who had been lucky enough to get away from Them. And those who were not so lucky were even less likely to talk.

Did that mean that he, Nikolin, had not only a present but also a future? Probably not: this whole affair had drained all emotion out of him. What kind of a writer could he be if even at such a moment he was unable to feel anything much – no relief, no freedom, no joy? Not even regret for his lack of feeling.

Right, he'd go home. It was four hours yet before his guests would be arriving, he'd give Auntie Xenia a hand. With typical resolution, he bought a loaf of bread and spent the next hour feeding the dusty sparrows in a square near by.

It was already mid-July by the time Nikolin managed a trip to see Grandpa Klim.

Interestingly, from the moment Nikolin decided that his novel had been lost, he wasted no regrets on it. True, there had been other matters to worry about. But even later – when he'd been writing the screenplay, for instance – the knowledge gave him no pain. They had it, and that was that. As though someone had removed it from his conscious mind with a giant eraser. If he ever thought about it, it seemed like some business long since finished.

Yet now, the matter began to nag again: the second copy! He could reread it, at least. It wasn't lost for ever. It was lying where he'd hidden it, waiting for him to retrieve it some day. And decide its fate.

The city was like a hot-house, and tempers were frayed. The lucky owners of Moscow residence permits did their best to escape. Writers, too, were at liberty to get away: they could scatter to dachas or 'creative houses'. Others, like Nikolin, took off for less predictable places. Only Pushkin remained in the sweltering heat of central Moscow, brooding on his pedestal. Dreaming of Africa, most likely.

Auntie Xenia was frankly bewildered: why should anyone want to leave Moscow? Hot? Nonsense, call this hot! Now at Stalingrad it had been *really* hot, she could remember it as if it were yesterday. A bit of heat never hurt anyone. So when

Nikolin asked her, was she planning to go anywhere, she looked at him in genuine perplexity.

'If I go, who's going to look out for Moscow?'

But she saw him off good-naturedly, as always.

'Go and give yourself a break. I'll look after everything.'

Grandpa Klim greeted Nikolin with his usual affection. He struck a colourful figure, wearing a long black jacket over a Breton shirt full of holes, and a jaunty straw hat. The sultry air hummed and shimmered with the movement of thousands of tiny bees' wings. Klim seemed impervious to the heat. He was delighted to receive a new undershirt, as he was down to his last one. Life isn't life without an undershirt, and the army ones he favoured weren't sold to civilians.

'That's a fine one there, my boy! Where did you manage to get that?'

Generally speaking, Nikolin didn't have the knack of acquiring goods that were hard to come by, but he had noticed that every time he went to get something for Klim, it seemed to drop into his lap. Unfailingly.

There was a huge old tree stump beside Klim's house, much older than the house itself, the apiary and everything else for a hundred miles around. It rose in intricate, mighty swirls from the ground, covered with lichen. The branches of surrounding trees met and twined above it, and it was in this cool and shady spot that Klim had his summer living and dining room in one.

Nikolin sat on a sawn-off log, enjoying forgotten smells. Klim had thrown a piece of sacking on the stump and was busy making new frames for the hives with a wicked-looking knife. As he worked, he boasted of his latest exploits. He had gone into the nearest town after the thaw had set in, to buy tobacco and various other supplies. When he returned – Mother of God, what did he see? His door wide open, and three strangers poking around, two outside, and the other coming out of the house just as Klim arrived. It was too early for the bees to have left the hives, so there had been nobody to stop them . . .

Well, Klim had grabbed a stout stick, and went straight for them!

'Got one of them across the back – he practically lost his footing, then ran like hell. The other two got clean away, though, the bastards. If I'd had both my feet, I can tell you, I'd have shown them a thing or two!'

He'd shouted at their retreating backs, hurled a few insults to make himself feel better, and then taken himself off to the collective farm office to warn the chairman that there were thieves around, and not locals from the looks of them. Could be fsi's or plain criminals. No, they didn't seem to have stolen anything, even the mead was untouched. As if Klim would let them get away with that, ha, ha! They'd managed to escape in one piece, so they could be grateful for that.

Nikolin could no longer feel the heat. A cold tremor ran through him. However, he couldn't head over to the cellar there and then, for no apparent reason. Klim wouldn't understand. So he stayed where he was, chatting.

When he finally found an opportunity to slip away, he knew that what he was doing was futile. There was nothing there, he was certain. The old man's place had been searched and the manuscript found.

And so it turned out.

Nikolin re-emerged, covered in cobwebs, the sun hurting his eyes. A wave of bitter hatred filled him: towards Them, himself, and the whole lousy world in general. If one of Them had been there right now, he would have killed him without a moment's hesitation. Strangled him with his own bare hands. Ripped out his throat.

A passing bee flew by on its own business. And, although Nikolin was standing motionless, the bee swerved from its course and dived. And stung Nikolin right in the eye.

*

Klim pulled the sting out of Nikolin's rapidly swelling eye and wondered aloud at such a thing:

'What could have got into the little beastie? Maybe you took a swipe at it – not having been here for a while? You have to be careful around bees, they're God's creatures and sensitive to atmosphere. It wouldn't bite just like that, because they die when they lose their sting.'

One of Nikolin's eyes sealed up completely, the other was a mere slit. His nose resembled a ripe plum. He sat on the log peering at what he could see through the slit of Klim's little paradise and the blue, cloudless sky. There was nothing behind him now: Nikolin and his past were quits. He had no strength to start anew – and what was there to start?

Klim brought over some fresh cucumbers from his vegetable patch, comforted him the way one would a child. Then he poured them both a glass of mead.

'Well, here's to our health!'

'Our health, Klim Vasilyich!'

And healthy they were, while summer continued to roll by, rustling and chirping.

That autumn Filipp Savich was much exercised in regard to his main object of concern: the Nobel Prize for Literature had been awarded to Solzhenitsyn, and there had been no way of preventing this hostile act. We had not taken adequate measures in time. Why?

Because a cholera epidemic had broken out in Odessa in the summer, and threatened to spread further. The epidemic was as much the business of the Fifth Directorate as it was of the doctors. Steps had to be taken not only in connection with the sick. Filipp Savich travelled there personally, and remained there till the end of September. Slaving away getting to the bottom of the epidemic, employing his best people on the job, until they had located the source of the infection, devised a suitable terminology and explained and suppressed matters as they saw fit – that had been his first priority; an epidemic's no joke. Everything had worked out fine. It would all be forgotten in a year's time. But Filipp Savich could hardly be expected to tear himself apart and be in two places at once. Officially, he was engaged on other tasks. But not in practice, only on paper.

Now the chickens had come home to roost. The Swedes had gone and awarded the enemy-in-chief, the Spider, the Nobel Prize. Furthermore, the Nobel Committee made its announcement two weeks earlier than usual, not in the autumn as is customary, which meant two weeks less for any last-ditch efforts to bring the panel to its senses. Now, the Spider was the enemy to some and a Nobel Prize winner to others. The news resounded on all the proscribed radios: universal applause! Truth penetrates the Iron Curtain! Yes, he's accepted it! No, he hasn't refused it! No, he doesn't intend to leave Russia!

Moscow heaved under a wave of emotion. Some could not conceal their joy: judging by the expressions on people's faces, the smiles exchanged on public transport, half of the population of Moscow could be charged with harbouring anti-Soviet sentiments. Others seethed with impotent fury. Yet others held belated conferences to determine what had gone wrong. Why had the situation not been averted?

But it would be wrong to think that Filipp Savich lost his job or even suffered any permanent damage. He had warned, he had called for urgent measures, he had even suggested which measures. This was all reflected in clearly dated documents. It was not his fault that no delegation had been sent to Sweden in time. Filipp Savich came up with a suggestion: pressure could be brought to bear on the Swedes even now, to prevent them turning the matter into a political circus. Our regime is just: Filipp Savich was not punished for something for which he was not responsible. Keep up the good work, Filipp Savich.

So he did. He ordered a new, imported cream against eczema (the central heating would be coming on all too soon) and immersed himself in his work. The matter of individual psychiatric re-education, if it were to be carried out on a mass scale, required a new analytical approach. There was an almost superstitious fear of the psychiatric hospitals, but how long would it last? It was essential to achieve maximum effect in one bold move, but the men at the top were jittery. As the old saying goes, they wanted to have their pleasure, and preserve their virginity at the same time.

As if that were not enough, there was an upsurge of nationalist sentiment in the republics, scientists and academics waxing over-confident, Jews and their emigration demands to contend with. Yes, the 1970s promised to be full of opportunities for creative endeavour!

There are no moments in time sufficiently powerful to halt it. It stops for nothing, presses on regardless. Only some meter in unimaginable spheres marks the passage of a month, a year, ten years, twenty. Meanwhile, learned men argue: must we all pay according to that meter, or is there a chance of slipping past for free? And if we must pay – then how much? The more far-sighted add a further question – in what currency?

Epilogue

THE MAJORITY OF our heroes were still alive in August '91. Only Brysik was no more, after a long and fruitful life, during which he enriched the genetic fund of succeeding generations of Moscow cats with his coat of three colours – to bring their owners luck.

Nikolin did not get another cat. He now had a dog, Yapsy, of indeterminate parentage. They were to be seen every morning and evening in the neighbouring square. Nikolin had a few lean years after these tumultuous events, then his work began to appear in print once more. He even wrote the scenarios for a number of cartoon films. When his financial situation was at its worst, director L— got him a job as an extra on various films. In fact, Nikolin was even singled out in a number of episodes, because it turned out that he was very photogenic. He and L— made a few more attempts to push through their first scenario, but it was turned down in the '70s, then again in the '80s, so was put aside to wait for better times.

Nikolin also remarried. His wife was a quiet little librarian with a mild expression and gentle hands. Despite his friends' fears, her hands remained gentle. She welcomed Nikolin's friends, accepted him unconditionally and never reproached him, even at those times when her salary was their only income. She and Katerina became best friends – not a common occurrence among writers' wives. At first Auntie Xenia had been as jealous as the traditional mother-in-law, but she settled down in time. His new wife kept an eye on her, and did her shopping: Auntie Xenia's legs got worse with every year.

At the time when the situation erupted, Nikolin was out of Moscow. He was away at Grandpa Klim's funeral. Klim had died not from illness, but from sheer old age. Feeling his time was near, he'd sent Nikolin a telegram: 'Dying. Come.' He must have sent it to others, too. Some twenty total strangers eyed one another, marvelling at the diversity of the old man's circle of acquaintance. One of those present wore a priest's cassock. Those who had arrived while Klim was still alive said that he had died quietly, a smile on his face. He had left a hand-written set of instructions on the table about how to tend the bees, then lain down for a rest. Nikolin was too late to say goodbye, but came in time for the funeral. It was the first time he had seen Klim not in an undershirt, but in a proper white shirt. He lay there with a naïvely triumphant look on his face, and it seemed inappropriate to stand round him and pro-nounce speeches. Even the collective farm president felt this and didn't try to push himself forward. So a quiet service was sung, Klim was lowered into his grave, and a simple oak cross was erected over it. The collective farm appointed a new bee-keeper.

Whether Nikolin had recreated his novel from memory, or whether he had written anything else 'for the bottom drawer' by that August is not known, nor does our story go beyond that point. However, he retained the habit of waking around four o'clock in the morning, and a man must occupy the time somehow. So maybe he wrote. Or maybe he simply sat there, immersed in his thoughts.

Dima was released after serving one and half years of his sen-tence. He did not recognize Stella when he saw her again, she was so bloated and aged. She drank inordinately even by the standards of the most bohemian circles. She cried on Dima's shoulder, promised to get herself 'patched up' so as to stop drinking, but didn't get round to it. Dima's only desire was to leave the country, and forget about everything that had happened. Including Stella.

He married a young economics graduate, and no obstacles were placed in the way of their application to emigrate.

So by that August Dima was living in New York, and working as the driver of a school bus. His attempts at literature hadn't worked out for some reason, even though he had acquired a good knowledge of English and did the rounds of the publishers with his poems in his own translation.

We have no way of knowing whether or not Dima did anything in the camps to justify his undertaking to cooperate with the KGB – that is, to inform against his fellow-prisoners. One is free to guess, but there is no hard evidence. It is a known fact that those who had signed such undertakings were not left in peace in the camps by the KGB, but were required to report. In written form. Reports, in their turn, were filed away in the archives. There have been four waves of archive destruction in the history of the KGB, and the last one, started shortly before that fateful August, was the most comprehensive. After that, much will have to remain for ever a matter of guesswork.

For the same reason, many still think, quite unjustly, that Belokon had been right in his assessment of Kir, and can't believe that he really managed to slip the leash. Moreover, soon after the business with Nikolin, rumours were to be heard throughout Moscow that Usmanov was a KGB agent, and had played an active part in the attempt to destroy him. These rumours soon spread right across the country, along with smoked sausage, Italian boots and other such goods in short supply. Nikolin denied these rumours hotly, but people would only shake their heads: the poor fellow had been under enormous stress, after all. He'd been in no shape to work out who was who.

Kir travelled to the north for several years, to engage in

seasonal work, as he laughingly described it. Then he surfaced in Moscow again, with a new volume of poems, undiminished energy and unquenchable loquacity. He was such an impulsive personality: ready to storm the barricades one moment, hiding his head in the sand the next; out of favour one day, then back in print, and with *perestroika* – suddenly abroad. Normally, when someone is over fifty years of age, he is taken more seriously than when he's twenty. With Kir, it happened the other way round, such was the nature of his talent. But even those who thought little of Kir in literary circles never cold-shouldered him: they drank vodka with him, shook him by the hand. It is only the young who adopt strong positions; with the passage of time everyone gradually becomes reconciled to others.

Kir was not on the barricades: he was making his way back to Moscow from his dacha at the time. But seeing them pulling down the statue of Iron Felix, he climbed up and started reciting his poem on the subject to the surrounding crowd. But nobody was really listening: people were laughing, dancing, yelling, tugging at the ropes. Kir gave up and joined in. It would be better to wait until the statue was down, when everyone started hugging each other and crying. With luck, he might be able to clamber up on the fallen giant then.

When Petya Nizov sailed back from the South Seas he told his mother that he would not be returning to the Institute. What would he do? Serve God? How? He didn't know yet, but God would show him the way. It is not hard to imagine the stress it caused Natasha meanwhile to see Petya working as a porter or a boiler-room stoker.

A few years later, however, the situation clarified and Petya began to prepare to enter holy orders. Strangely enough, Filipp Savich made no move to interfere: either he felt that this was an acceptable occupation, or he was afraid to make matters worse. So when Petya became Father Pyotr, Filipp Savich applied to him from time to time to baptize the children of his professional colleagues. His own daughters had been baptized long ago.

That was a fashion that swept through Party circles: to baptize one's children. At home, of course. Some believed that this would ensure the children's health. Some did it because they had heard that baptized babies don't wet their beds. Others reckoned that if Ivan Petrovich had his child baptized, why shouldn't we? Moreover, one could gain very useful connections this way, having someone influential to stand as a godparent. Father Pyotr carried out these baptisms gladly, turning nobody away. What might only be a fad for the parents, he reckoned, was still salvation for the children. A miracle, a divine mystery, the armour of God.

That was what he did that August, on the barricades. The crowd had gathered there with one aim: to die if They started something. And many thought for the first time: we've lived as non-Christians, brothers, shall we die like that, too? Father Pyotr had no time to wonder whether They would or would not start something. He baptized, blessed, and smiled at each one: go with God!

Filipp Savich took little interest in all the goings-on around the White House. He had enough inside knowledge not to be alarmed. In any case, it would have been senseless to try and keep the System running along present lines. How could a monopoly of information be maintained with people getting computers on all sides? Once they hooked up to the Internet – goodbye, control! His people had worked it all out: there was nothing to be done, either by taxation or by spreading disinformation. Well, you can't keep track of everything. 'The Web', how's that for a laugh? He couldn't help being reminded of the code-name he had once thought up for his enemy-in-chief. He'd think of it every time he logged on. However, all that was in the past.

Nowadays, Filipp Savich was engrossed in something completely different: it was time to go into big business. Viktor Stepanych had proved to be an apt pupil: he had realized the possibilities even before Filipp Savich. He was already a member of the board of a bank, and promised Filipp Savich his support. Unbelievable opportunities were at hand, unimaginable prospects for the future. The initiative had to be seized.

Denis Usmanov was on the Tibetan plateau at that time, taking part in a joint Soviet-Mongolian survey. Summer means field work to a young geologist. His mother Olga was secretly delighted that he was so far away. She spent that night on her knees before an icon of the Virgin Mary, asking for forgiveness and protection for one and all. Her inflexible nature, so like her father's, had mellowed considerably over the years.

As Belokon had surmised, the main factor in this was Denis, a child with a decided will of his own. He had been just over thirteen when, raised as he was by his mother in the spirit of the Russian Orthodox faith, he rebelled against her unchristian embargo on seeing his father. There was an unholy row, and Denis stamped out, slamming the door behind him. He phoned later that evening telling her not to worry: he was at his father's place, would be back in the morning, but wouldn't be going to school that day. Olga was grateful that he had phoned. When she used to storm out of the house at that age, she would stay away for a week without a word. Since then she had resigned herself to Denis's meetings with Kir, and their obvious affection for each other, and even to the presents Kir made to the household (something Kir had been wanting to do for a long time). She even forbore from mentioning her disappointment at the choice her son had made, for she couldn't accept that he could love them both, it had to be one or the other!

Yet to her amazement, Denis managed this without any obvious difficulty. Well, she should have thought more carefully before instilling into him the notion that one should not sit in judgement on others. Yet how could she not teach him that? Now she was reaping the reward, having to surrender one position after another. Kir started turning up at the house, and she was polite, if reserved towards him. So as not to upset the boy.

She decided to let events run their own course, and seeing that this did not cause the world to collapse, continued to treat life as it came. She became well known as an illustrator with a gift for graphics and etching. She had toyed with the idea of icon-painting, but Father Nifont did not approve.

'It's not a woman's occupation.'

She obeyed. He commended her obedience.

Mitri of ESP fame engaged in no more healing. He claimed that he had been attacked by hostile entities from the astral plane, and they had breached his defences. Every time he tried to enter the more rarefied strata of consciousness, he would find his fingers clutching his throat in an iron grip and he would start to choke.

For the time being, therefore, he was studying various books and meditating. He was getting ready to reanimate the Kundalini centre and waiting for an onset of pains. He continued to appear in public but held himself aloof. When he spoke, it was about entering a new era, about the law of ascendancy and similar lofty matters. His listeners tried to look understanding. A new era – nobody could argue with that.

Andrei Mikhalych Belokon sat drinking vodka with his cronies. Everything the Leader had built was crashing down, and the wildly cheering crowd was threatening to destroy the last vestiges of all that was sacred. In fact, they were already going at it with gusto, and Belokon could only clutch his head and wonder: how did we let it come to this? How can this be?

He looked at his friends in confusion, and they stared back at him: what now? What could they, who had remained faithful, do about it? The youngest of them was sixty-three, most were over seventy. Still, it wasn't a matter of age: each of them would give his life to save the great cause, confront any obstacle. But where were they, these obstacles?

They listened to their beloved records: was it possible that these records would now be subject to confiscation in house searches? They drank. They cried, unashamed of their masculine tears. They sat there all night. Were it not for this close circle of friends, they might as well put a gun to their heads straight away. As it was, they were there to support one another at this moment of crisis. They were as one. Sitting there in a tight little circle, in the light of the lamp, singing the old songs. While outside, there was nothing but darkness and fear, and the final destruction of everything.

It was already dawn when Belokon suddenly stood up, as if he hadn't drunk a drop. The others looked at him with hope: there was something in his stance reminiscent of Stalin, a will of iron gathered into an iron fist. Without saying a word, he went into his bedroom and took down the portrait. He brought it out, carrying it with care.

'Come along,' he said. 'To the square. They claim there's freedom.'

They brightened, drawing themselves up as they rose from the table. Not one of them hung back, took fright, or even asked, which square? They knew.

Belokon looked at them with pride, they were the generation that would not bend. Mishka had come out of hospital after a heart attack just three months ago, Tolik had been wearing a hearing aid for two years now; even the youngest, Sashok, was coming out in liver spots. But the spots seemed paler now, as chins were raised and they set out. Before leaving, they phoned a few others whose names came to mind.

They were on Red Square with the portrait by 10 a.m. Not in

a huddle, but standing shoulder to shoulder, like a parade under review, heads up and shoulders back. Go on – arrest us, grab us, kill us if you want to, right here. The day is yours. Your folly triumphs. But justice is ours!

But nobody made any move to seize them, or even drive them away from the square. A few militiamen strolled by, looked them over casually. Well, they were not creating a disturbance. They were exercising their civil rights. Freedom of conscience. It's democracy now, right?

Some passers-by grinned, a few shouted rude remarks. But nobody approached them or tried to start a brawl. They remained there, shoulder to shoulder. A couple of foreign journalists turned up, cameras clicked busily. After so many years, a pro-Stalin demonstration! On the first day of democracy, too. It was quite a sensation.

So they stood there, with the Leader smiling slightly down from the portrait. The one that Belokon carried: the one with the slight smile.